D1198791

The Enthusiast
Josh Fruhlinger

Josh Fruhlinger & Associates

THE ASSOCIATES ARE ALSO
JOSH FRUHLINGER

*For Amber, who always thought I could do it,
even when I wasn't so sure*

Acknowledgements

There are a lot of people without whom this book would not be in your hands and/or e-reader. Primary among them is, of course, my wife Amber, who supported me emotionally, logistically, and (let's be real) financially while I wrote it. She has always encouraged me to write and be creative, all the way back to when I started my blog, The Comics Curmudgeon, which became more than a vague idea at her urging. I only started letting her read the book late in the process, and when it turned out she actually *liked* it, I finally started letting myself believe that writing it would turn out to be a good idea. She has a sharp eye and great taste, and gave me critiques, suggestions, and help with some of the narrative corners I had painted myself into. She also suggested names for the some of the characters.

I also need to thank all my parents and step-parents. Over the course of my weird career and life path, they have always encouraged me and talked me up to their friends and never told me that it was about time I settled down and got a real job. And I am extremely grateful for everyone who's ever been kind enough to tell me they enjoyed the things I've written online, especially the community that's grown up around my blog; without their years of positive feedback, I never would have thought I was capable of writing a novel.

Lots of smart and talented people helped turn my manuscript into a real book that I'm proud to have people read. Emily Gordon was my editor and gave me notes and suggestions from the conception stage to the finish. Bill Peschel was my redoubtable copy editor who helped polish the book into its final form, and his wife, Teresa Peschel, offered valuable feedback as well. Matt Lubchansky drew the amazing art that you see on the cover (or the endpapers, if you're reading this in hardcover); Catty Donnelly created the gorgeous train poster that you'll see in a bit; Don Sparrow brought the Ladies who Lunch and Sons of UNIVAC to life; and Alexis Simpson took my author photo. The good people at Make That Thing!, including Holly Rowland, Sara McHenry, David Malki !, and Christopher Kallini, were responsible for the book design and for getting the final product printed and into the hands of my Kickstarter backers.

And, oh yes, I *really* need to thank those Kickstarter backers. I was overwhelmed by the number of people who chose to contribute to the Kickstarter for this novel. My initial estimate of how long it would take me to deliver the book was wildly optimistic, and, sometimes, when I worried I wasn't ever going to figure out how to finish, my main motivation was a desire to not let my backers down. Thanks to everyone for their patience; it's two years late, but here it is! And a huge thanks to Francesco Marciuliano, who donated his cartooning services so that I could offer some extra-cool rewards to backers.

For one of my Kickstarter rewards, I offered the opportunity for one lucky and generous contributor to become a "patron of the arts" and write a paragraph in the acknowledgements. That lucky and generous patron is Brian Christoffel, and here is his contribution. Thank you, sir!

When I was first approached in 2012 to fund The Enthusiast, *I didn't hesitate to reply, "I would be honored,*

Mr. Chabon!" It was only after I had been chained in the rat-infested basement of a Baltimore housing project that I began to suspect Josh Fruhlinger's deceit. I like to think that our frosty relationship has thawed since then, a process that was only helped by Josh's relocation to Los Angeles during 2014 in search of movie contracts with lucrative "kill fees." As I have not been fed since last year, I fear my remaining time is brief, but I must use the last of my strength to dedicate this novel to my lovely wife Eek, and our children Squeak and Squeak.

And, honestly, I consider everyone who backed the Kickstarter to be patrons of the arts. At the end of the book is a big list of everyone who contributed, under the names Kickstarter supplied. Thank you all so much!

1

ALL FOUR OF THE RAILFANS FROM THE INTERNET were standing at the fence when Kate and Mesut got there. This was not the plan. The plan was really quite clever and well thought out, but this wasn't it. They didn't want to be first, which would have involved a certain amount of awkward standing around and wondering if they were at the right spot, and also would have given them an edge in establishing themselves as *de facto* leaders of the group, if they wanted that edge, which they didn't. They also didn't want to be last, because then everyone who was eager to get moving (which was everyone, they were working on the assumption that it would be everyone, that's why they were here) would resent them. And besides, who wants to be last? Cool people, probably. Kate and Mesut were trying very hard not to be cool.

The actual precise right moment for Kate and Mesut to arrive would have been after at least one other person had shown up but before the last person had arrived. This would have put them in the middle of the group, literally and metaphorically, which is what they wanted. The metaphorical one. They didn't want to come across as a gang of two. They wanted to blend in.

"What would be really good would be if we arrived at different times," Mesut had said the night before. Kate had invited him to Pickles Pub, a bar near her apartment. It was her favorite place to go, and yet she had a moment of panic about it when she got there and saw him standing out front. It was raining and something about the cut of his pants (narrow) and the length of the sleeves on his jacket (a little short) reminded her that he was European. Europeans thought American things were lame, right? Especially American chain restaurants? Pickles probably wasn't famous enough for Germans to know about and make fun of (she imagined Mesut at home with some shadowy German friends, watching a TV show where dumb Americans go to a TGI Fridays and are stupid, with all the Germans laughing uproariously at how dumb the Americans and their restaurants were). Still, there were three or four Pickleses around D.C. and maybe he'd seen another one already. Was there one at the airport? Oh, God, she was pretty sure there was one at the airport. He probably saw it. It had the exact same decor as the one they were sitting in now, except one wall was missing, confronting diners with the terminal concourse and Dulles's dingy carpet. Surely he had seen it. The jig was up.

But once they were inside, Mesut seemed completely uninterested in harshly judging the decor, which was all wood paneling and old-timey colored glass. What Mesut was primarily interested in was beer and talking about the next day's live-site.

"They don't know we know each other outside the message boards," he said, drinking beer number three, "and I think perhaps we should not tell them that we do."

This was going to be the first live-site where Kate was the lead, and she wished that she were doing it with another Agent. Mesut knew in broad strokes what they were up to, of course, but he was thinking about it all engineer-y, or at least all engineer-after-three-beers-y. He wasn't showing any signs of intoxication, and yet he was saying things like this: "Ideally, one of the other people should get there first, then I will show up, then another person, then you, then the last one. That way we are seamlessly integrated into their group. Like the teeth of a zipper." He pulled the zipper of his jacket up and down a bit, in what he appeared to believe was a meaningful fashion.

Kate started to explain how hard it would be to hike to a remote location and slot their arrival amongst a group of people whose precise arrival times they had no way of knowing in advance, but the thought of it gave her a headache, so instead she just said, "But we're meeting four of them. The way you described it, it sounds like there's only three."

Mesut looked crestfallen but respectful that she had found a fatal flaw in his math. "Another beer, please," he asked the waitress as she walked by. She was no longer fazed that he wasn't asking for any particular brand.

Even though they knew they couldn't time their arrival with teeth-of-a-zipper levels of exactitude, they at least had high hopes of not being first or last. These hopes came to nothing when, parked in front of Mesut's hotel the next morning, Kate began to program their destination into her phone, only to have the sinking realization that "where the chain-link fence angles off to the east along the Orange Line a quarter-mile north of Addison Road" was not something that Google Maps would understand. She began to worry less that Mesut would think she was a dumb American and more that she was just dumb, in a nationality-neutral kind of way.

He made a muffled noise that Kate assumed was judgmental,

until she saw that he had a mouth full of candy bar and was peering at the archaeological layers of textured sugar making up the half that he hadn't eaten yet. This was, apparently, his breakfast, or maybe an after-breakfast snack. "This is very much like a brand of chocolate bar we have in Germany, except"—he chewed thoughtfully—"I think this has less peanut butter?" He looked at the label. "Why is it a 'Clark Bar'? Who is Clark?"

Kate began to think that Mesut might not, strictly speaking, be the *coolest* kind of European they had on offer, which was just fine by her.

They did, eventually, find an abandoned gas station on Addison Road where they could park, surrounded by tall grass. From there it was a short hike along the shoulder to the path that led uphill through the woods. It was still early in the morning, and the grass and branches were a little wet and the cuffs of their pants were getting damp. They only hit one dead end—to be fair, it was the one that the description she'd printed out from the message boards said they'd hit—and it was around 7:10 a.m. when they abruptly emerged from the trees and saw the chain-link fence along the ridgeline and the four railfans standing along it.

Only ten minutes late, but still late enough to be last. So much for plans.

"Hi! I'm Kate. kmac1987." She gave her board name even though it was obvious who she was. She was the only woman here. *Mac* was as in *MacAlister*, her mother's maiden name, not that she had told anyone that, and she was actually born in 1989—you try not to give anyone anything they could Google—but when the forums software asked her whether she was male or female, she had been honest, out of necessity if nothing else. She knew other people at the Agency who juggled online personae of different genders, the better to gain trust or social currency or just alleviate boredom, but this was an obvious bad idea if there was a chance that things would progress to a live-site.

Still, introducing yourself was good protocol, as was smiling and making eye contact and a whole host of other things that she wasn't entirely sure her fellow trainspotters were going to do. She was pleasantly surprised on three out of four counts. Charlie, aka Rail-Fanner, was a portly, grinning, bearded white man in his 50s; his coveted board nickname was a testament to how early he had joined the community. Darius, who went by foamerguy, was younger, shy, tall and skinny, African-American—just a kid, really, and Kate knew that he and RailFanner spent a lot of time skulking around train yards. They were generally the instigators of in-person outings.

Jack, aka The_Real_Jack, was small, stooped, white, bearded, somewhere in his 40s or 50s. It was hard to tell. He looked suspiciously at everyone while tugging on his mustache and didn't say much at first. His username was the end product of a battle for dominance with a different Jack on the boards on the question of whether Federal Railroad Administration rules ought to be relaxed for commuter lines in order to accommodate new diesel multiple-unit trains coming over from Europe, and also on whether the now-vanquished Other Jack had any business talking about trains with anyone, anywhere. The fight had ended as the stuff of legend, with Jack as The_Real_Jack. Finally, there was Rajiv, aka Rajiv, a thin Indian-American almost as young as Darius, who was also making his first organized raifanning trip. He had a camera that was impressively enormous, though he kept fiddling with it as if he weren't sure what its many buttons were for.

For a moment she tried to see herself as they might: short, white, red hair pulled back in a ponytail, glasses that weren't intimidatingly chic and weren't outright dorky but also weren't hipster dorky. She had agonized more about the glasses than any other part of the outfit, since for the rest—anorak, comfortable jeans, white sneakers—she had decided fairly quickly that clothes that conveyed a message of simple functionality would strike the right note, not draw attention to her, and also be, in practice, simple and functional.

"And I'm BerlinZug," said Mesut. "Real name's Mustafa." This brought Kate up short. Live-site best practices were that you used your first name or a variation of it, because otherwise you risked reacting unnaturally in conversation. She was sure she had told Mesut this at Pickles, though that might have been around beer three. As she looked him up and down, it occurred to her that his clothes, which had seemed so European last night, might just be the wrong size.

"You a Siemens guy, Mustafa?" asked Charlie, jovially. "Deutschland über alles?" Kate's stomach tightened and flipped. She was under the impression that Germans didn't like being needled with Nazi slogans, especially Germans like Mesut whose parents were from Turkey. And Mesut *was* a Siemens guy—specifically a junior engineer for Siemens SA, Rail Systems division, which was why he was here with Kate and the others along the Washington Metro Orange Line tracks in the first place.

Live-sites are not under strict control. So went the wisdom from Christine, the Agency's founder. *They are minimally managed by design. Be prepared for potential ancillary awkwardness.* This was one of the scariest and most important things about live-sites. Mesut, to her relief, did not look surprised or offended. He blinked quickly a few times, but he did that a lot anyway. "It's mostly Siemens equipment on the U-Bahn and S-Bahn in Berlin, though there's some leftover stuff from the DDR times here and there. But I came out here because I want to see what WMATA has in use. Breda and CAF, right?"

Charlie grinned. "Yeah, though most cars on this line are from Adtranz—before Bombardier bought it. Stuff from the early '90s. Ugly sons of bitches. Shitty seats, too, and the speaker systems are always on the fritz. If we're lucky, though, we might get to see the railcars WMATA has from up your way in here for testing this morning."

Mesut and Kate remained poker-faced.

While they had been talking, Darius had turned his back to them. Kate had filed this away—*notice, but do not judge, unusual social behavior* was a helpful Agency guideline—but now she realized he was taking the fence apart. Some of the links had been snipped, probably a long time ago; to a casual observer, the fence looked sturdy, or as sturdy as a chain-link fence ever looks, but when Darius unlatched a makeshift hook, he was able to peel some of it away, revealing a portal just big enough for a person to squeeze through. Like a door for elves, she thought, except instead of a twee little world of miniature shoemakers on the other side, there were enormous pieces of machinery purchased with millions of tax dollars.

"Gentlemen," Charlie said, then caught himself. "Sorry, it's usually kind of a sausagefest out here. Ladies first?"

Kate smiled and nodded and slipped through the fence, then moved to her left so the other railfans had room to stand. The fence ran along the top of a ridgeline, leaving her standing precariously at the top of a steep hill, which ran down around fifty feet, through tall grass and prickly bushes and the occasional tree, to the railroad tracks that ran along the lowest point of a little valley. On the other side of the tracks, there was another, gentler hill, more heavily wooded. It was a pretty scene. The green of the trees was starting to fade into fall colors. Then you looked more closely and noticed the strewn bits of trash, wrappers and mysterious abandoned piles of paper. On the other side of the tracks there was a toilet, lying on its side in a puddle.

Mesut was the last through the hole in the fence, Kate noticed; she hoped this satisfied whatever need he had to arrange the two cuckoos symmetrically among the real baby birds in the nest.

The portion of the rail line that they could see was a long arc through the woods, and they heard the train coming before they could see it. Thousands of pounds of metal, thousands of moving parts, rattling against each other and cruising along steel rails at sixty miles an hour. It was early in the morning commute. Inside the train were eager office achievers who were going to get so much done on their spreadsheets before their lazy co-workers rolled in at 9, or people who worked under the careful eye of the clock and needed to be in at 8 so they could take their hour-long unpaid lunch later. Maybe some shift workers were making a reverse commute from the suburban office park where they sat behind a security desk to their little apartments in the District, where they'd draw the curtains and try to sleep. They read or listened to music or stared into space or napped. Most of them probably didn't think about what it was that was taking them where they were going. It was grubby in there. The colors were what WMATA's low-bid branding consultants thought were cool in 1991. Some of the passengers didn't like the look of some of the other passengers. In at least one car, something or someone smelled like urine, and everyone was trying to figure out who or what it was without being obvious about it.

And yet. When the front of the Orange Line train to Vienna turned the corner, Kate gasped, because it was still amazing. Charlie waved his hand, gesturing for them to crouch in the weeds, and they did in a half-assed way for form's sake, but mostly they just gawked.

This was Kate's favorite part of a live-site: the part where everyone shut up and loved it. All six of them silently watched six hundred feet of train go by, not so silently. It was different from being on the platform in a station, when people have places to go and you have places to go and you're trying not to trip over anybody and the train is just a box that gets you there, hopefully soon. That morning, none of them wanted anything from the train except for it to be itself, metal and loud and fast. It was, Kate thought, the difference between seeing an animal at the zoo and seeing it in the wild. It wasn't here for them. It was in its element.

Part of Kate's brain could feel the joy vibrating off everyone else hunched awkwardly in the tall grass. That part vibrated along with the resonant frequency; that part was key to making this live-site work. *It only takes a few minutes for an enthusiast to spot a phony.* But as she enjoyed feeling the train's roar in her guts, other parts of her brain were assessing each of the trainspotters in turn. The client was going to make a multi-million-dollar pitch to a regional transit agency; this was way beyond a consumer-level play where you're trying to pick out who in the gang was the coolest, for whatever definition of "cool" had emerged from the group dynamics. Which of these guys was going to go to a public meeting at a middle school auditorium on a weeknight? And of those, which of them would come across least like a crazy person? Darius had barely made eye contact with anybody but Charlie, and Rajiv hadn't taken his face away from the camera from the moment the train had come around the bend. That left two candidates.

The train rounded the curve and disappeared behind the trees, heading in the direction of its distant terminus. Jack was the first to break the silence: "What a cheap pile of garbage."

A little bell started ringing, loudly and insistently, in the back of Kate's head.

"Way to kill everyone's buzz, Jack," Charlie said. He wasn't unkind about it. This was a conversation that, as Kate could tell from the discussion boards, had been going on for years.

"If you cretins want to go gaga over an ugly train that cost too much and breaks down all the time," said Jack, "be my guest. I'm sure the WMATA assholes who signed that purchase order are thrilled you're all fans of the worst decision they ever made."

Action opportunity: When an enthusiast's affection for a category and his disdain for a specific instance of that category combine to cause internal dissonance—

Charlie shrugged. "Yeah, yeah, they're ugly. Not gonna argue. Doesn't mean you can't enjoy the moment."

"The air conditioning's out in how many cars in that train, do you think? Two? Three? I'm sure all those sweaty chumps are really enjoying *their* moments."

—he is open to having his category affection rekindled by a new instance, even if he doesn't know it. Kate remembered the first time Christine had told her this. She had been cheerful, conspiratorial, as if letting Kate in on a great secret.

Charlie shook his head and gingerly picked his way down the side of the hill. "Whatever, man. We should get moving if you wanna get a good look at the new one. How else are you going to decide what you hate about it?"

Kate positioned herself to make sure she was closest to Jack for the hike down. Darius, who had been mostly silent, was excited, or maybe anxious, or both. "My friend told me the new train is running on schedule block 1456. That's the next block."

"That's if your guy is right," Charlie said. "They might have put it off for a few days."

"1456," Darius said. "Next block."

The six of them made their way down the slope to get closer to the trackbed. They could have covered the distance in a run if they didn't mind possibly stumbling onto the tracks, so they took it in a sort of slow trot. Kate was aware that Mesut was brushing past her to catch up with Charlie, but she stuck by Jack. "Did you see the pics of the S360s online?" she asked him.

He snorted. "Glamour shots. Taken inside a factory. I think most of the pictures of the interiors are just for show, not even installed in a car body."

"Someone's gotta be the first. I mean, we need new railcars. You said it."

Jack looked at her, brow furrowed. "What do *you* think of the pictures? You ask a lot of questions on the boards, but I never hear you offering much by way of opinions."

She shrugged. "I like the materials they're using for the interior. The surfaces have some give but are still impermeable. The rugs, the cushy seats on the Adtranz—God, they get disgusting. And the nextstop display looks awesome. Huge screens. They can put up pictures of the tourist stuff so that even the dumbest people can't miss it."

"What d'you think of the braking system they use?"

She shrugged. "I don't really know much about brakes."

Jack's mouth twitched in what was probably a smile. "Neither do I, to be honest. I was hoping you might. Read something about how they've had some trouble in France. But in France they put rubber tires on subway trains, so who the hell knows what goes on there."

They were almost at the bottom of the slope, and Kate could see Mesut gesturing grandly as he talked to Charlie. She was hoping he wasn't overselling the S360, or at least wasn't overselling it in a way that sounded like *selling*. There was always the potential for a live-site to get unstealth in a hurry, especially when a client was involved.

"You know they bought S360s for the new metros in Dubai and Mecca?" Kate said to Jack.

"Hope the air conditioning works."

"I know, I thought about that the other day when I was on the Orange Line and the AC was on the fritz, so I looked it up. The systems they use have crazy uptimes, 98 percent or something like that. Siemens does design-build-operate there, so it's written into the contract."

"Is that right." *Click,* she heard in her head.

They had gotten as close to the tracks as they dared, about five or six feet away. Kate had caught up with Charlie and Mesut. They were talking about brakes, though Kate was surprised by Mesut's take.

"Oh, absolutely the design Kawasaki uses is much more clever," he said. "You can run several tests on it and find it scores so many points better on whatever brake quality score you come up with. But, you know, they're both quite within every country's safety parameters. It is the difference between a one-in-a-billion and two-in-a-billion accident rate. Twice as good, but both fine for the real world."

The only client-employees allowed on live-sites were people who worked on the products, engineers like Mesut, not sales or marketing. *Genuine enthusiasm is not totalizing and can accommodate criticism*, another oft-repeated Agency maxim.

"Well, you better hope those brakes work," said Charlie, "because here it comes."

The Siemens S360 emerged suddenly around the turn. This was the train that Mesut had helped design, that Siemens wanted, with the Agency's help, to sell to WMATA. They had paid who knows how many millions to ship a prototype to Washington for test runs. It was the train that, with any luck, an unusually large number of interested, well-informed, slightly obsessed citizens would praise on their own accord at informational meetings, and would say nice things about in letters sent in response to Requests For Comments put up on obscure websites.

It was much quieter than the older Adtranz train they had seen from up above. If they had really wanted to get a good look at it, take in its details, their original vantage point would have been better. But then they might just as well have watched and rewatched the videos on the Siemens YouTube channel. The point of driving out to a pre-arranged spot near Addison Road and slipping through a hole cut in a chain-link fence was to have a more visceral experience.

"1456!" shouted Darius. "That's my guy!" The cab window on the Adtranz train had been a tiny portal, but the operator at the front of the S360 sat in what was almost a fishbowl. This was one of the many WMATA employees whom Darius had cultivated through his awkward, irrepressible love of trains and buses and everything else, and he nodded and smiled at the trainspotters as the S360 barreled towards them. It really was beautiful, all curves and sleekness where the Adtranz train was boxy and clunky. And someone at Siemens, in a charming but surely expensive gesture, had decided the whole thing should be orange—orange for the Orange Line—a more muted version of the color than what you saw on wayfinding signs, nothing garish.

Despite the S360's quieter motors and improved aerodynamics, the wind howl still quickly built up to near unbearable levels. Kate realized that some of the noise was coming from her because she was shouting. They all were, Rajiv behind his camera, Darius jumping up and down. Even Jack was smiling. And then the train was on them, flying at top speed, a huge orange blur, and Kate, who was by far the smallest one there, felt herself picked up and knocked to the ground by the blast of air that the train pushed ahead and around it. It was the difference between seeing an animal at the zoo and having it charge at you in the woods.

Mesut did a double take and kneeled besides her. "Are you all right?" she assumed he was shouting. She gave him a smile and a double thumbs up. "This is amazing!" she shouted. If before she had been experiencing joy vibrations, now she was feeling joy in her lungs. She was breathing it in and out. They all were, and it felt fantastic. Joy, joy, joy, joy.

The train passed by and Kate jumped up and everyone was laughing and talking at once. Darius high-fived everybody, then hugged Charlie. Kate scrambled to pick up the stuff that had tumbled out of her purse. They had been trespassing long enough, and it was time to scram. They ran up the hill, that-was-greating and did-you-seeing and I-can't-believe-you-fell-overing, heading for the hole in the fence. Left behind on the ground, difficult to spot among the trash, was a card that had fallen out of Kate's purse, which she was lucky none of the trainspotters had seen. It read:

KATE BERKOWITZ
SUBCONSCIOUS AGENCY
ENTHUSIASM IS OUR BUSINESS

2

KATE WOKE THE NEXT MORNING when the sun was beginning to filter through her bedroom curtains, and the fuzzy grey heaps of dirty
clothes on the floor were coming into focus. She looked up at her
nightstand and saw the round hump of her bedside clock, its face
pointed away from the window and thus still illegible.

"This is the most pointless thing" was how the last guy she had
slept with had described the clock. Kate had thought that maybe the
second time you spend the night at someone's apartment was a little
early to start criticizing their stuff, but Max was uninhibited about
sharing his functional-aesthetic opinions. "It doesn't light up, so
you can't see what time it is with the light off, and it ticks all night,
so it annoys you when you're trying to sleep."

"When the light is off you shouldn't be constantly checking to see
what time it is. That's bad for your sleep," *or whatever else you might
be doing with the lights off,* she thought but did not add because she
was irritated now and didn't want to turn things in that direction
again. "If I really want to know what time it is, I can turn the bedside
lamp on. But it shouldn't be as easy as just opening my eyes."

Silence from the other side of the bed. "It helps me sleep better," she said. "The no light."

"What about the ticking?"

"I like the ticking." That had been eight months ago, and, as it turned out, Max had only a couple more chances to be annoyed by the clock. Now she woke up by herself, which she liked, for the most part. She liked the gradualness of it, the reverse effect where her brain suddenly started organizing the sound waves coming from the clock into something she recognized as noise, which meant that she was awake. The clock—made in France sometime in the 1950s, a find on eBay—had a real mechanical alarm bell, but she almost always woke up before it started ringing. She had beaten the alarm this morning, too. She reached out in the darkness and felt the cold metal of the alarm switch on the back of the clock. She switched it off and it made a solid mechanical *clunk*. This was back when they really made things! Kate wasn't much of a nostalgist, but she did like her clock.

She let her hand drift and felt the cool, empty expanse of the rest of her nightstand. Empty was good: it meant that Nighttime Kate had again done the right thing and left her phone in the kitchen. Had it been here at her bedside, Morning Kate would not have been able to resist it. As it was, she was awake with nothing to entertain her, so she got up and headed for the bathroom, which was the order of events that she was trying to make into a habit. She hadn't left the phone on the hall table either, where she might have been tempted to grab it and scroll through the morning news while sitting on the toilet. *Good job, Nighttime Kate.*

By the time she got to her phone, she had gone to the bathroom and brushed her teeth and showered. She was still in her bathrobe. And her coffee was brewing but it wasn't done yet. Let's not expect miracles.

The phone powered up with the screen pointed away from her: This too was the ritual. There were no windows on this side of the apartment—her kitchen was nestled up against her neighbor's in the mirror-image unit next door—and only the dim counter lights were on. The phone's screen lit up the far side of the room like the sun. This was not a metaphor, or so she had been told: the screen was designed to mimic the spectrum of natural sunlight and fraudulently stimulate in the lizard-brain the good feelings that natural sunlight elicits, the way the Splenda she put in her coffee tricked her brain into thinking she was drinking sugar. Kate felt the glow (she knew she couldn't really feel it, but her lizard-brain told her she could and she allowed herself to believe it); after a moment, she felt the buzz that meant she had text messages. She never wanted to read them in the morning or even think about who they'd be from, which is why the ritual always began with the phone facing away from her. It was too early for information that wanted something back from her. She made a practiced swipe of her thumb that dismissed the text alerts so she didn't have to see them yet.

Start with her newsfeeds: they only wanted to be read. Articles pushed out by newspapers, blog posts from people she liked or hated or had heard about once and never taken out of the reader, the robotically culled results of Google Alerts she had set up months ago and then forgotten. Blah blah coup, blah blah earnings statements, blah blah divorce, blah blah tentative agreement reached, blah blah. Once in a while, she would spot a headline relevant to one of her projects, or to something that she thought would make an interesting project, and she'd throw her thumb into reverse so she could read the article. The world's news was pretty thin this morning—a few transit agencies around the world were buying new

28

railcars; participants from a multi-user text game from the early '90s were planning a live-action recreation of their old CRT-screen world, built out in the Arizona desert—so she was already reading her email by the time the coffee was done. Mostly mass-mailed nonsense from PR houses, each a personal affront with its cloying lack of subtlety. A note from Christine, typically gnomic. "I'm feeling great things about yesterday's live-site," it read, and "feeling" could mean anything: *Your First Impressions report sounded promising*, or *I've talked to people who you didn't realize had overheard you talking enthusiastically to other people*, or *Positive outcomes result in positive energy that is palpable, if difficult to quantify.*

Finally, she swiped over to her text messages, the most intrusive communication she could handle at this hour. There was already one from Miriam, her best friend since college, whom she hadn't seen in over a month:

> Hey I know it's last minute but I'm having a little get together w ppl from my office tomorrow night and some other folks too. Not just lawyers! Please come?

Miriam was a lawyer at the EPA and, in her precise, lawyer-y way, when she said "not just lawyers" she meant "at least one non-lawyer, but probably not many more than that." Kate looked at the time stamp—sent last night, which meant "tomorrow night" was tonight, and Kate could legitimately beg off because she had to client-sit Mesut. She didn't have to come up with a polite way to explain the dread inspired by a party full of environmental lawyers making dark jokes about their inability to stop climate change.

The other text was from her work friend LaMont, sent about 10 minutes before she had turned on her phone.

> oh god i have so much to tell you abt new TL and none of it good. let's have lunch. pickles???

LaMont worked for the Thought Leader Alliance, the other side of the Agency. TLs were what they called their clients, and his new TL was Mesut's boss, which made this fair-to-middlingly complicated. But Kate loved a good horror story. She headed back to her bedroom to pick out some clothes.

⊞⊞⊞⊞⊞⊞⊞⊞

Christine Marver, the Agency's founder, had spent most of 1992 as an unsettlingly effective get-out-the-vote coordinator for Bill Clinton's presidential campaign. "I would watch her phone-banking and be mesmerized," James Carville said years later. "Just speaking in this low, even voice about what voting meant to whoever she was talking to, about the physical experience of voting—she had looked up what the booths were like in different states, so she would know. Other stuff, too. Their lives. What they thought of the campaign so far. A couple people she asked if they'd ever had a sex dream about Bill, or Hillary, or Tipper, or Al. We cross-referenced later. Ninety-four percent of the people she talked to voted. Spookiest thing I ever saw."

After the election, she arrived in Washington, D.C., with family money and the Rolodex of contacts she had assembled during the campaign. Her plan was to start a lobbying and political consulting shop for the new Democratic era, but instead of renting space on K Street with everybody else, she found a warehouse near the Navy Yard around the corner from a dance club called Tracks and within walking distance of a just-opened Metro stop. She bought the building with cash and renovated it. By the time the Republicans swept Congress in the '94 midterms, half of the warehouse was habitable and only a third of the Agency's clients were political. Christine let her lobbyist license lapse, and Marver and Associates became Subconscious Agency, and became fully itself.

The neighborhood had changed a lot since, and Kate wasn't sorry to have missed it. There were people who had been there for years who liked to tell newbies about being solicited by prostitutes or mugged on their way to work in the morning, back in the '90s. Terrifying stories from the distant past of an institution are part of what Agency hands were taught to recognize as an *authenticity rundown* when other people were doing it to them, but "being conscious of a behavior pattern does not remove the social and psychological usefulness of performing that pattern," as Christine would say.

"Everything was supposed to be a learning experience," said Tim, a guy from the Thought Leader Alliance who had worked with Christine on the campaign and came to D.C. with her to start the Agency. "We were supposed to use our Agency techniques, figure out what their motivation was and channel it in the direction we wanted it to go. Eventually we compromised: we'd try it with the hookers but not the muggers."

Among the video segments playing on continuous loop in the Agency's lobby was a clip from a local news broadcast in 1993 with

Christine, looking remarkably like Christine did today only with slightly bigger hair, shaking hands with then-Mayor Kelly in front of the warehouse, which had just opened for business. The newly power-washed and painted exterior made the Agency's headquarters the nicest building around, the sort of thing that would get the mayor to come out and smile on camera.

Now, as Kate walked towards it, it was a hulking relic of the neighborhood's past, surrounded by condos and new townhouses, even though it looked exactly the same. *Objects and people and abstract concepts all exist within a cultural context. This makes it possible for signifiers to change meaning while remaining constant from the perspective of an isolated observer.* This was a Christine maxim that Kate tried out on LaMont to explain how odd the warehouse made her feel; he laughed and said Christine had bought the building just to make that point obvious when everyone showed up to work every day. Most people at the Agency half-seriously attributed that sort of prescience to her, but Kate didn't buy it, and didn't think Christine deliberately cultivated that kind of mystique. "When you figure out a useful way to describe the world," she overheard Christine saying to a client once, "you shouldn't be surprised when the world behaves as described. But it's not *magic.*"

The lobby of the Agency was the part that still looked most like a warehouse. The vast metal roll-up door still opened and could still accommodate three tractor-trailers abreast; it was lowered only on those rare occasions when the Agency was really, truly closed: hurricanes, snow emergencies, the week Christine gave everyone off between Christmas and New Year's. There was a wall of glass occupying most of the portal now, nearly invisible from far off, with an even subtler sliding door in the midst of it. This was an addition from 1996; in the first few years of the Agency's existence, the front-line receptionist had sat behind a desk exposed, more or less, to the elements, and so had clients, until finally there were enough clients to pay for the glass wall.

Not much else had changed. The receptionist still sat behind the ornate, battered desk that Christine had had ceremonially plunked down the day Marver and Associates opened. It had belonged to the private secretary to Tsar Nicholas II, according to a Russian émigré Christine's father had bought it from in Paris in the '50s. While that hadn't been proven, it was covered in gouges that could have been the product of some violent revolution. The chair behind the desk looked like a robotic bird and was the latest in ergonomic design. There was a nostalgic pleasure in the continuity of institutional surroundings, but the proper care of human bodies and their lower backs was a higher priority.

"Hey, Kate," said Stephanie, sitting in the robot-bird chair. Stephanie worked in Accounts Payable. The Agency didn't have a full-time receptionist; this was one of the other things that hadn't changed since 1993. Everyone was expected to man the front desk for a few days at a time, though the Agency now had enough employees that each person's turn only came up once a year or so. Christine's justification for this practice wasn't particularly profound. "If you see everyone coming in every day, it helps you learn their names," she told Kate during her first stint of desk duty. "And we don't have to pay for a full-time receptionist."

"Hey, Steph," said Kate. Her voice echoed through mostly empty space, bounced back from the rafters 30 feet up. There wasn't much by way of furniture; the desk, the chair, a square of sectional sofas defining a little wall-less room in the vast interior. "Who's here?"

"Me," she said, sounding a little put out about the early hours those on receptionist duty were expected to keep. Her laptop was on the desk, in the spot where some long-ago Russian functionary had his papers laid out as he decided which anarchist dissidents should be exiled to Siberia and which should simply be executed. Next to it, she had set up a little frame with a picture of her husband and toddler daughter, but at the moment Steph was staring at a spreadsheet of vendors, trying to figure out how many could be fobbed off with excuses about money they were owed by the Agency, and for how long. "Josh. Felicia in HR. You, now. Oh, and your guy got here ten minutes ago."

"My guy?"

"The German guy. Mohan or whatever." Steph was not even looking up.

"Huh, kinda early."

"Maybe he's still jet-lagged."

Kate sighed. She had organized her schedule so that she could gradually increase the level of enthusiasm expected of her from the people she interacted with. She tried to get to the office by 8, an hour that did not match the temperament of most of the Agency's staff. Subconscious Agency was largely free of the chipper go-getters you'd find at other companies in their field (not that any other company was *quite* in their field). The warehouse offices were full of grad school drop-outs, restless anthropology majors, dabblers in neuroscience, people whose ideas were too weird for the Big Four consulting firms. Almost none of them liked getting up early. This gave Kate sixty to ninety crucial minutes to herself most mornings.

But not, apparently, today. Kate started to say something to Stephanie, but she already had a thousand-mile spreadsheet stare and was closed off to the world. Instead, she walked past the desk, heels tapping on the concrete floor, until she reached the far wall. There were three nondescript metal doors there, the middle unlabelled, and each of the other two bearing a neatly stenciled sign:

THOUGHT LEADER ALLIANCE   **ENTHUSIASM CHANNEL**

She pushed through the one on the right.

▥▥▥▥▥▥▥▥▥

Clients came with checkbook in hand expecting results, of course. They paid hoping that a thing would happen. But Christine was more interested in process. *What most people would call an outcome is really just the shape a process makes when it's completed,* Kate remembered Christine telling her during their very first conversation. For a moment, she had thought, *This woman is the boss? This woman is nuts.* But Christine kept talking and the more she talked the more Kate's heart filled with increasingly manic joy. She had been 23, and was working at the Agency as a temp after abruptly quitting her first post-collegiate job. SourceCater provided catering services to working lunches and lobbyist meet-and-greets and think-tank symposia around Washington. Its HR manager—Kate's boss—was a wild-eyed devotee of the Metricized Management Paradigm that was a registered trademark of Mendex Private Solutions, the sprawling services firm and defense contractor of which Source-Cater was a wholly owned tentacle. Kate's job as an assistant benefits manager had been to deny low-level SourceCater employees benefits to which they were entitled. "Of course, we say yes eventually," her boss told her. "But some people just won't ask a second time, and if someone doesn't ask for something twice, they don't really need it. That's how we beat our assigned metrics. HR *always* beats its assigned metrics."

Her old boss would not have taken the time to speak to a temp doing data-entry and low-level sentiment analysis, but Christine talked to her. Los Mundos Del Cielo, the second-most popular avatar-driven social virtual reality environment for teens in Latin America, had rolled out a major update and needed to know how much of the complaining on site forums was transient resistance to change and how much was genuine discontent. Kate had squeezed her ability to read Spanish onto the resume she filed with her temp staffing firm. That led her to a cube at the Agency, with the CEO explaining how the names of the columns she would choose for her Excel spreadsheet would help get them closer to their goal, which was making sure the kids in Buenos Aires who were too shy to talk much in school kept experiencing camaraderie and happiness online. "Think about using a color spectrum for one of the sentiment axes you come up with," Christine had said. "Do you ever wonder why the people writing software tools for accountants added in color options? That's an accident you don't let go of. Use it to shape the results."

Process wasn't something just clients experienced. It was something that shaped how Agents did their work for clients, visible in the outcome only to the trained eye. There were different kinds of process Agents would experience, but one kind started like Kate's did the day after the live-site with the trainspotters: with a manila folder lying on her desk that hadn't been there when she'd left the previous evening, and a Post-it note with *You'll want to make time for this today* in Christine's handwriting stuck to the front.

"You know about comic strips, yes, Kate?" Christine had said two days previously in the break room. She was musing to the handful of people who happened to be in there about a potential client, an insurance company that was considering bidding on a portfolio of intellectual properties at a corporate bankruptcy auction that included some once-beloved comic strip characters—a sassy cat that predated Garfield by decades, and a can't-win husband who always seemed on the verge of a murderous rampage.

Was this a trick question? "Like the ones in the newspaper? Yes, I ... I mean ... yes? I'm aware that they exist, yes."

"Did you know I'm turning 56 this year?" Christine asked. "Eventually you stop assuming that your cultural competencies match up with young people's." The other Agents there, Monika and Rene and Conor, were all Kate's age, or not much older, and they smiled a little awkwardly. Christine never wanted you to think for very long that she was referring to your failings or inadequacies. With a little conversational shift she'd move to self-deprecation, though you were left wondering.

Perhaps it had been a trick question. Kate opened the folder on her desk and saw comic panels and assumed, just for a second, that she'd be tasked with patiently explaining to insurance executives from Connecticut who wanted to whimsy up their brand why jokes about domestic violence might've been very popular in the 1950s but probably wouldn't help sell term life policies today. But this too was a trick: Kate had steeled herself for an unpleasant task before the drawings in front of her bloomed and unfolded into ... something else. There were no household pets thought-ballooning wryly or adorable toddlers who tried and failed to speak idiomatic English. The drawings were something out of the ideas book of a fashion designer in the mid-'60s, or at least what Kate imagined such a thing would look like. *You could have such a clear image in your mind of a thing that you had never seen and that might not exist,* she thought, *and here it was, right in front of her.* At the top of the page, written in meticulously hand-drafted script:

LADIES WHO LUNCH

This was one of the ways the process of preparing for an assignment could start at the Agency: document bait. It worked best on the curious, the self-taught, which is why most of the people hired at the Agency were curious and self-taught.

"It's a soap opera strip. A *continuity* strip is what they call it in the industry," she told Mesut. By the time he came by Kate's cube, she had drilled way past the first page of Google results for *Ladies Who Lunch,* and was deep into the primary source documents that the strip's surprisingly detailed Wikipedia page drew from. Mesut, who had come by to show her the chatter about the live-site on the railfan forums, smiled nervously as Kate talked more and more quickly.

"There were translation rights, too," she said. "Very popular in France."

"Ah," he replied. "France."

"I mean, don't you think it's *beautiful?*" Kate said to Monika about forty-five minutes later. Monika was short, white, and blonde, with tattoo sleeves and thick glasses. She was one of the top culture people in the Enthusiasm Channel, usually tasked with driving the buzz groundswell that would land some hip but still easy-to-listen-to new band the car commercial that would subsidize their next two money-losing albums. She was extremely cool, professionally, and thus often made Kate feel vaguely stupid. But Kate was in too deep

at the moment to hold back, not that she didn't appreciate it when Monika agreed, and enthusiastically, leaning over Kate's shoulder as she scrolled through images culled from the newspaper archives that Google had mass-scanned in the '00s.

Three women, three faces, cycled through on the monitor, over and over: a blonde with variously elaborate hairstyles and predatory facial expressions; an ever-smiling brunette, whose outfits were simple and tasteful but not, to the extent that one could make this judgment about a drawing, cheap; and a redhead with a bob who seemed so committed to tomboyish pursuits—hiking up a mountainside, riding a horse in Western gear—that her occasional appearances in slinky cocktail dresses were all the more striking.

"Those boots are fucking rad," said Monika.

"Which?"

"I mean, all of them."

Then: an actual photograph of a woman who looked a lot like the strip's redhead, with a dash of the blonde's calculation. "This is Marie Redmond," Kate said to LaMont, later that morning. "25 years old in 1964." LaMont was short, African-American, and stubbly, with a round face that made him look vaguely like he was smiling even when he was a little irritated, which he was at the moment.

"Are you going to listen to me about my—"

"Not till lunch. I promise at lunch."

LaMont sighed and rolled his eyes. "Fine. 25 years old."

Marie Redmond was married to Ted Redmond, a psychiatrist who, under the pen name Hollis Houston, had created and written *Health of a Nation* and *I Object!*, wildly popular continuity strips about a heroic doctor and a crusading lawyer, respectively. Monarch, the syndicate that distributed these strips to newspapers, asked him for a "woman's feature"; Redmond, already overstretched and considering the gig beneath him, had fobbed the job off on his wife, who he had begun to worry was getting bored, alone all day in the big modernist house they shared in the Chicago suburbs.

"This guy, Stan Gieselman. He was a friend of Marie's from college." LaMont, Mesut, and Monika were all standing around her cube now. Other people were prairie-dogging over their cube walls to see what was happening. People always wanted to see enthusiasm start to catch fire at the start of the assignment, even if it wasn't their assignment. They were hounds who had caught a scent. "He'd already had a couple of jobs doing sketches for couture houses and *Vogue*. Monarch had grabbed artists from the superhero books for the other Redmond strips, but Marie convinced them to bring in Stan. Or, well, she convinced her husband, who convinced Monarch."

Marie Redmond, or some version of her, was starting to come into focus in Kate's mind: 25, younger than Kate was now, married to a successful, older professional, living in a clean house with floor-to-ceiling windows, not an apartment building with walls that rung hollow when you knocked on them, clothes neatly hanging in the closet rather than lying in piles on the floor, and glamorous grown-up clothes at that. But also: spending all day in that house, husband at the office, liquor readily available, surely. Always afraid to seem too melancholy because your husband is a psychiatrist and he might have plans. He comes home and complains, in that laughing, half-proud way that the successful complain, that Monarch wants *another* strip, can you believe it, they think I've got the golden touch, I guess. Something that would appeal to women, the money's right but when would I have time to spend it? And a woman's strip, I don't know. They wanted the lawyer in *I Object!* to be young and single and handsome, but I think they're getting at something else with this. Do you know what they're getting at?

Ladies Who Lunch went out under the Hollis Houston name. It was Ted's photos that appeared in the press materials that accompanied the strip's launch, scanned versions of which Kate found in an obscure directory on Monarch's website, not linked to but somehow found by Google in its remorseless webcrawling. This was a PR blitz like you'd get at the launch of an HBO prestige drama; there were newspaper interviews, magazine articles. Ted had insisted on a pseudonym for his comics gig—to protect his academic career, he said—but he apparently thought that nobody would recognize him in the pictures. He wore glasses, horn-rimmed frames with no lenses. "Like Clark Kent!" he probably thought, and probably thought that was funny.

Still, *Ladies Who Lunch* was really Marie and Stan from the start. In an interview with a comics archivist in the early '80s that Kate found later, Marie had claimed that the title came from something her husband had said when she was planning to meet up with some other wives in the neighborhood. "I didn't even like them," she said, "They were older than me and they didn't read books. But Ted was so keen on my having some sort of gang to pal around with. And then when he left for work that morning, he said, 'Have fun with the ladies who lunch!' Which is exactly what I had been calling them, but I didn't like it coming out of his mouth. I thought, fuck him, what's wrong with ladies having lunch? It's the only time they let us out of the house."

There were three ladies in *Ladies Who Lunch,* all perpetually but fuzzily between 27 and 35, all chums from an unnamed East Coast women's college they had attended for very different reasons. Carol, the brunette, had gone to get her Mrs. degree and had succeeded. She was married to a doting, bearish up-and-coming business executive; all her material needs were met, and she kept trying to fill her time with projects and volunteer work, but nothing ever seemed to hold her interest. Eve, the redhead, had studied architecture, then shocked her friends by getting a job as an architect. Marie had originally written Eve as having married young and then divorced a year later, but Monarch thought this was too scandalous ("Ted could've made it stick if he pushed, but he didn't believe in divorce," she complained). So Eve became instead the widow of a dashing young officer who had been killed in Vietnam. This allowed her to occasionally date but then discover anew her emotional unavailability, which prevented any strip-disrupting developments.

Then there was Maureen, the beautiful blonde heiress. Maureen's wealthy industrialist father had sent her to college in another state because he was terrified of her, and because he hoped she might meet a young man at the Ivy League school up the road who could tame her or at least take her off his hands. Instead, she broke a series of fraternity boys' hearts, and when she found out her two best friends were moving to Chicago after graduation, she insisted that her father send her there, too, with the vague promise that she would "look after" his Midwestern business interests. Maureen alternately terrorized and ignored the bewildered businessmen at the Chicago office, tried to steal away the husbands of every society girl she deemed too mousy to deserve domestic happiness, and cooked up self-aggrandizing and wildly unrealistic business schemes funded by her generous allowance. Everyone—the characters in the strip and the people who read it—was crazy about her.

Ladies Who Lunch was, by the admittedly forgiving standards of newspaper continuity comic strips, a quick hit. Maybe "sensation" was a better word. *Ladies Who Lunch* left marks everywhere. It was a *thing*. The strips were collected into digest-sized anthologies sold in supermarket checkout lines (battered copies of which were available on eBay). *Cosmopolitan* did a feature that included a quiz to determine if you were a Carol, an Eve, or a Maureen. ("I'm definitely a Maureen," said Monika. Kate hoped she was an Eve but worried she might be a Carol.) *Vogue* did a spread on the casual yet impossibly classy outfits the ladies wore. *Ladies' Home Journal* did a more practical take on the clothes, explaining how you could, say, chase a wayward puppy across the park, or sneak out through a villain's basement window, or ride in a handsome aviator's open-cockpit stunt plane, all without wrinkling your blouse or mussing your hair beyond what most people would find adorable.

There was even a movie, released in 1967 at the peak of the strip's popularity, put together quickly but with big names nonetheless: Shirley MacLaine as Eve, Natz alie Wood as Carol, and Tuesday Weld as Maureen. It bombed, and the studio hadn't bothered to release it to DVD, but there must have been a VHS version at some point, because some true obsessive had uploaded a few grainy clips to YouTube. The film's most painful irony was immediately obvious: the costume budget had been sacrificed, perhaps in the name of paying the stars' salaries, or perhaps because nobody understood how important the clothes were to the look of the strip. But there was something off about the performances, too. Carol should've been sensible and straightforward, but Wood played her like a simpering dope. If Eve in the comic had announced at lunch that the three girls would be spending the afternoon at the racetrack, it would be because she had some plan up her sleeve, not because she was flighty and impulsive.

And Maureen: "Ugh," said Mesut, wincing when Weld opened her mouth and aimed for the kind of clench-jawed boarding school mid-Atlantic accent that was already going out of vogue when the movie was made. "Maureen does not talk like that. Maureen hates the people who talk like that."

Kate, LaMont, and Monika looked at him, surprised.

"This is not obvious?" said Mesut. "We just read a comic strip where she said she hates people who talk like that. It was only five minutes ago."

The trove of promo material for the strip's launch also included material for the film's rollout. Hollis Houston was still billed alone as the strip's creator; his name appeared before the trio of studio hacks who had actually written the script, and in a much larger typeface. But on the promotional tour, "Hollis" was now accompanied by his wife "Ruth." Ruth, the studio let on, had been an invaluable help to her husband, offering the "woman's perspective" necessary to making the characters come alive on the page—and, the studio promised, on the screen.

In the photos that accompanied these thinly rewritten press releases, Ruth/Marie had her own presumably prop glasses to wear. Sometimes she had on a pair of Browlines that reminded Kate of Flannery O'Connor, impossibly square juxtaposed with her simple, chic haircut. Sometimes she wore Wayfarer sunglasses, even though the pictures all seem to have been taken indoors.

She never smiled in the pictures.

The movie flopped but the strip continued. The newspaper industry was making tons of money, and so was its remora, the syndicated comics business. A strip, once it had become a permanent part of a newspaper's landscape, was impossible to dislodge without prompting an irritating letter-writing campaign, so papers just kept sending Monarch checks.

Ladies Who Lunch did try to keep up with the times. In 1970, Carol took a group of prankster hippies under her wing, much to her husband's horror. The kids wore polka-dotted shirts and huge, droopy bow-ties, and looked more like London mods than scruffy American college students—*it would've killed Stan Gieselman to draw jeans with holes in the knees,* Kate thought. Carol's success in channeling the hippies' political activism to save the local park made Kate cringe, but it was a kinder treatment than the counterculture was getting in the other Hollis Houston strips, where square-jawed doctors and lawyers gruffly explained the social dangers of unchecked facial hair. There was even a subtle implication that Maureen had helped the kids score some pot; the syndicate editors apparently didn't catch this, but the writers of several angry letters to the editor certainly did.

A new plot in 1972 might have raised even more controversy: Eve, suddenly remembering her dead husband, who hadn't been mentioned in the strip for years, joined an anti-Vietnam War march on the Pentagon. But by the time that ran in newspapers, there was only room for one story in the "drama involving a continuity comic strip" space and that was Ted and Marie Redmond's ugly divorce. Film excerpts from the impromptu press conference Marie's lawyer gave on the steps of the Cook County courthouse had made the CBS News, and, improbably, had been uploaded to Dailymotion. Mr. Redmond could keep the car, he declared, along with the stock portfolio and that damn pretentious house; Mrs. Redmond just wanted what was rightfully hers, which was the share of the marital assets deriving from the highly popular and lucrative *Ladies Who Lunch,* along with complete ownership of the strip and rights to future revenues pertaining thereto.

In court (*God bless whatever grant had digitized 100 years of Cook County legal records,* Kate thought) Marie's lawyer argued that "Hollis Houston" had ceased to be Ted's pseudonym and became marital property from the moment that Ted deferred day-to-day creative control of *Ladies Who Lunch* to his wife. Ted's lawyer brandished the contracts with Monarch, which, no matter what name appeared on the comics page, identified Ted Redmond as the strip's creator, named Stan Gieselman as the contractor hired to do the art, and mentioned Marie Redmond not at all. Marie's side countered with her meticulously kept diaries and correspondence, demonstrating that she had developed all of the strip's storylines and, once the strip had been launched, communicated with Monarch without her husband acting as an intermediary.

The revelation that did the most to affect the outcome of the case, and yet was relevant not at all to the ownership of the strip, was this: Marie and Stan had been having an affair almost since the strip was launched. Stan had been called as a witness to corroborate Marie's claim that she was the sole writer of the strip; Ted's lawyer picked up on an off-hand comment Stan made during cross-examination and hammered him relentlessly until he admitted the relationship. He had intended to embarrass Marie with his on-the-fly legal detective work, but the revelation turned out to be more humiliating to his own client than to anyone else. ("Never suspected it," Ted said in an interview later. "I always thought that guy was ... funny, you know?") To prevent still more dirty laundry from being aired, the Redmonds agreed to a deal that nobody liked: Ted and Marie would sell *Ladies Who Lunch* to the syndicate and split the (not insubstantial) profits. The strip would still run under the "Hollis Houston" name, but Monarch would hire new writers and artists. The last strip written by Marie and drawn by Stan was published on January 4, 1973. Eve had been jailed for chaining herself to the White House fence, and Carol was paying her bail. "I didn't think you had it in you," said Maureen.

"This is all very interesting," said Mesut, after some thought. "Though I do not see how it will result in more trains being sold. I realize your agency is unorthodox, but..."

"It was a mystery folder, right?" said Monika.

"Yeah," said Kate. "This morning."

"It's her new assignment," Monika told Mesut. "These things just appear, from heaven." She gestured meaningfully in the direction of Christine's office.

"So you are trying to sell ... comics? To somebody?"

"Oh, she doesn't *know* yet, that's half the fun," said LaMont. "She's supposed to get excited about the thing before she knows exactly what she's being paid to do about the thing. Otherwise it distorts her enthusiasm into, you know, *commerce*."

"What you all do here ... it's very non-linear," said Mesut. He sounded respectful, but wary.

"That's what *they* do," said LaMont, taking in Kate and Monika with a sweep of his hands. "What *I* do is..." His eyes suddenly twinkled. "Mesut, do you want to go to lunch?"

"Hey!" said Kate. "You're going to lunch with *me*."

"Will there be curled french fries?" said Mesut.

"There can be anything you want, son. You're about to become my secret weapon."

3

"You know who was a great TL?" LaMont said as they slid into the booth. "Chuck Gindhart. Let me tell you, I miss Chuck Gindhart every damn day of my life."

This isn't good, Kate thought. *We haven't even ordered yet.* Whatever reason LaMont had for so aggressively inviting Mesut to lunch clearly involved the tale of Chuck, maybe for no other reason than that Mesut had never heard it, and Kate had heard it a *lot*.

Mesut, the chosen target, was oblivious. "Say," he said to her, "this is the same restaurant as the other restaurant, yes? The one near your apartment?"

Normally this would have been an opportunity for LaMont to make fun of Kate for eating at Pickles constantly. As it was, he plowed ahead, talking to Mesut and acting as if his question, with its obvious and hopelessly banal answer, had never been posed. "I'm so glad Chuck was my first big client, because at least I found out I could do well with a TL, and that the whole program wasn't just some of Christine's woo-woo. But I have to be honest; he totally spoiled me."

LaMont had been handling Chuck during Kate's first year at the agency, when she knew next to nothing about the Thought Leader Alliance. This ignorance was deliberately cultivated by Christine, who felt that Kate and her Enthusiasm Channel cohort should begin with no deeper understanding of the Thought Leaders than the general public had. "What's the point of being an insider," Christine would say, "if you don't begin on the outside?" Or, another time, at a meeting for new employees: "Knowledge should be offered up only in response to curiosity and discovery. There's nothing in your orientation binder really worth *knowing*," she said, and a few people sheepishly stopped looking at the paperwork. "HR is only here to help you on your financial journey. Your intellectual voyage must be self-directed."

Early in her time at the Agency, Kate and LaMont realized they were kindred spirits and started lingering together in the break room. But at first he was cagey about what exactly he and the other Agents in the Thought Leader Alliance program did. "I'm not *alloooowwed*," he drawled. "Christine'll kill me, and it'll ruin your fun. But just let me say one thing: Chuck Gindhart. That's all. Don't even Google it. Just keep that name in your head."

Her first Chuck sighting had come earlier that week, and she hadn't even known it. She was working on her first research assignment. This mostly consisted of playing *Lords of the Ashes*, a massively multiplayer online game in which characters fought for dominance in a post-nuclear hellscape. The task was definitely in line with Christine and the Agency's philosophy of radical self-guidance, in that she had very little idea what exactly she was doing or why she was doing it. She assumed that she had been given the job because she noted on her extensive Agency intake form that, for six months, she had been part of a *World of Warcraft* guild in college.

She had been embarrassed enough by the fact at the time that she had never mentioned it to any real-life friends, but when faced with so many spaces on the paperwork, she found the thought of leaving them blank even more embarrassing, and felt compelled to fill in as many of them as possible.

Kate thought *Lords of the Ashes*'s graphics were so-so and found the aesthetic almost completely derivative of the *Mad Max* movies, but the in-game economics caught her eye. Her gameplay hadn't been *entirely* without guidance: "Look for dynamics that generate value," Christine told her, "for any definition of 'value' you can think of. Camaraderie, joy in deep play, personal achievement, but also money, and things other people might pay money for." The *Lords of the Ashes* economy was based on gold coins minted by the various post-nuclear warlords; a cut scene at one point depicted the last few soldiers guarding Fort Knox being overwhelmed by chainsaw wielding mutants with pink mohawks riding motorcycles. What interested Kate was that players could spend coins not just in the game—for more gasoline, say, or for food that was only slightly radioactive—but for real, physical items that would be shipped by the post office to the non-virtual location of your gaming lair. At the moment, you could only buy T-shirts and bumper stickers put out by DeathHug Games, *Lords of the Ashes*'s creators, but the lucrative possibilities for this were clear. The question that piqued Kate's curiosity was not the obvious one of how DeathHug and its future corporate partners would make lots and lots of money off this system, but rather how people would play the game differently when there was real money at stake.

That was how she met Chuck Gindhart. In the midst of one of those long, semi-directed voyages of Internet clicking that occupied substantial portions of her days, she found herself on the Web site of a middle-tier news network, watching a video of a panel discussion about gaming. The very serious moderator looked to be around 65; he was dressed for the job he wanted (the elder statesman of a network news division), not the one he had (a guy on cable who had to stop angry people from strangling each other), and he handled his panel with a bitterness that led Kate to conclude that the segment had been originally broadcast either at noon or 2:30 in the morning.

The panel was stacked with about two-thirds anti-gaming crusaders with big hair and a third hardcore gamers with black jeans and *Duke Nukem* T-shirts. But one guest, a middle-aged white man whose shaggy haircut, bushy mustache, and rumpled green suit were barely in sync with each other and not at all with current fashion, sat back and listened to the escalating moral panic with a look of amusement.

Finally, he broke in. "I'm just really curious," he said, "if you've ever had a bunch of people in here talking about art, and they basically have to decide whether everything painted on a flat surface is either Rembrandt or terrible. You guys"—he gestured at the antis— "sound exactly like the people who fought against everything fun ever invented, back to dice and playing cards, probably, and you"— he rounded on the gamers, who were starting to look smug—"ought to admit to yourselves that improving the graphics for *Halo* isn't a 'bold new paradigm' or whatever."

Everyone looked at him in shock, including the moderator. He used the silence as an opportunity to talk about the games he loved, mostly sandbox games like the *The Sims* or world-building titles like *Civilization*. "It's all the parts of your brain that get activated by playing with model railroads and that sort of thing. It's good for you!" He rambled on enthusiastically for nearly a minute and a half, which was almost certainly some kind of cable panel fight record. It was mesmerizing, and Kate bookmarked the link, partly because he touched on virtual economics in his talk and partly because she liked it when the panelists stared at this strange guy, unsure whether he was even arguing with them.

So when LaMont told her not to Google Chuck Gindhart, she obviously did as soon as he walked away from her cube, and there was the link to that video, marked in purple, and she realized she knew who he was talking about. Watching it again, she focused on the chyron that came on-screen when the odd mustachioed man started talking:

CHUCK GINDHART
DIGITAL LEISURE EXPERT

"Oh, my God," said LaMont, "That was the best day! That was, like, our breakthrough. I told him, 'All these people are here to either push for new laws or sell video games. You're here to do nothing, and that gives you all the power. Something comes into your head, as long it's on topic and not a swear word, just say it.' He was so pleased at how it went, he took me out for milkshakes after."

After that, Kate saw Chuck Gindhart everywhere, always talking about something vaguely related to computers. He was quoted in *The Wall Street Journal* about managing twentysomething software developers: "Under no circumstances let them work from home. Human beings are generally their weak point, so they need to experience a public restroom once in a while to remind them that the code they're writing is for people." In the wake of a major hacking scandal at the Department of Defense, he did a stand-up with CNN, and when Wolf Blitzer asked him how companies could protect themselves from similar attacks, he said, "Wolf, nobody watching this show right now works for the Pentagon. They shouldn't be worried about some kind of superspy from *The Matrix*, they should be worried about some guy who walks into their office in a UPS uniform and leaves with a laptop." He went on *The View* to talk to the ladies about back problems caused by spending too much time in front of a keyboard. "Have you thought about standing up and walking around once in a while? Try standing up and walking around. Maybe go outside if it's sunny."

"Barbara Walters loved him," LaMont said in the break room as they watched. "She wanted to eat him up."

"I don't get it," said Kate. "Why is he on all these shows?"

LaMont flipped from channel to channel on the break room TV, going through the afternoon mix of talk shows and cable news shouters. "Do you see all this? They need people, they need real people who will talk to them about whatever bullshit they've decided the folks at home want to watch. Only look at the people they get!"

Click. A retired general stood stiffly in front of a map on MSNBC. "Blinking too much," said LaMont. "Knows what he's saying isn't true."

Click. A tiny brunette was mixing cake batter in a studio kitchen next to a neatly stacked pyramid of cookbooks with her picture on the cover. "Look at that smile. It's being held in place with drywall screws. I don't know where she wants to be, but it sure as shit isn't there."

Click. Back to *The View*. Chuck and Whoopi were laughing about something; he reached out and touched her hand in mid-sentence, and she brushed it away flirtatiously. "Now, look at this. He could come back once a week for the rest of the year if he wants."

"But..." Kate started again. "Who's *paying* us? What's the job?"

"Huh? Oh, Chuck's paying us. He's some kind of high-level tech ... consultant ... thing, I dunno. Every time some executive with a contractor budget sees this happy guy saying halfway sensible things about computers on television, they might call him to solve whatever dumb problem they don't want to think about. Happens often enough that he keeps us on retainer. Though I'm done coaching him at this point." LaMont shook his head as Chuck positioned Elizabeth Hasselbeck in an ergonomic chair. "Look at that magnificent bastard. He can barely match his clothes. It just makes them love him more."

Now, three years later, Kate idly swirled a mozzarella stick in marinara sauce while she listened to all of this rehashed for Mesut's benefit. LaMont even had his phone out and was showing Mesut the video of Chuck talking about video games, which was probably his finest hour. Mesut seemed mildly intrigued, an attitude that he had adopted for as long as he had been in the U.S. Kate wondered when it would wear off.

"This is all very interesting," said Mesut. "But so ... now you do not work with Chuck anymore?"

"Now," said LaMont, "I work with your boss."

Mesut looked alarmed. "My boss?"

"Yes."

"My boss Sigmar?"

"Yes."

"You want to put my boss Sigmar ... on television?"

"That's the plan."

"Why would you do this? You should not do this."

LaMont slid his thumb across the surface of his phone a few times and came up with a new video. A sandy-haired man in his fifties was on the screen, still handsome if starting to sag a bit around the jowls. He looked like someone who had just seen his whole family shot. "Trains," he said, "are ... an important part ... of transportation."

LaMont switched off the phone.

"What he says is ... true, at least," said Mesut. "Why are you doing this to him?"

"Your company is paying us to do it."

"Have you seen how small my hotel room is? I doubt this very much."

"Look, you have to help me," said LaMont. "The whole point is that we find out what the Thought Leaders like, and then we find them an audience that wants to hear about it. But he doesn't ... like ... anything." He growled that last sentence through gritted teeth. "He says he likes things, he's given us a whole list of things that he says he likes, but then he talks about them like he's in a hostage video. I think the thing he likes best is for us to stop asking him what he likes. I can't work with that! What do you think I should do? What's his deal?"

Mesut thought for a moment. "Sigmar is a very nice man. And a good boss."

"Give me something I can use," LaMont said.

"Sigmar is a very nice man," said Mesut. "And I think you maybe are fucked."

4

"Christine wants to see you," Stephanie said as the three of them walked back into the Agency's lobby. "Not you," she said to LaMont when she saw his eyes widen with panic. "Kate."

"Oh, thank God," said LaMont. "I have literally no idea what I'm going to say to her about Sigmar."

"You should tell her that doing this to Sigmar will be … will be … *mean*. And also will not work. And she should give Siemens their money back," said Mesut.

"OK, *usually* we don't give clients' money back when we've already done work for them."

The Agency did give refunds, Kate knew, but only early in assignments, and only with an elaborate exit interview that was secretly a sales pitch for another custom-designed program that better fit the client's needs. "Your misgivings are completely understandable," Christine had once said to a group of bros who were starting to go bald and were convinced that their undrinkable energy beverage was the natural fuel for fraternity mixers everywhere. "Corporate media appearances aren't going to give you productive opportunities to get your message out about PartySweat. I'm sorry we've wasted your time with this. We'll get your deposit back to you, of course.

"Thinking about it now," she'd said, looking over at Kate, who hadn't been sure why she was in a meeting with Thought Leader Alliance clients, "what seems obvious is that this should've been about the grassroots from the beginning. You mentioned that you planned to franchise sales out to the college kids who you're also targeting as consumers?" And that was how Kate began three months on multilevel marketing message boards, chatting up aspirational entrepreneurs (a phrase she made up and was very proud of) who everyone else was turning away as too young. A year later, the original investors had been able to cash out after selling the brand to a Belgian beverage conglomerate, beating by ninety days the report on PartySweat's dangerous interaction with vodka and the subsequent recalls.

But once you go on TV, you're committed to the program you've paid for, and Sigmar had already been on TV. *Christine must have some plan for this,* Kate thought. *Is it a meta-sincerity play? Maybe he's so unpolished he's persuasive?* But she had seen the video; he was way past meta-sincere, and meta-awkward wasn't a thing.

"Please," LaMont said to Mesut, "Just come with me and help me brainstorm Sigmar ideas. For, like, fifteen minutes. Ten minutes. *Please.*"

"No, I do not think so," said Mesut. He wasn't making eye contact now. "I'm sorry, I just feel it is wrong." He started to walk off, then paused and turned back. "Thank you for taking me to your lunch. I do not mean to be upsetting. If something comes into my head I will let you know."

He walked a few more steps, and then turned around again. "I do not think it will, though." Then he pushed through the ENTHUSIASM CHANNEL door.

"Well, I tried," said LaMont, his desperation evaporating. "Oh, God, I talked about me and Sigmar the *entire* time, I am so sorry. How are you? How'd it go yesterday? Was The_Real_Jack as crazy as you thought?"

Kate laughed. "He was fine. I mean, yes, but he was fine. It's not a crime to care a lot, you know?"

"Just don't make him mad. I don't want you to end up, like, turned into a mannequin in his basement, with model train tracks winding around your feet."

"He's harmless. He liked the train. They all did. The train was awesome, actually. Mesut got a kick out of watching them watch it."

"Well, I hope he didn't blow your cover. We do not need another one of these Germans ruining our lives." He held up a hand. "Sorry, I'll shut up. Do you think Christine wants to talk to you about the girls? Sorry, the *ladies*. In the comics."

Kate sighed. "I guess? Or maybe the live-site, I don't know. I sent her my report on that."

"It's the first live-site that you ran! You know Christine wants to *process*."

Kate made a face. "I don't have time to process anything. I have to go make sure all the trainspotters are posting convincingly enthusiastic things on DCRailTalk. Serious business."

"Pfft. Come find me after work, and we'll go get a drink. Nelson's working late, and I don't want to go back to Hyattsville by myself and watch TV. Don't bring the German. I won't talk about me, promise."

"OK. You can talk about you a little, but only when I'm done talking about me."

"Deal. Don't keep her waiting!" LaMont vanished past the THOUGHT LEADER ALLIANCE sign, leaving Kate by herself to walk through the third, unmarked door, the one that led to Christine's aerie.

卌卌卌卌卌卌

Kate got to Christine's fourth-floor office and found it open to the sky and bathed in sunlight. When the Agency had been founded, the roof in this section of the uppermost level had been missing altogether, a victim of the building's last dodgy days as a warehouse when—depending on who you asked—either industrial chemicals or actual dynamite was stored in an improperly ventilated room, with predictably violent results. Christine had this damage repaired and installed a jerry-rigged system that would open a motorized hatch that took up about a quarter of the curving ceiling of her office. When the ceiling was closed, the room was windowless and felt a little snug; when it was open, you were practically working outside, and could clamber up a tiny set of stairs to step out onto the edge of the roof. This surely violated any number of OSHA workplace regulations, though not as badly as having barrels of explosive chemical solvents around would have.

"I'm coming down," Christine shouted. Her office was meticulously tidy—half-filled bookshelves, a desk with a very large monitor on it and nothing else, some couches arranged so a mid-sized group could sit and talk, and that was it. "I can't have any messy piles of papers," Christine had told Kate at their first meeting in the office, "because they'd blow away when the roof's open. That wasn't *why* I built a retractable roof, but I enjoy serendipitous opportunities for systemic improvement."

The view that most people would've found interesting, of the Capitol and other monuments of the Federal City, was on the other side of the building. Through the gap in the roof that Christine emerged from, stepping down the stairs, Kate could see the south-eastern fringes of the city and the dense, twisty sprawl of Prince George's County.

"Good, good, good, you're here," Christine said. She was tall, white, thin-faced, her hair chin-length and blonde fading into silver. She pressed a button at the bottom of the stairs and the roof rumbled shut. "Everyone said you had a positive and upbeat demeanor this morning, which means, I'm guessing, two things: the Siemens live-site went *great,* and the new assignment's got your interest. What's occupying more of your mindspace at the moment?"

This was not an atypical way for Christine to start: she asks to see you, and then asks what you want to talk about. Kate felt like she had a handle on her next moves with the trainspotters, and worried that if she asked for advice, it might be so oblique as to be indecipherable: "This public meeting you're planning to attend with them ... can you be present, without being *present?*" Or, worse, the advice might be understandable but uncomfortable: "The self you offer your new friends can be your *real* self without being your *whole* self. And they are your new friends! But not *whole* friends with your whole heart. So help them with the part of you that loves them." *It's not fair to have to slice up your affections for a paycheck* (she, objected, silently), but her mental picture of Christine laughed and said, "You do live in the world, don't you? If you do something every day anyway, why not do it for the Agency?"

Kate shut down mental-Christine, then shut down the next intrusive thought process that it had spawned, which was that she spent too much time talking to Christine in her head. None of it was going anywhere promising.

"Let's talk about *Ladies Who Lunch*," Kate said.

"I thought you might go there," Christine said. She was trying to pull down a battered projector screen from its hiding place in the ceiling. "They stick with you, don't they?" Christine moved through the world gracefully, efficiently, with no wasted movement, and Kate was queasily fascinated by the minimal awkwardness of her momentarily struggle. Her feet didn't wobble on her chunky heels, and her ivory skirt didn't ride up past the limits of decency as she squatted and then stood up and then bent again. The office was still a little muggy from the outside air, but she didn't sweat. Her skin looked great. Kate took mental notes, as if watching it happen were the same as learning how it was done.

"It might not be obvious," she said, the screen's rattling mechanism finally catching on the fourth try. "But I think there will be some useful reinforcements as you work on this assignment and Siemens in parallel." Christine looked at Kate as she walked back. "Non-congruent but moderately overlapping headspace territories. Work on one when you're hitting a wall with the other. I promise: new possibilities will start to unfold in your midbrain, waiting for you to come back to them."

"More online community work?"

Christine's eyebrow went up. "Did you already find..." Kate's ears grew hot: she hadn't already found. "Ah. Well, how far did you get?"

"1972. The divorce, the trial."

"You're very interested in background. Authenticity. I like that. It's crucial for this. But there's a long afterlife that's crucial for our current purposes."

Christine was slowly pulling down a rusty metal lever that stuck out between two bookshelves; this turned out to be connected to the ancient-looking light bulb dangling from the ceiling, which dimmed to candlelight strength. Next to the dimmer was a projector, and she flipped a switch on the side of it, illuminating the screen across the room with an empty square of light. Kate thought she was meant to contemplate the meaning of its blankness, but Christine muttered, "Oh, poop, that's not supposed to happen," and walked back to her desk. "Sorry, I know it's vain, but I like a little showmanship." Her computer's monitor was pointed away from Kate, and Christine's irritated expression was illuminated by its soft glow.

After a moment, the faces Kate had been looking at all morning popped up: Maureen, Carol, Eve. Christine swiped through them rapidly, until they shifted, melted into something not quite themselves. Maureen looked less hungry, Eve less mischievous, Carol a little dumber.

"You know the strip still exists, of course," said Christine. "It's still in newspapers."

"Sure. When you Google it, today's comic is the first thing that comes up. It looks ... not so good."

"Well, this is how we arrived there."

For most of the '70s, the strip's artist was a devotee of the original style, though clearly he couldn't match Gieselman's skill. Or she couldn't? Or they? Tracking down the names of the artists that Monarch hired to toil on the strip turned out to be remarkably difficult—it had occupied several days of some Agency intern's work. Clues showed up in LinkedIn profiles: the resumes of various commercial illustrators and graphic designers boasted of spending a couple of years drawing the strip, adding flavor to otherwise unbroken professional careers of designing corporate logos and trade-show banners. At least two major comic book artists, people who worked on prestigious projects that were published in hard-backs filed under "graphic novels," spoke fondly in interviews of the time they spent in their early 20s drawing *Ladies Who Lunch*. "The strip, the memory of it, still has juice," said Kate, as they watched a clip of a balding, goateed man in a too-tight Green Lantern T-shirt laughingly describe how he had cut dozens of pages out of *Harper's Bazaar* and hung them around his studio after Monarch hired him. "In the industry, anyway. However you want to define the industry. It's a weird gig for them, but it's, like, proud-weird."

"Mmm-hmm?" Christine said. Kate couldn't decide whether this meant *That's a detail I hadn't noticed* or *I'm glad you're finally picking up on that*. She hoped it was the former and was a little embarrassed about that hope.

"Of course," Kate added, "it's a small industry. In-group nostalgia isn't going to be anywhere near enough to support a broad-based sell." She paused, and then ventured: "Like a theatrical release?" *Why not,* she thought. Why else would someone be paying the Agency to think about a 50-year-old comic strip? Sure, *Ladies Who Lunch: The Motion Picture* had flopped in 1967. 1967 was a different planet.

"Mmm-*hmm*," said Christine. "But as a seed?"

Kate shook her head. "You'd need another angle."

"What if you could use the seed as a pattern for the sell? Don't depend on the in-group, but make the consumer feel what the in-group feels."

"You embed the seed pattern in the marketing?"

"You embed the seed pattern in the *content*."

Kate was briefly taken aback. "So they haven't started making this movie."

Christine laughed. "Oh, Kate, you're too smart. I wanted to keep product specifics out of your headspace for a while longer, but I need to be cleverer around you. No, they haven't started making the movie yet. But hold that thought."

The slideshow of *Ladies Who Lunch* panels had blown through the Reagan years and arrived in the 1990s. The ladies' faces and wardrobes wobbled and waxed and waned as artists and fashions changed, but Kate could see a consistent direction: every year the characters' faces took up more and more of the panels, and as the focus got tighter and tighter, there was less room to dedicate to their fabulous clothes and quirky decor. Eventually, all you were left with most days was the hint of a funky collar that implied something interesting going on with the unseen remainder of the jacket, and the sketchy implication of an abstract impressionist painting hanging in somebody's apartment. Even though the faces took up more of the panel, they weren't any more detailed, and you were left looking at unsettlingly vast and undifferentiated expanses of forehead and cheek.

"The panels were getting smaller," said Christine. "We're looking at each one on the same scale here, but that's not true to context." A slide on the screen showed two comics pages from the *Washington Post* side by side, one from 1972 and one from 2001. The juxtaposition was shocking. The physical page had shrunk, and there were more comics crammed in around more advertising space. The strips were half the height they had been three decades earlier. "You can't put in a wealth of detail in the newspaper anymore. It requires a shift in the visual language. You always need faces to make the action legible, so the panel becomes all face. And lettering needs to be bigger too, so there's less dialogue, and it takes up more room."

"What about online?"

"What *about* it?"

Kate had hit a conversational milestone on Christine's schedule rather than running off ahead. It made her feel claustrophobic. "Don't they have ... online comics sections now? I mean, who reads newspapers on paper anymore?"

"Old people," said Christine, then quickly pivoted: "Old*er* people. But print is where the money is. Newspapers pay to physically print comics, and pay decently. Then they pay next to nothing to run them on their websites. So they have to tailor for print. Monarch has a site where you can pay to see all their strips online, with really huge images, but not many people do it. You're just getting a blown up version of a strip designed to be an inch and half tall on easily smudgeable newsprint."

"They're in color," Kate suddenly realized. "These newer strips you're showing me. Every day is in color, not just the Sunday ones."

Christine flicked a few strips forward to settle on a panel in which Eve and Maureen were arguing about whether Maureen had designs on Eve's new boyfriend. "It's too bad you wore a red scarf today," Eve said, "You're going to look like Christmas when you go green with envy." Maureen's scarf was quite obviously orange.

"Yes, the strips are in color when they put them online. I think they outsource the process. Maybe to people who don't speak English. It causes problems." She jumped a few slides and paused on a drawing of a clean-cut, dark-haired young man who was getting perhaps a bit too friendly with Carol and appeared to be wearing a vest. "Do you recognize him?"

"Do I recognize ... this drawing of a person in a comic strip?"

Christine silently flicked back to a strip in which Maureen showed up at a charity ball with a mysterious new beau on her arm. The gentleman was sandy-haired and dressed in a tuxedo with an unsettlingly large bow tie, but ... "Wait, is this supposed to be the same character?" He had the same pointed chin, the same broad smile, the same slightly fleshy nose.

"No. And neither is this." Now Carol's husband, bearded and avuncular, was awkwardly making conversation at a cocktail party with one of Eve's love interests from a storyline in the mid-'00s. He was a student at the Art Institute of Chicago, so naturally he was wearing a striped sweater and a beret and sporting a rebellious tuft of hair below his lower lip, but otherwise he was pretty much the same guy. "The current artist for the strip seems to have a, let's say, limited palette when it comes to drawing men. You have the big, bearded model, you have the stooped old man, and then, if he's between 20 and 50 and supposed to be good-looking, you have this fellow. But, what I want to know is, do you *recognize* him."

The comic panels were replaced with a photograph of a handsome man with a pointed chin and a broad smile, and Kate very much did recognize him. She'd watched him in movies and on television since she was in high school.

"Mitch Landers? All the dudes in *Ladies Who Lunch* are secretly Mitch Landers?"

Christine was now flipping through highlights of Mitch Landers's comedy career: Mitch in a shaggy wig in a '70s cop show spoof, Mitch playing opposite Kate Winslet in a dry, Oscar-nominated British comedy, Mitch getting punched in the balls by a seven-year-old in a Funny Or Die video that got over a million views.

"I don't think the relationship is *linear* in that way," Christine said. "That is, I don't think these male figures are meant to be directly modeled on Mitch. For one thing, Rex Bargeman, the current artist, has been on the job since 2004, which was before Mitch was quite so omnipresent. And his male template was pretty much set even then. Plus, if you look at the character and background designs, I don't think ... well, it doesn't seem like he spends a lot of time consuming contemporary media."

Rex Bargeman has never seen the inside of a house that's been redecorated after 1975 is how Kate would've put it, but she decided to follow Christine's lead on not making explicit out-of-touch old-person jokes about someone that she might be working with.

"But I admit the resonance is uncanny, uncanny enough to have drawn a certain amount of attention from the media-savvy," Christine continued. "You've done assignment legwork in MovieSpace communities before, right?" Kate had, and had spent way too much time tracking down its fascinating and largely forgotten history. The site had been started in 2000 by a largely unsupervised division within the newly merged AOL TimeWarner. The idea was that it would provide space for user-generated content about current and upcoming Warner Bros. films that could be surfaced into professionally directed marketing campaigns. It was completely ahead of its time.

It was also run by four overworked people who were counting down the days until their stock options vested. Traffic to the message and image boards quickly overwhelmed MovieSpace's ability to monitor them, and the site degenerated rapidly into communities that mocked terrible movies in particular and the entertainment industry in general. One of the most popular boards, Winners and Losers, was dedicated to tallying each week's most and least profitable films; users would Photoshop the faces of the producers, directors, and stars into scenes of Depression-era hobo jungles (for flops) or '70s cocaine orgies (for successes). The images inevitably got emailed around Hollywood and eventually filtered up to Warners executives who went predictably ballistic. By then, the site was too popular to shut down. In 2003, after multiple rounds of screaming fights between old- and new-media executives, it was sold at a dot-com-crash fire sale price to a Russian oligarch with an odd sense of humor. He stuck the site under the corporate umbrella of BerezhneCo, his oil refining and aluminum smelting conglomerate, and hadn't done much with it since, other than add increasingly intrusive banner ads for increasingly dodgy advertisers.

"Yeah, I've spent some time on the MovieSpace boards. They can be a little rough."

"Hostility—"

"—is inverted enthusiasm. Right. Nobody ever posted a full-length script for a porn parody of *Interstellar* to MovieSpace because they didn't *care* about *Interstellar*."

Christine looked up from her computer. "What did they..."

"*Dick Her Stellar.* They called it *Dick Her Stellar.* So, does someone on MovieSpace know something about an upcoming project, or...?" Enough industry people lurked and occasionally posted on MovieSpace that site denizens often got wind of new films before anybody else, which meant that some movies had their porn parody scripts completed before their screenplays were green-lit.

"Not exactly." Christine minimized PowerPoint on her desktop and projected a browser window on the screen. It was pointed to a MovieSpace discussion zone whose title banner proclaimed it to be "LaWLChat: The World's Greatest Bitchfest For Ladies Who Lunch, The World's Greatest Comic Strip."

"Hello," said Kate.

The MovieSpace archives hadn't been pruned since the BerezhneCo takeover, so that afternoon Kate was able to trace

LaWLChat's origins. In 2008, Monarch had rolled out a paid comics portal that touted "collaborative community features," which was a fancy way of saying that readers could post comments under each strip. Most mirrored the character of the strips closely, and critics were quickly driven out by a consensus established by five to ten very, very dedicated superfans. But *Ladies Who Lunch* didn't have superfans. There were a few cranky old-timers (or cranky young nostalgists; it was always impossible to tell online) who mainly complained about the degree to which the art and writing had declined since the strip's glory days forty years ago. There were people who had spent years marveling to themselves or to their tolerant families about this weird, semi-comprehensible cultural artifact in their newspaper, only seeking it out online when that newspaper stopped running it, or they stopped reading the newspaper. Every time Monarch gamely ran *Ladies Who Lunch* as the featured strip on the front page of their site, some drive-bys showed up to ask "What in the name of God is this?" and a few of them kept coming back.

Then, nine months after the Monarch site launched, the commenting feature abruptly vanished. *Fall Semester Forever,* a theoretically zany strip about college life, was under the control of its artist-creator, and it had attracted a hard core of haters who became his personal obsession. He demanded that either the comments go or he would; his strip was one of the syndicate's most popular, and the site hadn't been built to allow comments on some strips but not others, so the shared paratextual universe that the *Ladies Who Lunch* hangers-on had created—a world where Maureen was an actual cannibal, Eve an increasingly not-so-secret lesbian, and Carol a friendly wife-robot who had replaced the biological original in the mid-'80s—vanished into the ether.

The *Fall Semester Forever* trolls had gotten more and more persistent as they realized they were successfully antagonizing the artist, but once banished found better things to do with their time, or maybe worse things, but certainly *different* things. One guy started a hate site at fallsemesternever.blogspot.com, but stopped updating after a few weeks. But the core group of *Ladies Who Lunch* commenters had already exchanged email addresses and managed to hang together long enough to land at MovieSpace, where one of them was an unpaid moderator and had the power to set up a new set of themed message boards and fend off BrezhneCo's occasional desultory attempts to keep the site focused on film. By the end of 2009, LaWLChat was getting over 450 posts a day across six discussion and image boards.

Christine clicked on one of the more active threads, titled "LANDERPALOOZA XVIII: THE MITCHENING." It was entirely dedicated to strips in which a Landers-esque character appeared (a "Mitchengänger," they called them); posters would try to find a picture of Landers online in which his facial expression matched the look in the strip, and Photoshop his face—or, better yet, his entire body—into the relevant panel. Some of the posters were very, very sure that Rex Bargeman was using screencaps and promotional stills of Mitch as models; to find a precisely matching picture became a community holy grail.

"So now here's something on this board from a few months ago that's relevant to our interests."

Posted by
handsome_dan
Jun 18 02:37 am

lol you guys these are amazing

Posted by **handsome_dan** *Jun 18 02:49 am*	for real though i could get you a bunch of pictures of mitch landers for this site. im not so good with photoshop but maybe you could do something with them?

Posted by **handsome_dan** *Jun 18 02:53 am*	probably pics you haven't seen before ... probably pix mr. rex hasn't seen before either, though, heheh

"Oh my God," Kate said, "He Googled himself."

"Everybody self-searches," Christine said. "Trying to assess the shape and volume you occupy online is not a character flaw."

"I guess. But this has to be pretty far down the list of search hits, right? Someone this famous, this board's probably on the fifth or sixth page of results. And he's doing it at three in the morning."

"Well, he lives in California, so subtract three hours. And the link's at the bottom of the second page, actually. Gawker linked to the board a year ago, so it still has some search engine juice." Christine breathed in and held it for a moment. "I'm not denying it's a little bit *silly*."

"I guess it's harmless," Kate said warily. On the screen was Mitch's face crudely pasted onto the professional mountain biker/dot-com millionaire who had spent much of 2011 trying to woo Carol away from her husband. His stern, serious expression was, Kate suddenly realized with almost embarrassing clarity, taken from one of Landers's few dramatic roles, in a period piece that had flopped badly a few years back.

Posted by **handsome_dan** *Jun 20 12:04 pm*	lol serious face serious FAAAACCCCEEEE so serious you guys, this is serious business

"So who's the client?"

"Mitch Landers. I thought that was clear? You didn't know that's who we were just talking about?"

"No, yes, I knew that. I mean, who's *paying*."

"Mitch Landers."

"Mitch Landers, like, Mitch Landers personally is paying? With his own money?"

"He wants to start a production company to develop projects for himself, of course—he's at that stage now. Last I heard he was having a hard time coming up with a funny name for an LLC, so I believe he's just writing us checks from his personal account at the moment. You can ask accounts receivable if you're interested in the details."

"That's not ... exactly ..." She changed tack. "So who's the target?" Kate suddenly began to panic at the thought that she'd be expected to do a subtectonic groundswell job on the LaWLChat posters. *There's 100, 150 people who post in this group tops*, she thought. *They wouldn't fill a single showing of this movie.* (Later that week, she would take a census and come up with 123, which made her pretty proud of her ability to quantify community membership at a glance.) But then she remembered.

"This," she said, looking up at Mitch Landers's face, his endearing face, handsome but not threatening, almost always smiling, eyes glinting with joy and not too much self-awareness. "This is the seed pattern you were talking about."

"Mitch wants to do a movie where he plays all the male roles."

Kate laughed. "That's ... OK, that's funny. To me anyway. Who else is going to get the joke, though?"

"How long ago was it that you had never heard about *Ladies Who*

Lunch? About five hours now? Millennials in particular are primed for quick media educations."

"So we're going to be explaining to America why Mitch Landers playing multiple roles in a movie adaptation of a soap opera comic strip that's been running on nostalgia for more than thirty years will be funny."

"America," said Christine, "is a big target, and a little beyond our capacities. You know we don't do mass sells. But if you could bottle this enthusiasm a little bit. Digest it. Put it into a form Mitch could take to money people, the ones who'll eventually hire the people who do the mass marketing."

Posted by **divalicious** Aug 20 12:04 pm	guys maureen's new man makes me feel all tingly downstairs. is that wrong? am i dying?
Posted by **Mirthquake-1** Aug 20 12:21 pm	I don't know, but I now desperately need to know whether he's scamming her or not. Damn you, Ladies Who Lunch. Damn you for making me care about you.
Posted by **Darayavahus** Aug 20 12:33 pm	I don't think he's scamming her, I think he is in love!!!
Posted by **handsome_dan** Aug 20 12:41 pm	its not wrong to feel tingly everybody, not wrong at all. lol

"These people love *Ladies Who Lunch,* even if they wouldn't say it." Christine said. "And they're just the ones whose media journey happened to lead them there. They're not different from anyone else, statistically speaking. This love is latent in enough people that

Ladies Who Lunch: The Movie will make its costs back even if it goes direct to video on demand. You'll help them recognize that."

Kate started to see the energy lines in her head, the network of potential affection—from the strip to LaWLChat to Mitch to the studio to the world. The Mitch-studio link was her business, but to create it she'd also have to create an image of the studio-audience link that was real enough to touch. It was a higher degree of difficulty than she'd tackled before, and the rhythm of Christine's declarative statements about her future success made her breath quicken.

"When do I start?" Briefly, she was worried that she sounded too eager. She had to remind herself that nobody within the Enthusiasm Channel division could ever be too enthusiastic.

Christine smiled. "You've already started. I hope you don't have plans tonight?" She did, but LaMont knew that sometimes Agents had to work evenings on short notice. "Mitch is in town to testify before Congress about his art education charity. You've got"— Christine looked at her watch—"three or four hours to get ready for a dinner meeting with him. Start with IMDb, would be my advice."

5

KATE WASN'T SURE WHY she had asked Mesut for help. She had been staring at a yellow legal pad across the top of which she had written:

How To Interact with an Attractive Famous Person

And beneath it:

1. Don't Babble
2.

And that was it. She tapped her pencil eraser against the desk and idly chewed on her fingernail, then added:

2. Don't Chew Fingernails

before crossing everything out. *Why not just call these "tips for interacting with all sorts of humans,"* she thought. And then: *What would Maureen do?*

That was an odd thought. The Agency taught you to hold on to your odd thoughts, especially if they're related to the subject at hand—*let content and process intermingle*—but she wasn't sure taking advice from a sexually aggressive comic strip character was helpful. Maureen would overpower Mitch with her charm and make him her thrall, which was not on the table for her. Maybe she should think more like Carol: open-hearted, honest, chaste.

Carol never gets what she wants, she wrote on the pad, surprising even herself.

Mesut at least had the advantage of being a real, actual human being, one who, when she left her cube to find him, was poring over some exquisitely dull-looking small print.

"These are Automatic Train Control safety regulations from your Federal Transit Administration," he said. "They are very involved."

"Can you handle not looking at them for a few minutes or are you too enraptured?" she said, sitting in the spare chair.

"In a sense," he said, "they are actually very interesting, because they are attempting to achieve the same goal as the German regulations, but they try in a totally different way. But, in another sense, they are quite boring, because ... because they are regulations, I think. Also, I don't understand many of the law words. Basically what I am saying is that the idea of them is interesting but I don't want to read them. So, yes, tell me about something that is not this."

Kate wasn't sure if Mesut spoke in paragraph-sized chunks because he learned English by reading it or because that was just how he operated, but she had decided it was mostly endearing. "Do you know who Mitch Landers is?"

"Yes, he is a comedy actor. The country I come from has cinemas and also television."

This was one of the easier calls in the mental game Kate had made up for their conversations, *Sarcastic or German?* "Well, he wants to make a *Ladies Who Lunch* movie." She raised a hand. "Yes, it's absurd. It's also absurd that I'm having a meeting with a good-looking movie star on half a day's notice. I'm probably going to make an ass out of myself because he'll be funny or flirty or something. Charismatic. Charismatic people don't know they're being charismatic half the time."

"Well, he will be used to people making asses of themselves, then. Do you know who Petra Trottenberg is?"

"Should I?"

"Not unless you are a fan of the contemporary German electronic dance music scene, which, as I say this, I recognize you are not. She is an important DJ. Some of my friends were bringing her in from Hamburg to perform at a show they were organizing in an abandoned Stasi barracks, and they needed to find a place for her to stay. 'Mesut,' they said, 'you are bourgeois, you have a second bedroom in your apartment.'" He looked mildly ashamed of the exchange. "This was, I think, about three hours before the show started."

"Did you do it?"

"Yes, of course. But I didn't enjoy the music as much as I should have because I worried about what I would say to her when we will go back to my apartment. If I talk about music, maybe she will be bored, and if I talk about something else, maybe she will be insulted. And if I don't talk, she will think I don't like her. And if I talk a lot, she will think I like her too much. She is also very pretty, did I say this?"

"Yes, see, OK, this is exactly it. And all you had to do was make conversation after some rave. I have to have a professional relationship with Mitch Landers."

"Actually, it was a very well-curated electronica show," he said, "and it was important that I not make her uncomfortable. I did not want to make the Berlin scene look bad."

"So what happened?"

"Well, we dated for the next eight months. Now and then. She travelled often."

"Yeah, not helpful," she said, standing up.

"Do you want to know what we talked about?"

"Not helpful!" she said, walking away.

‖‖‖‖‖‖‖‖‖‖‖‖

"Everybody in the industry has a charity or cause that's their thing." Mitch Landers was shorter in person than Kate had expected, and she hadn't expected him to be particularly tall. He was still very nice to look at. Blue eyes, lively, not too deep-set. Great smile. Nice lips. Good mouth all around. What she could see of his arms told her he was in shape without being some kind of workout freak. Dark hair a little shaggy, in an adorable way, though she supposed that was professionally sculpted. So, no credit to him for the hair, though maybe *credit* was the wrong word. He wasn't responsible for the eyes or the mouth, either.

Kate was 5'3" and didn't think that a guy had to be tall to be interesting. When she had walked into the restaurant and spotted Mitch, he had stood up to greet her, and her assessment—5'8", maybe 5'9"—was more information-gathering than judgmental. Still, it was a noteworthy fact. Humanizing, a little. Grounding herself in the humanizing was helpful in this scenario.

They were meeting at National Table, a trendy and pricey new restaurant near the Capitol that touted its commitment to local organic sustainable free-range everything. The inside was dark, rough-hewn wood—the walls, the floor, the tables—with enough variation to give the impression that it had been built out of whatever nearby trees came to hand. The lighting was dim and supplemented by real fires burning in brick fireplaces on all four walls. Those were an engineering achievement, since the restaurant was on the first floor of a high-rise office building that dated from the early 1980s. Where was the smoke going? It worried her a bit.

What would Maureen think of this scene, or Carol, or Eve? She couldn't get the question out of her head. She supposed it made sense: she was face to face with a real-life Mitchengänger, after all. This could be a plotline ripped from today's comics section. Carol would coo at the effort put into it all. Maureen would think it was tacky, inauthentic, trying too hard. Eve ... Eve was a harder one to get to know. She hadn't gotten her read on Eve yet.

They met at 5:30, early enough on a weeknight that she hadn't had to drop his name to get the reservation. Still, Washington ate early. Middle-aged men in suits everywhere, along with older people in more casual but still very expensive clothes. Dotted amongst them were younger couples on early dates looking nervous or excited or both, boys in blue blazers and khaki pants, girls having changed into something little and black before they left the office, backpacks at their feet giving off a vaguely collegiate air. Kate felt a bit of vertigo realizing she wasn't their age anymore. She was a little surprised that nobody was visibly impressed by the movie star at the next table. It was D.C., she supposed. Maybe if he were a senator running for president there'd be more whispering.

"What do you think of when you think of Clooney?" Mitch asked her.

"Uh..." She thought of his Italian villa and his new wife and the series of vaguely famous and extremely pretty girlfriends who had preceded her.

"Darfur, right?"

"Sure," she said, though she was mildly embarrassed to realize that it was the other way around: when she thought of Darfur she thought of George Clooney, and she hadn't thought about Darfur for a while. She toyed with her bone marrow appetizer, not sure if she was supposed to use her fork or pick it up and suck the marrow out or what. Mitch had ordered them, and she had planned to follow his lead, but he had become so engrossed in his spiel that he hadn't touched his.

"And Laurie David? Global warming?"

"Wait, didn't they get divorced?"

Mitch looked sheepish. "OK, fine. This is mostly an internal scorekeeping thing, I guess. Not that I'm in Clooney's league."

"I think you could take Laurie David, though."

He smiled at her, a genuine smile, as near as she could tell. Actors were masters of the genuine smile, so it paid to be careful, but she could only spend so much energy second-guessing. "You're saucy," he said, "and I don't know where that word just came from. Do people say 'saucy'? I think I'm auditioning for a pirate movie in my mind. You always gotta be ready for the call. 'Mitch'"—he pantomimed holding a phone to his ear, thumb and pinky finger out, and did an accent that could double as Mid-Century New York or Stereotypical Hollywood Agent —"'they want you for that new pirate comedy, huge payday. How's your old-timey jargon?'"

The smile unfolded into a grin that was impressive to experience. Kate was sure she would remember the glow of it for days. Mitch's

81

charisma was industrial strength. This was not unexpected. There were several kinds of famous people whose success could be aided by charisma, but Mitch was the kind of famous for which charisma was a prerequisite.

Agency guidelines for dealing with the famous urged a certain amount of internal segmentation of consciousness. Part of you needed to be receptive to this charisma, to experience it as an ordinary person who had no stake in the famous person's success or failure. You needed to understand its contours, because the other part of you, the part that you've segmented off, will be figuring out how to help your client channel that charisma towards fulfilling their goals.

"Anyway," he said, "My deal is not Clooney-level Darfur-level business. A couple years ago, some people tried to recruit me for an advocacy group for refugees from the Azerbaijan-Armenian war. I thought, hey, here's a tragedy that nobody else has locked down! But it turns out there's two sides to *that* story."

"There are people who are ... against the refugees?"

"There are two different groups of refugees. And they *hate* each other. They fought each other in a war and all, so it makes sense. What if I had picked the Armenians and, like, Anna Faris picked the Azeris? And then we couldn't do a movie together? I bailed before they had a chance to put my picture in any of their literature." He smiled. *He knows this is absurd,* she thought, *but he's not making it up.*

"Anyway, the thing that I'm here for is pitching increased funding for after-school arts programs for kids. Zero controversy. I did theater at a community center in Indiana where I grew up, so I get to talk about the topic in the first person without having to fly to a refugee camp, which is a plus."

She smiled at him. He was funny. She genuinely found him funny. But from the part of her brain she had segmented off, the part that wasn't soaking in Mitch's charisma, she heard *I wonder if he ever gets to turn it off.*

"The hearing was ... well, I don't want to say it was boring. But meetings of most House subcommittees don't even rate C-SPAN 3 coverage. Which I guess meant that the congressmen weren't making speeches for TV and were listening to what I was saying. Everyone seemed to like me, anyway, which was good."

"But no cameras. Sort of defeats the purpose."

"Kate," he said, and it was the first time he had said her name, and it was suddenly obvious having an attractive famous person say your name in his trained voice, a voice you were used to paying $10 to hear in digital surround sound, was pretty great. "The *purpose* was to boost government funding for after-school arts programs, and we didn't need cameras to do that." He kept a straight face for a beat. "Plus, my publicist had someone taking video. Took them about twenty minutes to get through security. If ISIS thinks they can murder several mid-level members of Congress with a machine gun disguised as a camera, they are in for a rude surprise."

They both laughed. Here was another thing the Agency guidelines had to say about charismatic famous people: *You may find that your meeting with the Famous Person evolves such that it takes on the shape of a date. This can happen regardless of the configurations of genders and orientations involved. There is no bright-line boundary between charisma and the process of attracting sexual partners. Powerful charisma is not under the moment-to-moment control of the charismatic.*

"So, blah blah blah, me me, I'm fascinating," said Mitch. The table wasn't large, and his hands drifted into the neutral zone between them and closer to her space. "What's your story? What do you do?"

Judge for yourself the extent to which ambiguity on this point can be useful and safe. This was the moment at an initial client meeting where an Agent might say, "The thing you want to happen? I make that happen." She had seen Christine do it, and it made people melt, all the more because it was often the first sentence they heard from her that wasn't dreamy, hypnotic jargon. But there was the danger that it some clients would find it too assertive. "Well, at the moment, I work for you," is what she settled on. "You want to make a movie; I want to help you make that movie."

He leaned back, re-establishing the distance between them. "Right. OK. So, you've worked with movie clients before."

"Nope." A couple of months after Kate had started full-time at the Agency, after she had gotten through most of *Lords of the Ashes* and taken meticulous notes on the permeable wall between its internal and external economies, she and Christine had flown to San Jose. They were going to meet the programmers and marketers at DeathHug Games and spell out how enthusiastically customers would be injecting real dollars into the game, assuming Death-Hug's legal team could convince the state of California that this didn't technically constitute online gambling. They had prepped in the hotel the night before the meeting. Christine dropped her usual soothing affect, making her voice deeper and more nasal, and peppered Kate with sarcastic, probing questions about her gaming history. She had played more video games than most, certainly most women, which is why she was on this job in the first place. But under the simulated onslaught, she felt like a fraud.

"Kate," Christine finally said, back to herself and exasperated, "all your replies start with 'No, but.' You are letting them frame the terms."

"But they're right," Kate said. "I'm not a hardcore gamer the way they think is important." She felt sheepish, realizing that "they" weren't there. "Or that you think they'll think is important. Do you think it's important?"

"If I thought it was important, I would've brought Enrique," Christine said. Enrique was an Enthusiasm Channel Agent who was extremely enthusiastic about first-person shooter video games, which he played throughout his lunch break in his cube and sometimes well into the afternoon. Kate had wondered if this was part of an assignment or not. He was polite about wearing headphones and not shouting, but she could always hear him hammering on the keyboard five cubes over.

"So, should I ... exaggerate my experience? It's not like there's going to be a quiz, right?"

Christine pursed her lips and turned down the corners of her mouth just a little bit. It was the most disappointed Kate had ever seen her up to that point, and her stomach dropped. "We don't misrepresent ourselves on non-stealth assignments. Even on stealth, we stay as close to personal reality as we possibly can. Misrepresentation is not the solution here. The solution is to provide an accurate but dissonant counterpoint."

Kate looked at her, blank and anxious.

"These questions are framed with two possible outcomes in mind. If you say yes, the questioner is emotionally reassured. If you say no, they've established dominance. So you come at them with a dominant no. You need to make it clear that no is not the wrong answer. They have free access to any number of people who play video games. But they hired us, and that was the right decision."

It was a revelation that Kate never got tired of. You have to make it their problem that they wanted an answer different from what you gave them. It was one of the most powerful feelings in the world, sitting there steadily while you watch them rearrange the scenario in their head.

"So…" said Mitch. He picked up his drink and swirled it, then set it down without drinking. "But your … company does work with film people? Are there colleagues of yours we'll be dealing with?"

"We have entertainment industry clients. And lots of institutional knowledge to draw on. But. Mitch." She tried to say it with at least a fraction of the power with which he had said her name. "You have an agent."

"That's what 15 percent of every check says." He was being funny again, but it was wary, a little defensive.

"And a publicist."

"I have an agency I work with, yeah."

"But you hired us, not anyone those guys know. You don't know us. They don't know us. We're in Washington, D.C. But…?"

"Yeah, but," he said. "You know, you guys are like, this weird rumor in Hollywood. Nobody understands you. But they whisper about you. Did you work on the whole *Necronomicon Realm* thing?"

"No, that was a little before I started. But we all know about it. It's pretty legendary."

"Fuck right it is," Mitch said. *Necronomicon Realm* had been born in the late 1970s as a multi-user text-gaming environment hosted surreptitiously on an MIT mainframe. It was based loosely on H.P. Lovecraft's Cthulu mythos, but was much gorier and hadn't gone commercial the way *Zork* and some of the era's other text adventures had. It had been shifted from server to server over the decades and was still a going concern in 2009, when *Airlock,* a cerebral sci-fi thriller written by a former engineer and longtime *Necronomicon Realm* player, won an unexpected Golden Globe for Best Original Screenplay and snagged an Oscar nomination to boot. The resulting clout got the writer's dream *Necronomicon Realm* script green-lit, leading to a troubled production and a film that limped into limited release three years later.

"I mean, I don't know if you know how they felt about that movie in the industry," said Mitch. "It wasn't bad, exactly, but it was one of those shitpiles that wasn't making anybody any money, which is the Hollywood equivalent of deadly radiation. Nobody who worked on it wanted to admit it. Not actors, not publicists, not makeup people, nobody. Definitely nobody new wanted to come on and try to save it. Except you guys."

"The game had a cult Internet following," said Kate. "Those guys hadn't been engaged, not even a little."

"I still don't think it made its budget back, at least not in pretend Hollywood accounting," said Mitch. "But it made so much more than usual on digital downloads, it was nuts. Nobody had seen anything like it. Being slightly less toxic was suddenly like being a hit."

"So do you just sit around with other actors and talk about digital download revenues? Kind of a disappointing image of the Hollywood lifestyle."

"Not other actors. You know, I'm trying to get into this production thing, so I've been talking to ... producer ... people. They kept dropping your name. I mean, not your name, not Kate..."

"Berkowitz."

"Right. Subconscious Agency is who they talk about. But not Kate

Berkowitz, because you haven't done any work with the industry."

"Yet."

"Yet."

Their entrees arrived: hearty, basic American fare, meat and potatoes and root vegetables. They sat on slightly mismatched but still very nice plates. The presentation was a testament to the local small-scale farms that had long been plowed under and replaced with broad boulevards and subdivisions of suburban homes of varying scales. The menu vaguely promised that this food was from Maryland's Eastern Shore or maybe not too far off in Virginia. Kate put a bite of chicken in her mouth. It really was very good.

"Look," she said, cutting up her asparagus, "I'm not going to pretend to be an expert in what you do. You already know those experts. You *are* one of those experts." Mitch managed to put on an expression of exaggerated and deliberately false modesty while he chewed his steak; Kate appreciated the effort. "What you've hired us to do is the stuff that L.A. hasn't figured out."

"Yes, please. What do we not know? Teach us, wise one." He pyramided his hands and slowly nodded, *Kung Fu* style. He was back on her side again, she decided; he was sarcastic, but not mean.

"Well," she said, "You already have an idea of what we're going to do together. At least handsome_dan does."

Immediately she realized that had been a mistake. His face went white, then very red, and it wasn't part of his shtick. *Jesus,* she thought, *he didn't tell Christine.* Christine had culled handsome_dan's posts on LaWLChat to show to Kate, and Kate had understood why as soon as she looked at them. The part of her brain that she had walled off from Mitch's charisma had built an elaborate backstory about how Mitch had come to hire the Agency; she had been visualizing Mitch, puppy-dog eager, showing Christine the Landerpalooza posts on LaWLChat, and he would talk about how he'd been posting to the boards.

Except he hadn't. He thought he'd been stealth. Now she was seeing Christine going through the discussion threads; the handsome_dan posts would jump out at her as aggressively as they had jumped out at Kate. Maybe Mitch had been in the room with her at the time. Maybe she had flown out to L.A. (Christine would vanish from the office for days at a time, meticulous about replying to emails promptly but cagey about where exactly she was) and was sitting in Mitch's ... house? office? Kate didn't feel like she knew Mitch, or Los Angeles, well enough to visualize it. Probably had good light. Maybe some concert posters on the walls. Anyway, there Mitch was, pulling up LaWLChat on his laptop, and Christine's eyes fell on a few posts from handsome_dan, and she nodded, and waited for Mitch to say something, but he never did. And that was relevant in and of itself. Or, maybe they had communicated by email, and Mitch had sent her endless LaWLChat links—"see what I'm talking about, lol"—and she had stumbled upon those posts and eventually stopped waiting for the explanation.

Kate wished Christine had said something before she had met Mitch. Was it an oversight? Or a trap for Kate? Not a trap, an *opportunity*. A trapportunity. Sometimes Kate felt like she was being managed even as she was sent to manage others. She knew human beings tended to read design into chaos too often. But Christine was always two steps ahead, so it was hard not to expect it.

Too late to figure it out now, she thought. *Make it work.* She couldn't help but imagine she was face to face with a startled and embarrassed Mitchengänger. What would the Ladies Who Lunch have done? Carol would have apologized profusely; Eve would've let him twist in the wind a bit, let it play out. But Maureen...

Mitch had recovered and was smiling wanly. "Wow, are you guys, like, sorcerers? Internet sorcerers?" He made a mock-serious face. Goofing around was helping him find his bearings. "What am I thinking about right now? Wait, this isn't the Internet, so your powers are useless here."

Maureen would've acted as if the accidental reveal had been a deliberate power play, she decided. "It's not *magic*," she said. "We're just very good at paying attention to what people say, and what they're excited about. That's what we *do*. And you're excited about a weird old comic strip."

"They're all excited about it," he said.

"Yeah," she said, "but you're excited about it in a ... particular way. It's personal for you, very specifically. It comes through, if you know what to look for."

"I guess. Everyone on the boards is super-excited. Obsessed, really."

"Self-selected online communities intensify obsession, both inherent and apparent." He looked at her blankly. She started to hedge with "We say at the Agency..." or "That's what my boss says..." But no, she was an Internet sorceress who had sniffed out his secret identity, and she had to commit to it. She knew things, and that put her in charge. It made her a little sad the way the dynamic had shifted. She was going to have to spin a web of Agency woo-woo to reel Mitch in. She had to see it through.

"By inherent," she said, "I mean real. Maybe you read *Ladies Who Lunch* every day and enjoy it ironically, to yourself, and don't talk to anyone about it, because who would care? It's weird. Eventually, you get bored with it. You stop reading it. You stop subscribing to the paper, because who subscribes to the paper anymore?"

"But..."

"But Google doesn't judge your weird obsessions. It could lead you to other people who don't judge, either. Once you're posting things to make them laugh every day, you keep reading the strip to keep up. And then your paper cuts it, or you stop subscribing to the paper, but you figure out where you can still read it online. Everyone's enthusiasm has fed off of itself."

"And you go see the movie!" Things were syncing back up for Mitch, she realized. The girl who had shown that she was creepy-smart was now leading him to the very idea that he had come up with in the first place.

"Sure. But you have to keep the apparent nature of the obsession in mind, too. All the people on the LaWLChat boards—they have other hobbies, you know. Jobs. Families! You think they're fixated because you only see this tiny slice of their life."

Mitch rubbed his chin with his thumb. "I dunno ... some of those people, I don't think they could ever love a human being the way they love putting my Photoshopped head on the bodies of comic strip characters." But he had eased into the world she had created for him. *He should,* she thought, *he was paying enough for it.* "So ... will they go see the movie or not?"

"Oh, they'll see it," she said. "Maybe their families will go along if they haven't alienated them by posting LaWLChat memes on Facebook all the time. We have to convince some money people that there's enough of them, though, or that we can create more of them."

"Cool, cool," he said. "Wait, I have something for you. Someone to get in touch with when you're ready." He pulled various credit cards and slips of paper from his wallet and piled them up among the detritus of their meal. Kate felt a surge of affection for him when she spotted a hole-punched card that showed he was a few visits away from a free sandwich at some Los Angeles deli. Mitch commanded six figures a movie, according to the trade press she had read in her meeting prep, and he'd been making two or three movies a year since Kate was in high school. "Ah ha!" He handed her a card.

ZACH, THE PRODUCER
digital innovation in entertainment
(310) 555-0872 ❖ theproduc.er
zach@theproduc.er

"Is that a domain name from…" She worked through some geography in her head. "Eritrea?"

"I know, right? So it spells out 'producer!' I thought that was pretty clever."

"What does he produce?"

Mitch looked sheepish. "Oh, you know, a lot of things. It's kind of what he calls himself. We bounce ideas off of each other a lot. If he helps broker anything, he gets a cut. That's kind of how it works. Distribution ideas, digital … innovation …" He trailed off. "I met him when I did some Web shorts last year. Did you see those? The ones where I got kicked in the balls?"

"I'm familiar with the genre."

"Zach was working for those guys. Kind of. He always seemed to be around the office, anyway, and they listened to him, sometimes."

She suppressed an irritated sigh. "Well, I'll certainly let him know what we're up to," she said.

A waiter showed up and Mitch reached for the check. Kate

stopped him and handed over her Agency card. It was an American Express Centurion card, obsidian and terrifying. It still unnerved her to see her name on it. "You're paying for it eventually," she said after the waiter walked away, "but it's better for taxes or something if we do it this way."

"I don't understand that, but you sounded smart when you said it, so obviously it's true." He grinned at her. "You gave him the company card without even looking at the bill. That's a baller move."

Her face reddened. "Oh, I'm sure it's very large," she said. "I would never do that..." She almost said *in real life,* but that was wrong. They were talking about movies and money and Mitch's smile was still radiating across the table at full blast, making her aware of her skin and her body. It was all *very* real. "...normally."

Mitch laughed. "Oh, God, don't listen to me, I'm just busting your chops. I'm honored to have someone pay for my dinner without knowing how much it cost and then bill me for it later. Basically, my life is an episode of *Cribs.* I'll probably have my assistant pay that bill without telling *me* how much it's for, that's what a baller *I* am."

The waiter came back with the card and the receipt and started to return it to Mitch before correcting himself and handing it to her. She tried not to react to the magnitude of the total charges as she signed it and wrote in the tip.

"Where are you staying?" she asked.

"Wow, I know you're paying, but that's awfully forward," he said. She narrowed her eyes at him. "Sorry. The Ritz-Carlton near Foggy Bottom. You don't have to worry about driving me. I took a cab."

"Yeah, that's what I figured. Come on, I want to show you something else I'm going to make happen."

"Why does it have a *rug?*" Mitch asked.

"Nobody knows why," said Kate. They were on the Orange Line. There were only three stops to Mitch's hotel—they could've walked it—but she had a gut feeling it might make an impression on him. She thought about Eve, who startled the Italian playboy who was courting her by taking him on a biplane ride over Chicago. This wasn't the same, but Mitch had never been on the Washington Metro, either. "Well, somebody probably knows. Maybe they thought it would seem classier than regular subway cars."

"It smells really bad. Didn't they know how bad it would smell?"

"They do now."

Here, there was murmuring and surreptitious glances, and she wondered if she'd miscalculated the part where she was bringing someone famous into a situation that was both public and not easy to escape. If Mitch noticed, he played it cool.

"So you're going to fix this smelly carpet and also get my movie made."

"That's the plan."

"How're you going to do it?"

"Well, first, we're going to get together some LaWLChatters and see why they like you so much."

"No, not that. The train part."

"Oh. That's top secret and already in progress. It involves—" she lowered her voice, and without thinking about it leaned in closer to whisper "—*disguises and assumed names.*"

He raised an eyebrow, then mimed zipping his mouth shut.

"That's the spirit," she said. The train pulled into the station. *DEE-do-DEE-do. Doors opening.* "This is your stop. Can you figure out how to get out of the train station?"

"Despite my life of privilege, I think I can handle a door," he said, and hop-skipped onto the platform.

"Do you think you can make it out through the fare gates?"

DEE-do-DEE-do. Doors closing, the last syllable rising like a question. "No promises!" he shouted as the door slid shut. He stood there for a moment, and she watched him slide backwards as the train pushed on into darkness.

6

PICTURES OF THE S360 HAD STARTED going up just hours after Kate and Mesut's live-site with the trainspotters. The first wave of enthusiasm was not under anyone's control, certainly not Kate's. It would have happened anyway, except in the sense that they would not have been there, at the right place, at the right time, without the weeks of groundwork Kate had laid, a drip-drip of chipper enthusiasm and breathless revelations in the railfan forums. *I hear Siemens is shipping over a working prototype, it's unprecedented, they're going to do live runs, I don't know how they're getting around the testing requirements either.*

She had combed the archives going back to the mid-'00s and the endless now-forgotten arguments about the introduction of the 6000-series cars. Who was most interested in seeing those cars right away when they came out? Who posted the most pictures, the best pictures? Who figured out the best viewing spots? Those were the people whose threads she tracked, who she responded to with hints about the S360 wherever appropriate. Charlie, Darius, Jack (The_ Real_Jack). Rajiv had been a wild card, a newcomer to the boards, but she had liked his photos. A lot of this part of the play would be visual. They needed images, but not corporate glamour shots.

Their S360 pictures bloomed across railfan Internet. And the video, of course. Darius had taken it with his phone. It was shaky, and the wind blowing across the microphone made most of the talking indecipherable. Watching it on your phone or in the little YouTube window, you could feel a sliver of the power they had felt in the train's presence, seeing the gleaming orange train get closer and closer and suddenly veer off to the right, everyone's shouting still unintelligible but the joy coming across clearly. You couldn't see Kate's face in the video, which was a bonus; on a stealth assignment you can't expect to stay fully anonymous, but you take what you can get. You could see the back of her head, see her ponytail bob and flutter and see the push of wind pick her up and knock her down as the train goes by, see everyone else scramble to help her up.

Kate could hear herself laugh over the wind, but only because she knew to listen for it. She wondered if anyone watching thought she was hurt. The video ended before you could see her stand back up.

ArlingtonStreetcar 21 minutes ago

oh man this looks sweet. wish they had these on now.
fuck those adtranz craptrains.

mind_the_gap 37 minutes ago

These are just basically the same trains Siemen is selling in Munich and Singapore. Don't know why they have to give a new model number every time they build them for a new system.

foamerguy 33 minutes ago

Have you ever ridden on the trains in those systems? Are they any good???

kendall7 45 minutes ago

oh dag that chick totally eats it lol

IGotOpinions 1 hour ago

This looks OK but you can hear that brake whine as it takes the curve. AnsaldoBreda's doing some amazing things with metro rolling stock now in europe. Too bad they don't have deep German pockets to ship them all over the world to show them off.

jozy1992 52 minutes ago

breda are you kidding me lololololol

breda trains stink it up in san fran, boston. LA dumped them before they even delivered. please, no breda, i'm beggin you

The pictures Rajiv took weren't as good as his enormous camera promised—some were weirdly out of focus, most not even centered on the train. Maybe he thought he was being arty. They did the job. Darius and Charlie had taken some lower-quality stills with their phones, too. It only seemed to boost the appeal. There was a hunger for them. That grainy film of Bigfoot loping through the forest, Nessie's is-that-what-I-think-it-is neck breaking the surface of Loch Ness in black-and-white murk; they add to the drama, to the *atmospherics*. More and more light rail and streetcar systems were opening, and that was fine, everyone in the railfan community was all for that, but the Washington Metro—that was a real, full-on subway system, by God, and there weren't that many of those in the U.S., and they didn't buy new rolling stock very often.

What if you could see it before anyone else? Not as a stepping stone to any further goal or anything like that. What if you could just *see* it. See a shiny new train in a familiar setting. Those Brutalist concrete caverns, the Great Society's sci-fi vision, fading and cracking and looking worse for wear—but then something streamlined and beautiful pulls in, with digital readouts that the '60s architects couldn't have foreseen, splashed with a bold color to match the aesthetic of the '10s.

Fifty years from now, that train will look as dated and quaint as an avocado-colored refrigerator. The color will make you cringe. But right now, as you see it pulling around the curve in that video, it looks like the future.

The pictures first went up on Charlie's Flickr account. Most people had stopped caring about Flickr in the '00s when Facebook became your go-to website for sharing baby pictures, but it was still popular with specialized communities and people who were old and cranky and set in their ways. Kate had nearly a dozen Flickr tags monitored. You could fiddle with your account settings so that everything you uploaded was legally licensed so that anyone could share it. Charlie didn't bother, and maybe he didn't even know what the licensing terms were or meant. It didn't matter. People shared the pictures. Charlie was cool with people sharing the pictures. The whole point was that people would share the pictures.

The pictures were reposted on the local railfan discussion boards, and then on the national boards, and then on forums with an international readership, like Skyscraper City, which despite its name was a clearinghouse for pictures of infrastructure on the ground and under it. They spread to the amateur blogs, the ones still running on Blogger or WordPress and full of misspellings and cranky, unrealistic opinions, and you could feel the excitement in the wonky grammar. *Your going to crap yourself when you see what*

WMATA is running this month. It's not like any rolling stock theyve ever done. Next came the "professional" urbanist blogs, like Greater Greater Washington and BeyondDC—not professional in the sense of making money—Kate was pretty sure they didn't—but in the sense that they worked hard to conceal their enthusiasm under a layer of journalistic affect, which was what professionals did. These guys were invited to write serious op-eds about the Metro system in the *Washington Post* and appear on important panels about urban policy and transit planning; they couldn't jeopardize their gravitas by stooping to fanboy foaming. They discussed the aesthetics of the train in lofty terms, compared and contrasted it to the traditional WMATA rolling stock design, attempted to compare the technical specs to AnsaldoBreda's offerings in a way that sounded professional but—in Mesut's actually professional opinion—was only half-informed. They used adjectives like *sleek* and *game-changing* and *next-generation.* They made no explicit endorsements, but: *They want to ride that fucking train,* Kate thought, flicking from browser tab to browser tab, enjoying a satisfied glow. *They want to ride it to work every day. They want to ride it for fun. They're going to ride the hell out of it.*

"Did you make this happen?" Mesut said one day, stopping by her cube without any introduction or context. He sounded awed, and Kate was feeling pretty pleased about how the project was going, so she decided that she probably had, and was about to say so until she saw Sigmar was with him, looking less depressed than usual. Mesut tentatively held his phone towards her, screen first.

"What is it?" she said, taking it from him. "I don't read German." It was a tweet, a tweet with an image, and she recognized the picture: one of the first that Rajiv had taken, the S360 emerging from around the bend and barreling towards them. *"Der S360: Jetzt betriebsbereit in Washington DC, und danach bleiben Sie dran!"*

"That is the official Twitter of Siemens Mobility," Sigmar said. "It is run by the Public Affairs Department. We were curious who you sent your friend's picture to? Because I could give you the contact information of the executives there if you want to do this through the proper channels..."

Kate handed the phone back to Mesut. "I didn't send this picture to anyone," she said. She felt triumphant. "They must've seen the picture floating around the Internet and decided to use it. So, yeah, I made it *happen*. *We* made it happen," she said, looking at Mesut. "But organically. It emerged from the bottom up."

Sigmar looked dubious. Mesut looked impressed.

"Normally we coordinate campaigns very tightly," Sigmar said.

"Well, sure. But we do it this way. This is what you're paying for," Kate said.

"Yes, apparently," Sigmar said and walked off. Mesut lingered and gave Kate an impressed raised eyebrow before walking in the opposite direction; Kate actually winked at him, then felt mildly embarrassed about it.

It was a minor victory, as victories go. But when your own client can't differentiate subsidized from unsubsidized enthusiasm, you're doing it right, even if it makes them feel like they've lost control of the process. The process is, in fact, not supposed to be entirely under control. Control renders things artificial, fake.

Kate emailed a link to the Siemens tweet to Christine, with the note *photo taken by one of the trainspotters on our live-site.* Christine replied less than five minute later: *Nice, nice.* No jargon, no suggestions. The warmth could've stayed with Kate for hours if she hadn't been jarred out of it by an alert on her monitor:

THEY'VE FOUND YOU

This was a joke to herself, or she thought it had been when she had set it up. There were two mailboxes in Outlook that let her know when someone was interacting with one of her online personae. One had the boring name "Updates" and got new notifications all the time, so often that she didn't set up a screen-interrupting alert for it. It was dedicated to notifications sent when something she'd posted in public—on a Facebook group, on Quora, in the comments of some ancient Blogspot blog—had received an equally public reply. There was the expectation any content you posted in this way would be argued with, reblogged, praised, hated. That was the point. When she posted Darius's video in a few places under a few assumed names, she expected to hear (as she did) that it was "epic," "2 close 4 comfort," an exemplar of "germanic engineering," that "vertical phone vids suck." The commenters were performing, just like she was.

Someone sending you a note that only you would see, though: that was an act of intimacy. She almost never sent anything like that herself. There was a frisson of danger to it. It was sometimes necessary, productive even, but always nerve-wracking. Thus the "THEY'VE FOUND YOU" folder and its associated alert, though she wondered if it didn't make it worse. When she realized who had sent the note, she felt a stab of relief. It could've been scary. It was just irritating.

"Zach," she said to nobody.

"What?" said Zach DeLong, who worked two cubes over and specialized in seeding content on extremely high-end luxury parenting blogs.

"Not you," said Kate.

"Suit yourself."

In the days since she met with Mitch, Kate had pretty much stopped thinking about Zach, the producer, and yet here he was, sending her a direct message via the ancient MovieSpace forums software.

Message from **zach, the producer** Sep 19 02:14 pm	Kate. Spotted your name on the LaWL-Chat boards and recognized it from my last conversation with Mitch. Looking forward to this meeting of the minds. And making a very different kind of movie for Mitch. Send me your contact info: zach@theproduc.er.

".er? Is that even ... a thing? Is that a working email address?" LaMont asked as he looked over her shoulder. She had sent him a direct message in Slack asking him to come down to her cube, because she knew he was a connoisseur of the absurd.

"It's from Eritrea. It's supposed to be impossible to get if you don't live in the country. I don't know how he did it."

"Maybe *he's* from Eritrea. People from Africa can be smarmy Hollywood hangers-on, too. Don't make *assumptions.*"

Message from **zach, the producer** Sep 19 02:14 pm	Or we could make contact on Twitter. I'm @ zach_the_produc_er, and I #followback.

Kate pulled up his Twitter feed. In his profile picture, Zach was standing on the beach, ankle-deep in the surf, with linen pants rolled up halfway to his knees. His hands were thrust deep into his pockets, and he was decidedly white, a fact made obvious by his decision not to wear a shirt. LaMont pulled his glasses down and studied the picture with clinical detachment. "Mmm. People make interesting choices."

After LaMont had left, her phone buzzed. It was a text from Mitch, written with the cheery disregard for syntax, punctuation, and spelling that she would come to regard with affection.

> kate still super syched
> were going to work on this
> together. zach says he
> spotted you on LaWLChat?
> yr not wasting time lol. told
> him he could write you,
> hope you dont mind

Kate had, in fact, been spending a lot of time on the LaWLChat forums, getting a feel for what the community was like. It was fast, sharp, quick-witted; mean, though not usually at the expense of anyone on the boards. The main discussion thread was called HOT OFF THE PRESSES, where you would go to make fun of today's strip. The thread was hundreds of pages deep. Jokes were often short and sweet, written in a shorthand that you'd need experience or guidance to decipher. PLS stood for *possible lesbian subtext,* and usually showed up in discussions of Eve plotlines. If things got really overt, you'd get DLS, *definite lesbian subtext.* An MSL was a *Maureen sexual look.* When Maureen did something particularly awesome, like the recent storyline that concluded with Eve's stalker with a bucket over his head and Maureen holding him at Taser-point, there were rounds of MIOLAS; SSWA: *Maureen is our lord and savior; so say we all.*

Every once in a while, you'd get longer musings, or a short-story length post giving a backstory for some improbable character who appeared in a ridiculous outfit in a single panel. Sometimes, Eve would wear a silly hat, and then a poster named IM_A_HATMAN would appear and write a sestina about it. He never posted anything else.

After sprinting through the current *LWL* storyline on Monarch's site—Maureen had begun romancing an older man, only to discover he was her father's bitter rival from their prep school days—Kate started posting jokes of her own.

Posted by
KateBerkowitz
Sep 17 12:12 pm

Guys, I think there's been some kind of accident at the torso factory? There's a pileup on the conveyor belt.

"It's true," said Mesut, as he idly swirled a mozzarella stick into marinara sauce, a few days after her meeting with Mitch. They were eating at Pickles again, and she had gotten over finding it embarrassing; Mesut's love for fried cheese—"a technology America has truly mastered"—had made him a devotee. She was showing him the LaWLChat forums on her phone because she was tired of talking about trains, and because (she barely admitted to herself) she maybe wanted him to see her as someone who thought about something other than trains. "You do never see them from the waist down in the strip. This is a funny comment." He scrolled through the thread on his phone. "What does 'oversnarkpologies' mean?"

"It means you were so eager to post a joke that you didn't notice that someone else made the same joke earlier in the thread, and now you're apologizing for it."

"There is a very rigid set of rules they seem to have. I respect it. Why are you using your real name? I thought we were not supposed to use our real names."

"It's not a stealth assignment. I'm going to be putting together a meeting, a focus group of these people, using my real name and the company's real name, so I figured, might as well start being up front now."

"Well, none of them are as maniacal as Jack, probably, so you are safe. Ooh, except, who is this?"

Posted by **DOCTOR_FERRET** Sep 18 01:49 pm	you all still don't have anything better to do i see
Posted by **DOCTOR_FERRET** Sep 18 01:51 pm	@divalicious way to crap on what you don't get
Posted by **DOCTOR_FERRET** Sep 18 01:54 pm	@Mirthquake-1 eve's got a job, can't all be on line all day on welfare posting trash

"It's weird, right? He shows up like, once every other week, does some drive-by slams on a few posters, then disappears again."

"He is a—what do you call it in English again—a troll? Like Mr. LR?"

LR was someone Mesut had met the previous day in the comments of one of the higher-level DC-area transit blogs. He and Kate had been huddled together in his cube, checking out the first round of reactions to videos and pictures of the S360.

"Make the font bigger," she had said. She had to stare at computers all day and didn't like squinting. A lot of people—a lot of guys—told her they liked her eyes. It made her worry about crow's feet, which was ridiculous and paranoid and shallow, but there it was.

"You know, I think there is a reason that the comment font is usually smaller than the main article. It is because comments are all terrible and nobody should ever read them."

"Do you want to know what people think about your train or not?"

"Well, the nice man who wrote this blog post liked it very much, which is good because he is the one that normal people will read. As opposed to this person"—he touched a finger to the screen—"named 'LR,' who believes that cameras to catch speeders exist to steal money from drivers to buy 'fancy new choo-choos.' " Mesut shook his head.

"LR's a hater, a troll," she said. "He's deliberately trying to stir up shit."

"So he does not really believe that an order of rolling stock could be purchased for the cost of several speeding fines, you are telling me."

"No, but he really does think trains are too expensive and the government makes driving too hard. This is how he acts out about it. It's not healthy, but it's not *fake*. But he's an Other in this space—nobody's going to listen to him, and nobody's going to change their minds, which is fine by him because what he's actually after is to annoy people that he finds annoying. For our purposes, he's going to solidify the existing consensus. Halfway useful for drumming up counterenthusiasm in our direction, honestly."

Mesut looked at her warily. "This LR is not ... well, I am mostly joking when I say this, but he is not *you*, is he?"

Kate chuckled. "No. I've done it before, but it's not a ... *preferred* Agency technique. Don't tell them I told you this, but if I start doing a False Other thing for our project, it means we're in trouble."

A day later, and Mesut was seeing trolls everywhere. "DOCTOR_FERRET and LR, they are the same ... species you would say?"

She shook her head. "No, LR is angry about public transit being a waste of money, but he's angry, like, *theatrically*. Like literally, like he's on stage being angry for an audience. Not that there isn't an emotional truth to it, but he does it for our benefit and thinks about how it'll make us feel. This guy..."

Posted by **DOCTOR_FERRET** *Sep 18 01:59 pm*	@prettypug you think you're so funny, you should be on TV. oh wait, you aren't because you aren't funny.

"This guy's just *pissed*."

⊥⊥⊥⊥⊥⊥⊥⊥⊥⊥

Mesut was right about one thing: it felt strange posting to the LaWLChat forums under her own name. It wasn't something she usually did for work, and it left her feeling exposed. She hadn't been *happy* to hear from Zach, but she had already filed him away as, essentially, harmless. She had been worried when THEY'VE FOUND YOU flashed on her screen that the "they" would be DOCTOR_FERRET or someone like him, and that they might track her down in the real world. There had been a guy in high school who had had a painful and obvious crush on her when he was a senior and she was a sophomore, whom she hadn't rebuffed so much as ignored, mostly because she hadn't known what to do about it. She had forgotten about him by the time she got to college, until he started messaging her and her friends on Facebook, sending ugly, violent notes about how she had ruined his life and condemned him to an existence of involuntary celibacy. He stopped, eventually, and since then she had made sure that any social network account she had in her own name was as hidden as she could make it.

Even when she started at the Agency years later, Facebook still gave her a sour feeling of anxiety, and she checked her newsfeed with decreasing enthusiasm, dominated as it was by her relatives' political opinions and, lately, the first wave of pictures from the ill-advised weddings of her still-too-young college classmates. She was worried that this would disqualify her as an Agent, that her self-presentation as a media-savvy millennial had been fraudulent. Sure, she could navigate around the fan forums for long-cancelled CW teen romantic dramas, but she didn't have a Twitter account. She didn't know what to *do* with a Twitter account. Did she even *exist*?

Eventually, she had a Twitter account. Multiple Twitter accounts. Facebook accounts, too. LinkedIns. The list went on. The social networks didn't want you to do that, of course, but the Agency set you up with as many dummy email addresses as you needed to establish fake accounts. And Christine seemed pleased that Kate had few pre-existing social media habits. "You have nothing to unlearn," she said. Kate should have found that creepy, but she liked finding out she was good at things, or at least good for things.

It was freeing, she discovered, being other people on social media. She trusted the wall of anonymity the Agency's IT staff built for her, and trusted the long leash the Agency gave its employees to absolve her for the screw-ups she might make in her various disguises. The PartySweat job had involved pretending to be a college student interested in multilevel marketing both as a money-making opportunity and as a lifestyle ideology. So the Facebook account for Katie Berkshire was a Fan of pages that could loosely be categorized as inspirational entrepreneurship, with names like "Believe in Prosperity" and "Success Is In Your Grasp!" She Liked homemade knockoffs of corporate inspirational posters about Teamwork and

Leadership, and Shared images of frat guys semi-ironically re-enacting rap album covers, smoking cigars and fanning hundred-dollar bills, and posted links about *The Secret*. It was intoxicating and deranged. None of the ridiculous joy she felt reflected on *her*, because it wasn't really her, after all. It was Katie Berkshire. Katie shared Kermit Drinking Tea memes about the tax implications of freelance income. Katie got the electric thrill of every Like. Kate felt it too, one step removed.

She would burble on through lunch about PartySweat and multilevel marketing to whoever would listen, which, that month, mostly was Rick and Chiara, who, despite being longtime Enthusiasm Channel hands, seemed pleasantly surprised by her enthusiasm. At the moment, they were locked in a death struggle with another agency called Ouisseauhai, and this was how Kate learned that the Agency had a *nemesis*. It was the kind of death struggle where nobody actually dies, and you don't struggle that much. An office grudge. *WEE-soo-hi,* they would say, letting the first syllable whistle in between their teeth.

Their client was a web startup that promised to organize your life in ways that your email and calendar and contacts list couldn't, all in the cloud. You would, unfortunately, still need to *maintain* your email and calendar and contacts, because the web app, which began life as Gigr and then became Improvise, drew all its data from them. Their differentiation strategy—their gimmick—was that knowledge about the app was supposed to percolate from user to user across social networks, getting tried and used and promoted only by genuine organic enthusiasm. Naturally, nobody was doing this, because Web apps that combine your calendar and contacts and email are dull and pointless. This was the prison Rick and Chiara found themselves in: the prison of genuine online identity. Katie Berkshire would've posted on Facebook about Improvise with very little prompting. Katie was up for anything. But Kate wouldn't have, and neither would any of Improvise's customers.

"Ouissouhai *Partners* and *Associates*," Rick said over lunch one day. He and Chiara were in the break room at the same time every day: Improvise's employees were forced by the company's vaguely culty founder to all eat lunch together for alleged team-building and digestive benefits, which meant there was one hour a day when Rick and Chiara were sure they wouldn't be getting desperate emails or texts wanting to know if they'd convinced anyone to love Improvise yet.

"Ha, are they *partners* or are they *associates?* Let's just jam a bunch of boring words into the name of our company, right?" Kate said. Rick, a skinny white guy in his thirties who wore vintage Hawaiian shirts and shaved his head for what Kate assumed were male-pattern-baldness-related reasons, nodded and smiled at her, with an expression that Kate read as, *Yeah, this girl gets it.* Chiara, an African-American woman around Kate's age with curly hair, did not acknowledge her quip, just kept shaking her head and talking about Ouisseauhai *jackhammering away,* which made Kate want her attention all the more. Chiara was really leaning on the word *jackhammering.*

Ouisseauhai was working for Improvise's most successful competitor, a West Coast company called Chronos. Chronos also had the idea of expanding its customer base by going after its users' social media friends and friends of friends, but went about it in a different way: it sent spam invitations to every contact it could find in any of your address books, social media accounts, or cloud services. It was a move that Rick and Chiara called "classic Ouisseauhai" for its lack of subtlety. What's more, the app mined and analyzed your email and messaging outboxes (the fine print of the terms of service gave it permission and access) so that the spamvites it sent out were auto-generated based on your prose tics. The resulting messages were, as Chiara put it, "some serious uncanny valley shit," but—and here was what was giving the lunches an air of increasing anxiety—they were apparently working. Chronos was sending out press releases trumpeting its month-over-month user gains, which meant that people were signing up faster than they were quitting in disgust over the unexpected spamming. Meanwhile, Improvise's press releases focused on feature updates, each duller than the last (putting an exclamation point at the end of "improved cross-platform syncing!" was a crime against PR) because it had no user gains to speak of.

"Bob Byrd used to work here, you know," a tipsy Christine would tell Kate at the company Christmas party after his name had come up. Byrd was the CEO, founder, and sole proprietor of Ouisseauhai; there were, Kate was told, no actual partners or associates involved. "I held anger inside over it for years. I went to *therapy* about it, if you can believe that. Took me years to figure out why. It wasn't the poached clients. It wasn't even that he tried to reproduce what we do here. It's that he does it in a way that's so *banal*." She took a long sip of white wine and shook her head.

Rick and Chiara hadn't found Ouisseahai's techniques banal. They found them infuriating. "I mean, it's clearly not sustainable," said Rick. Kate wasn't sure who he was trying to convince. "Spambushing is such a dick move. Eventually, nobody will want to touch them."

"Improvise'll be dead by then, though," said Chiara.

"Fuckin' Ouisseauhai," said Rick.

"Fuckin' *Improvise*," said Chiara. "Some things people aren't meant to be enthusiastic about, you know?"

Kate had been full-time at the Agency for four weeks and three days at that point: a calendar month. This was how her life would go for her, that month: She would wake up every day before her alarm went off, on the lumpy mattress in the tiny bedroom in the Capitol Hill rowhouse she shared with Miriam. It was summer, so the light would stream in through the tall, narrow window that took up much of her one exterior wall, and she would pull the sheets a little tighter over herself, a little chilly because she had turned the air conditioning on full blast to fight the oppressive heat the night before, and now it was too much for the morning's mildness. She'd get up, turn the air conditioner off, and look around her cluttered little space, a bit bewildered as to what she was doing up so early. She'd grab her phone off the bedside table, look at her emails and text messages even though she wasn't at work yet, eat breakfast quickly, and find herself at the office before eight. By the time she had that conversation with Rick and Chiara in the break room, she had figured out what was happening: she liked her job. She thought that she had liked her previous jobs—her high school job at the public library, her college gig at the career center. She had even convinced herself for more than a year that her terrible HR job was all right. It turned out she had just been tolerating all those jobs.

"Some things people aren't meant to be enthusiastic about": To hear Chiara say that made Kate gasp. One of the worst sins, the Catholics believed, was that of *despair*. Four weeks after that lunch, Improvise had laid off its staff and was shopping its patents to get something back for its investors. Rick was gone, and Chiara had been transferred, humbled, to the Thought Leader Alliance. Even more than her college stalker, that was what Kate thought of when she thought of people using their real names online: Improvise and its users' failure to get enthusiastic, shackled by their actual identity. Improvise and Ouisseauhai and dreams being crushed.

‖‖‖‖‖‖‖‖‖‖‖‖‖

She let Zach stew a few hours before writing back to him something short and noncommittal. She screenshotted some of the funnier jokes from the LaWLChat forums—the ones at which she had laughed out loud, like the post where someone meticulously created an image database of the last ten Mitchengängers and matched each one up to a Republican presidential candidate. The ones she liked best she sent to Mitch, without accompanying text, because she knew he'd find them funny, and because she wanted to show him that she got it.

lol he texted back. yr gettin obsessed

She was, a little bit. She was digging way into the depths, following the trail of hyperlinks that the more meticulous LaWLChatters inserted into their jokes to explain obscure references to plot points past. MovieSpace never purged its archives, the cost to store data being radically less than the cost to pay someone to figure out what to delete, and you could click some of these links and find yourself on a page of the HOT OFF THE PRESSES forum that was years old, and none of the names looked familiar. You realized that there were distinct eras, that LaWLChat would sometimes be the best thing in somebody's life for two, three years, but no longer. Dip into the archives from 2009: Remember_Winter is there every morning by

7 a.m. on the East Coast. She (Kate guessed she was a she, she was pretty sure she was a she) was gentler than some of the other posters, an unironic reader before she stumbled onto LaWLChat and was drawn into the fun. *Eve's dress is what someone who doesn't know what nice clothes look like thinks nice clothes look like,* she might say, but then also *No, I can't believe Rick died in that avalanche! He could've been Maureen's whole world!* Remember_Winter was very invested in the ladies' romances. By early 2010, you notice she's starting to miss a day here or there, or posting later in day; by the end of the year, whole weeks go by with not a word from her. Her last post was in March of 2011. Had she grown bored with the strip, or the community? Had she just found something else to fill the time? Had she fallen in love? Her Irish exit from the boards left the question open.

Would she see Mitch's movie?

Later that afternoon, THEY'VE FOUND YOU popped up on-screen again, and she had another moment of panic, again unwarranted. Katie Berkshire had gotten her first direct Facebook message in more than two years. Long ago, she had posted in the MLM AND LOVING IT Facebook group in triumphant, bubbly tones about some entirely fictional success in extending her sales downline. Rusty, an MBA student at a second-tier college in the Midwest, was thrilled for her, and also not very good at reading dates on posts. *Good job, Katie, your doing great,* he told whatever version of her he had in his head, based on her long-dead persona and stock photo profile pic. *I love to see women get into business. Great for #America.* She felt a glimmer of all the fun she had had as Katie, bounced back at her from Rusty, like light from a distant moon.

7

NoVaLocomotive 7 hours ago

How many times are these pictures of this fucking
German train going to be posted here. We get it, it's
orange and its experimental and it's powered by angels
blah blah blah. Siemens has never done anything for
WMATA before and they don't know the system and it's
going to be a maintenance nightmare. Let some other
system do the experiment. This is how we got stuck with
the Adtranz cars they're trying to replace.

The_Real_Jack 7 hours ago

Boy do you not know what you're talking about. As usual.
The S360 isn't "experimental." They run basically the
same train all over Europe. Asia. Middle East. Amazing
uptime on all the systems. You know they run it in
Mecca, right. Saudi Arabia. Air conditioning runs all the
time. All those pilgrims packed in there. Think about
that when you're on the Blue Line in August. And the air
conditioning doesn't work.

NoVaLocomotive 6 hours ago

I don't know where the Saudis get their techs but there's
nobody in the WMATA yards who's ever worked on this
stuff. Nobody in America, either. Saudis probably aren't
union. Maybe they even bring in Germans. All I'm saying

is, AnsaldoBreda built the last three models, which were huge improvements over Adtranz, so why not let them build this one too. Our guys won't have to work too hard to figure them out, which is good, because they don't work too hard period. Just keep your head down and wait to collect your pension, boys.

The_Real_Jack 6 hours ago

1) Plenty of Siemens trains in the U.S. Mostly light rail. But all systems are built to be cross-compatible as possible. S360 has the same AC as the S70s in Charlotte or Houston.

2) The Breda trains are the ones with the broken air conditioning, dipshit. Saying they're better than the Adtranz isn't saying much.

3) You're an asshole.

Railyard Ape 5 hours ago

Jack's right that the expertise is available in the U.S. He's also right about you being an asshole. WMATA shop staff are skilled professionals and paid accordingly. Don't blame us because you don't have a pension.

The_Real_Jack 5 hours ago

Whoa there. I did NOT mean to defend WMATA's pensions. Yeah, let's build a system that encourages our most highly skilled technicians to retire early at full pay. Great idea. Works out great for everybody who has to ride the train.

Glad to hear you agree with me on cross-training however. They taking you down to Norfolk to see their S70s? That's what I heard.

NoVaLocomotive 6 minutes ago

Jesus fucking Christ, don't you people ever sleep?

There were several points on her trip to New York that would've been obvious, or at least unsurprising, times to run into Darius. Normal people with normal jobs run into normal clients in the normal world all the time, and they have to grapple with the social implications. It's awkward. You have this intimacy that you've established, a rapport that feels like a relationship, but you don't want to sell them anything or make them feel any particular feelings, and it's difficult to know where to go from there, or so Kate imagined. You have to make small talk. You don't care about this person in that context, even though they may care about you.

Normal people, of course, generally don't present a constructed yet plausible identity with a different name to those clients (Christine never directly forbade the use of the words *fake* or *lie,* but she never used those words, either, so they tended not to come up.) But aren't you presenting a different face to your coworkers than you are to your business partners? Not a fake one, but a modified one, a managed one? Katie Berkshire was not exactly the same person as Kate Berkowitz; but when Kate Berkowitz worked in HR, the Kate Berkowitz who tried to deny benefits to people wasn't the same Kate Berkowitz who went to parties with Miriam's lefty lawyer friends, either.

It wasn't the same thing, she knew. You don't get into as much *trouble* when you're using your business face if it goes with your actual name. But still.

The train station, for instance: that was a place where she would've expected to see Darius. He lived in the District, not far from Union Station; he was a subway guy, for sure, but that didn't mean he didn't like mainline trains as well. Kate hadn't heard him talk about them or seen him post on the subject, but nobody's enthusiasm was *that* specialized. The Union Station train shed was a great place for trainspotting: a huge covered space, lots of stub-end tracks, Amtrak trains plus commuter lines serving Maryland and Virginia, lots of people boarding and getting off, so you don't stand out too much if you're just looking. The only downside is that there wasn't usually that much to see: the commuter systems generally used the EMI and Bombardier equipment that agencies all over the country had standardized on, and Amtrak hadn't had anything new to look at in a long time.

Until this year, anyway.

Kate and LaMont were trailing behind Sigmar as he walked towards the front of the train, dodging passengers heading the other direction. "It'll be like we're on vacation with our dad!" LaMont had said to Kate when he found out they'd all be going to New York together, and she was sure feeling it now: he had thirty years and (despite the somewhat defeated slouch) six inches on them, and was insisting they go look at something that was a lot more important to him than it was to either of them.

"Ah ha, it is!" Sigmar said. They had arrived at the front of the train, the northmost end, the direction facing their destination, and were staring at the locomotive. It was aesthetically modest: boxy, mostly featureless except for the windscreen's gentle curve, that on-the-nose red-white-and-blue color scheme that Amtrak really pushed. It towered over them, but something about its proportions made it seem compact, petite. It was also unmistakably new: the metal frame was undinged, unmarked by years of grime.

Sigmar looked both ways to see if anyone was looking, then reached out to rest a hand on it.

"What is even happening here," LaMont whispered to Kate.

"It's one of Amtrak's new ACS-64 locomotives," she said. "Siemens makes them. They're brand new."

"They aren't that new, actually," Sigmar said. He had abruptly stepped away from the train and walked past them towards the passenger cars, and they fell in behind him. "They're a rework of our EuroSprinter platform to accommodate your train crash rules, which means they have to..." He looked back and caught LaMont's expression, then thought better of going on. "I have never seen the American model in person. It looks nice."

"What about that fancy one over there? Do you guys make that, too?" LaMont waved a hand at the bullet-nosed Acela train three tracks over.

"Alstom," Sigmar said. *"French."* He picked up his pace and pulled away from them.

"That was mean," Kate whispered to LaMont.

"Just trying to get him riled up. *Something's* got to."

So then, for instance: that would've been a time she would've expected to have seen Darius. Or maybe on the train itself. Railfans tended to neglect train interiors, in her experience—wheels and engines and destination signs had more of an appeal than seat cushions and tray tables—but Darius seemed thorough. It wouldn't have been out of the question. It would have been awkward, certainly, and maybe difficult to explain to Sigmar, but it wouldn't have been so bad. Probably not as bad as it was to stare at her laptop, pretending to review her notes and listening to LaMont trying to prep Sigmar across the aisle.

"Should I mention that I took the train to New York so that I could appear on this television program? With a Siemens locomotive? Would that be helpful for the ... the ..." He hesitated, then said it, sounding a little fearful. "For the brand?"

"Well, not if you just blurt it out," said LaMont. "Don't just be like, 'I rode a train!' Think about ... well, what's great about this train ride?"

Sigmar looked out the window. They were in the pitch-black tunnel underneath Baltimore, so he was looking at nothing. "Not much, to be sure. Your Amtrak—I'm sorry, it is just not very good. This tunnel we are in is very ancient. We are going far too slowly. The locomotive is not being used to its full capacity."

"Maybe there's something there." LaMont had a faraway look. "This new locomotive is a beautiful animal ... America's outdated infrastructure is holding it back, holding *her* back..."

"I would not call the ACS-64 beautiful. Or feminine. Would you? When we saw it, at the station? It is quite ... square? It looks like an actual square."

"It's a *metaphor*," LaMont hissed through his teeth.

Is what you like about this comic filmable? This was the only sentence Kate had typed in her prep notes document, and she had been staring at it ever since they left Washington. She drummed her fingers on the seatback tray, felt the train sway around her as it inched its way through the tunnel. *To what extent is your affection for this comic strip congruent with the necessities of the moviemaking process,* she typed, then frowned; that was just the same sentence again, except wordier and dumber. She deleted it, then typed: *Do you even like this comic strip?*

She thought about that, chewing lightly on her knuckle. That was the question, right? But a little too raw to present that way. Might make people feel uncomfortable. She could see them squirm. It was OK to make people feel awkward in a focus group, sometimes, but not over something close to why they were there in the first place.

Still, she didn't erase it.

Light suddenly burst in through the windows as the train emerged from the tunnel. Her phone buzzed in her pocket. A series of texts from Mitch had arrived while she was underground:

> hey i just got into jfk
> syched to see you soon!

She supposed "syched" was better than "siked."

> wait no i'm not at jfk i'm in
> newark. lol. gotta be more
> specific w my assistant i
> guess?

Then, a few seconds later:

> whats an easy way to get
> from newark to manhattan

This was the first time on the trip she thought about Darius. He had a weird fascination with the now-vintage monorail system that connected Newark Airport to the nearest train station. She didn't think he had ever been there, but every time anyone on the railfan boards mentioned train infrastructure in New York, which was regularly, Darius wedged it into the conversation, usually without much context. She typed an answer:

> there's this monorail called
> AirTrain, they built it in the
> 1980s

and then just as quickly held down the delete key as a flood of embarrassment washed over her. *Mitch Landers is a handsome movie star. He is not interested in train trivia.* She had been in this railfan headspace for so long—she was actually on a train right now, which helped, or didn't help, depending on how you looked at it—that it was organic. That was great, right up until you have to shift out of it, which could be abrupt and painful. *Traversing an enthusiasm gradient can be dangerous mentally,* Christine once said, explaining techniques for juggling multiple assignments. *Like a scuba diver getting the bends if they come to the surface too quickly. You'll find that the in-group social and mental norms you've cultivated won't serve you if you go out-group.*

Babbling about trains in front of a hot famous guy like a fucking *nerd.* It wouldn't do.

She started to type, casually, as if casualness were a quality that could come across via typing:

> I think there's an AirTrain shuttle that will take you to a station where you can

But before she could finish, a new text from Mitch came in:

> never mind i'm in a cab! see you soon! let's make movie magic happen

and he added airplane and taxicab emojis to the end of the text. She deleted her unsent text, less abruptly this time, and thought about how Darius would've gone on and on about that monorail, how he wouldn't have known what people thought about him and probably wouldn't have cared.

The phone buzzed one more time:

> hey where is the meeting again? oh and also when is it lol

Four hours later, Kate was alone in a shabby conference room in Midtown. The table was scuffed, the drop-ceiling panels were yellowed and chipped, and the fluorescent lights hummed at a frequency at the edge of human hearing. She was embarrassed about bringing Mitch into this aggressively unhip white-collar milieu. She wished some deep psychological gamesmanship had gone into the off-putting setting, because describing that planning process would have probably impressed him; but in truth it was just a co-working space that their office manager had found on the Internet that fit their budget, had decent Yelp reviews, and was available on short notice. She was frowning at her laptop, trying to figure out how to get it to recognize that the TV she had plugged it into was a monitor it could use, when she heard murmuring in the lobby up the corridor: a yelp of surprise, a shy greeting, some friendly acknowledgements. She couldn't make out the words, which made the emotional contours obvious.

A celebrity, she thought. *A celebrity is coming. Everyone's trying to be cool. Which I need to succeed at. Be successfully cool.*

Mitch walked in, in one sense normal-looking and casually dressed, but in another equally valid sense ludicrously handsome and impeccably put together. He was holding two Starbucks cups; both had "MAGILLICUDDY" written on them in Magic Marker. This was a character Mitch had played in his occasional *Saturday*

Night Live hosting gigs, a ruthless restaurateur who had to pretend to be a genial Irish barkeep as part of the marketing shtick for the chain he ran. The facade inevitably crumbled by the end of the sketch as he tried not to strangle his customers or rivals. Kate imagined the barista meticulously not acknowledging Mitch's identity as he ordered, imagined him winking as he gave the name, imagined her smiling and blushing. "They spelled it right," he said, grinning.

She honestly would've preferred a can of Diet Coke, but had been touched when he texted her to take her order. There's a coffee machine here, she had protested, but he insisted that nobody drinks from a shitty pot of ofice coffee on the mitch landers xpress, lol.

"So," he said, "should I be ... hidden or something? Is this a surprise?" He scanned the room, seeing only a conference table and some half-filled bookshelves, and seemed sad that there was no obvious hiding place. "If we had a little more prep time, I could jump out of a cake. A cake with Maureen's face on it, maybe. Or *my* face. The *Ladies Who Lunch* Mitchengänger. Just imagine my real face pushing its way out through a frosting version of my face, the fondant me sticking to the real me..." He trailed off. "I think this crowd would appreciate it. And it would work with what you guys do. The layers of, you know, artifice."

"This is going to be pretty, uh, straightforward," she said. "More so than a lot of what the Agency does." Mitch would occasionally text her out of the blue and ask her about what he called her secret agent train job. She tried to describe it in as matter-of-fact terms as possible, but he still seemed to have some baroque ideas about the Agency's methods. Or maybe he always wanted to jump out of a cake with his face on it. *You probably have to think about your own face a lot if you're an actor,* she thought. *At least it's a nice face.*

"We're just here to talk to some serious LaWLChat fans about the potential for a *Ladies Who Lunch* movie with you in it. See how they react, and how they react to you."

That last part had not been her vision for the meeting. "Mitch really wants to have direct enthusiast contact on this," she had told Christine when she was setting everything up. "Like, he *really* wants to. I told him I was going to arrange a focus group on the seventh and twenty minutes later he'd booked a flight. He didn't ask or anything." Kate had come up to Christine's office and found the ceiling open and her standing on the roof, and the two of them were staring over the Anacostia River.

"When someone has reached the level of success that Mitch enjoys," Christine said, "the things they want to happen generally happen without them having to ask. It's an occupational hazard."

"Should I have tried to stop him?" He had seemed so excited about it. Dousing enthusiasm ran against her personal and professional instincts. It struck her as cruel.

"Not at all, not at all. Think about what Mitch would represent to the enthusiast community you're gathering. Not a drawing that bubbled up out of the collective pop-cultural subconscious into the comics, or some image you can download and play with in Photoshop. The real Mitch. In the *flesh*," and Kate had been uncomfortable with how Christine leaned on the last word, but she got the point. "It will be profoundly strange for them, and their reactions will be immediate, intense, and instructive."

This turned out to be true. "Hey there," said the first arrival, a fiftyish white man with tousled grey hair, reading glasses, and a loud Hawaiian shirt. "I'm here for the *Ladies Who Lunch* discussion and Jesus fucking Christ is that Mitch Landers?"

Mitch smiled and waved from the other end of the long conference table. "The same," he said. "Or should I say ... Pete Mills?" He tipped his head forward and made what was apparently intended to be a very serious face. Pete Mills had been Eve's latest love interest in the strip, a passionate but humorless billionaire philanthropist whom the other girls hated and whose wedding to Eve was called off at the last minute when his dead wife turned out to be not dead at all, but an amnesiac who had taken on a new identity and eventually became CFO of Chrysler. Her memory's sudden recovery made the news the evening of Pete and Eve's exquisitely catered rehearsal dinner, leading to a tearful goodbye there that had lasted three and a half weeks in strip time.

Kate introduced herself and got the new arrival to sign in, which he did while maintaining nearly unbroken eye contact with Mitch. "Lyle Lewis," he said cautiously.

"What name do you go by on the LaWLChat boards?"

"Mirthquake-1. Is this one of those hidden camera shows?"

"Nope," Mitch said. His easy smile was not defusing anything, at least not yet. "I'm a fan of all your guys' work. You're one of the main Landerpalooza instigators, right?"

"Uh-huh," said Lyle, sitting down and still eyeing Mitch warily.

"Well, I know it sounds conceited, but I think the whole thing is hilarious. Do you remember the heroin dealer plot from last year? That guy in the vest who looked like me? He always—"

A younger Asian woman stuck her head through the door. "Hi, is this the *Ladies Who Lunch*—holy shit!"

It went on like that. She had been vague about the topic of the focus group when she solicited potential attendees in the forums— just that it related to something new in the *Ladies Who Lunch* franchise, something that wouldn't see fruition for a while. Most of the people who were up for participating in return for a $30 honorarium and free catered lunch were in New York—a surprising number of LaWLChat posters worked in publishing—so that's where she rented the space. Mitch was meticulously not mentioned in any communications with the people who agreed to come. He also didn't blink when the Agency sent him the bill.

The LaWLChat posters gathered in a wary clot at the far end of the table from Kate and Mitch. There were a couple of loud, laughing older guys, a wider spread, age- and exuberance-wise of women. One of the men was a little younger than the others, handsome, well dressed—he said he was a Wall Street trader and eyed everyone else warily—but most of their clothes were either bland or aggressively uncool. Kate spotted a couple of T-shirts from the online *Ladies Who Lunch* CafePress store that had appeared one day without fanfare, supposedly officially affiliated with the strip, though it seemed fly-by-night for a storied franchise. The floating heads of the three ladies on the shirt dated from the strip's glory days and were not drawn by the current artist.

There was a complex series of greetings and introductions and acknowledgements as people mapped identities onto each other. *Oh, hey, Mirthquake! Yeah, I post as divalicious.* Or: *Yeah, Jerry—he's the guy who goes by jeremiad, writes all those poems. He and I went to college together, and he got me into it. I think he's coming today?* It seemed that everyone there had met someone else from the boards at least once, and Kate could see those ties knit together in the larger group. *You work in downtown Brooklyn? SporkAndBeans and I get together after work Thursdays for drinks. You should come! We could do dramatic readings!*

Every time someone introduced themselves by their screen name, Kate caught Mitch out of the corner of her eye, looking like he wanted to say something. *I'm handsome_dan,* she imagined him announcing, and everyone would be … pleased? Amazed? Horrified? Outraged? So far, everyone had acknowledged him upon arrival, displayed varying degrees of gobsmacked, then mostly avoided eye contact, falling into their easy camaraderie as an excuse to not figure out what was going on here.

Kate looked at her phone. Ten minutes after the official start time, and seven of the nine people who had RSVP'd were there. Not a bad turnout. "Hey, everybody, let's get started—"

"Hello, is this the room for *Ladies Who Lunch?*" The voice was familiar, but so out of context that Kate's brain refused to process it. Then she saw the face: smiling, dark-skinned, eyes unfocused. He was tall, thin, wearing one of the maybe-official *Ladies Who Lunch* T-shirts and a fanny pack. "Darius!" she blurted out. She wondered if thinking about him on the train had summoned him out of the ether.

"Hi, Kate!" he said. "Wow! Mitch Landers! Hello, I'm Darius Young." He seemed to regard both of their presences there with equal, and mild, surprise, then turned to the opposite end of the table. "Are you guys on LaWLChat? I post as Darayavahus. I love it!" There were cheerful noises of recognition from the posters. "Kate, do you like *Ladies Who Lunch,* too? As well as trains? We have a lot in common!"

"It's important that even your untruths have a foundation in truth," Christine had said when explaining to Kate how stealth assignments worked. "And narrative lacunae are important for stealth assignments as well. If some aspect of your real life doesn't further your assignment identity, you don't need to disclose it, but don't replace it with a falsehood unless absolutely necessary. If a subject finds out information that you had intended to keep hidden, your assignment identity should grow incrementally more congruent with your day-to-day identity, not less. Don't build a bigger web of lies."

Kate laughed. She hoped it was convincing, because she was really glad to be sitting down. The world had suddenly shifted, like *she* was a high-powered Chrysler executive suddenly remembering that she was married to a dull man named Pete Mills and also obsessed with subways. "This is my job, Darius—I put this group together for a client. Wow, this is a weird coincidence." *Everything I'm saying is true,* she told herself. *I never told anyone on the railfan boards what I do for a living. I never even told them a last name.* She realized that she didn't know where Darius or any of the other railfans worked. There was a single context she had for them, and it was rails and brakes and route miles and grade separation, posting pictures of wheel trucks online and slipping through a fence to stand dangerously close to a train. She had a laser-focused image of all of them that was centered on the bright point of their enthusiasm. Who knew what other things they got up to? Maybe Charlie was a successful criminal defense lawyer. Maybe Jack was a Civil War re-enactor. Darius was apparently very much into long-running Photoshop gags involving Mitch Landers and soap opera comics, so obviously anything was possible.

He doesn't go by "foamerguy" on LaWLChat, she thought. She'd looked right past "Darius Young" when he RSVP'd, but she would've recognized foamerguy.

"Kate and I are railfans in Washington," Darius announced to the room. "We like to talk online about the trains they have there, Metro and long-distance. We went to see a new one they're testing a few weeks ago!" There was a long, quiet, moment where everyone looked at Darius and Kate, and she felt her cheeks turning bright red. Everything she was thinking was petty and mean: she had an urge to insist that she wasn't *really* a railfan, she was young and pretty and had a relatively active sexual life, and she resented that *these* people could be judging her, with their too-loud laughs and they liked *soap opera comics*, for God's sake. It was poison, she knew, it was all poison, and she had to get it out of her system or this afternoon was going to be a disaster.

"It's true," she said. "We did."

"Hey," said the young Asian woman, the one who went by diva-licious. "Remember like, two years ago, when Carol's husband was on that train trip that was hijacked by terrorists?"

Kate breathed out through her nose and felt the tension in her neck loosen.

"I loved that plot! Obviously!" Darius grinned. "They kept saying they were going to take the train to Mexico. That would've been pretty difficult! I figured out some routes they could take, though."

"Oh, God," said Mirthquake-1, "and at the end the terrorist leader takes his balaclava off for the big reveal, and it's supposed to be someone we know, and he looks like—"

"—Mitch Landers!" they all said at once. Mitch obligingly pulled his shirt up over his nose, like a bank robber's mask, then slowly pulled it down, looking mean, and everybody laughed. Darius, who had been hesitating about where to sit, walked towards the other *Ladies Who Lunch* fans.

Kate took 15 minutes to outline the idea of a *Ladies Who Lunch* movie via Powerpoint. There was a lot of excited muttering at first. When she told them it was going to be a comedy, the group turned on itself.

"The strip is not funny," said divalicious.

"The strip is *hilarious*," said Stockyard_Channing, a middle-aged woman with close-cropped hair and a leather jacket.

"It's not funny on *purpose.*"

"Like, it's purposely not funny, or it's accidentally funny?"

"Both, I think?"

Cool Story Bro, whose jorts Kate considered not particularly bro-like, said, "Can you imagine Mitch Landers doing all the male parts, though? With CGI effects so there are multiple Mitches on screen? It would be like my dreams came true, for real. I've been thinking of trying to make an *LWL* fanvid by stitching together scenes from your movies, but now ... I wouldn't have to." He sounded slightly disappointed.

"You know they already made a movie, right?" divalicious said. "It didn't do so well."

"Yeah, but that was before they invented irony," said Mitch. People chuckled, but didn't sound convinced.

"The problem with the original movie," said Kate, "was that it wasn't clear what register it was in. Was it a straightforward drama with these pre-existing characters? Was it supposed to be campy or knowing or over the top? I think Mitch is right in that there wasn't really a ... creative vocabulary back then people could use to think about how an adaptation could be pitched."

"You mean they weren't all up their own assholes thinking about movies about movies about movies or whatever," said Mirthquake-1.

Everyone was calling each other by their screen names, Kate had noticed, and she followed their lead. He was the loudest and most opinionated, which had made him the de facto leader, not that anyone seemed to mind.

"Look," said Mitch, "I'm just going to confess something. I Google myself, probably inordinately often. And I find a lot of weird stuff about myself on the Internet, right? A *lot*. Most of the time, I either laugh at it and then never look at it again, or send it to my manager to get a restraining order filed and never look at it again. But these things you guys do"—he had one of his favorite Mitchengänger Photoshops on his phone and was waving it around—"they're hilarious. They're *amazing*. I visit the boards all the time. I read the posts that don't have anything to do with me!" *I even post on the boards, as handsome_dan,* he continued to not say, and she wondered why he was holding back.

He was thumbing through more images on his phone. "Here," he said. "This is from eight months ago. Remember the whole thing where the girls thought Maureen's condo was haunted, but it turned out it was her neighbor, who always hated her and wanted to buy it and knock the wall down and make his apartment twice as big?"

"Literally a Scooby-Doo plot," said Stockyard_Channing. "The 'ghost' looked like you, and then they pulled off the mask and it looked like you with a pencil mustache."

"Right, and then you all had a contest to see who could come up with a better ending."

"Slow gas leak causing hallucinations," said Cool Story Bro.

"Eve's CIA agent ex-boyfriend testing a mind-control hologram on them," said divalicious.

"An actual ghost," said Darius.

"Right!" said Mitch. "What if we could do something like that with the movie? Like, cut to different, better plots. Like in *Clue*."

"Will it even make sense if there's not a real strip for people to refer to, though?" divalicious was still unconvinced. "These jokes are all like … parasite jokes. Para-jokes. They're jokes about something else. They don't live on their own."

Ding went the alarm in Kate's head. It was an obvious question, *the* obvious question. She would've asked it, so she had prepared for it. She could've just put it in her initial Powerpoint. But one thing she had learned from sitting through presentations in Christine's office is that it was more *impressive* to wait for someone else to bring it up first. She pressed a key on her laptop to bring up the file of survey responses.

"We actually did some random surveys about the strip," she said. "Not just among old people, either. The thing is, *Ladies Who Lunch* has a remarkably intense mental footprint in the culture at large for a fifty-year-old newspaper comic strip."

A single word appeared on-screen:

BORING

There was a burst of laughter from the LaWLChatters. *At least they're not offended,* she thought. Next came:

Those three pretty (?) girls in that weird strip

She began advancing through them, letting each linger barely long enough for people to read it.

Nothing ever happens

The blonde is the trampy one, right

Plots take forever

Does that still exist

Weird shitty art

I used to have a thing for the redhead

"Those are the free-form answers in the survey where we asked for people's impression of the strip. We also asked a more specific question: do you, or have you ever, actually read it?"

No

No

Not in a long time

No

Every once in a while I see it somewhere

No

My mom used to be super into it

No

No

"People already have opinions. Uninformed, unkind, and largely accurate. The parasite jokes can work without the host."

There was a silence that Kate read as impressed. Or cautious. Mirthquake-1 had a little smile and nodded. divalicious looked

135

sour. Stockyard_Channing was rubbing her chin. Call it 60 percent impressed. She was not entirely convinced herself, and that nagged at her. *Ladies Who Lunch* was cultural background radiation, like that distant, fuzzy radio signal that was the echo of the Big Bang. In the mid-1960s, a specific kind of hip young adult culture, a specific style of fashion drawing, and newspaper continuity strips had come together and burst and radiated *Ladies Who Lunch* lore throughout the country, and everyone was still warmed, just a little, in its dim, dim glow. It was one of those things you don't know you knew about until someone pointed it out to you. Helping other people find it would be the problem. Getting people to pay for movie tickets—or, more likely, log into whatever video on demand services would bite and let the charges flow invisibly onto their credit card—that was also the problem. But that was not her problem. That was a straight-forward enthusiasm-generation problem, so straightforward it was basically advertising. Her problem was getting these enthusiasts to direct their passion a few degrees in a different direction, so their display, their enthusiasm, their flowering good cheer, would attract more money, to make a movie that might make *more* money, to make the money Mitch was paying the Agency worthwhile.

She didn't like all this money flying around in all the connecting lines in the diagram in her head. She just wanted more people to smile the way Mirthquake-1 was smiling.

Darius broke the silence. "So if there's a movie, what do we get to do?"

Oh there we go she thought and then desperately wished that *this* was something she had anticipated.

"Like the contest you remembered," Darius said. "I came in third place in the contest. Do the contest winners get to be in the movie?"

Everyone was looking at her, including Mitch. She looked at him and tried to burn *This is your call* into his brain with her eyes. It didn't work.

"Well," she said, "the project is in a very early stage, but at the moment Mitch is working out the shape of the creative process, so..."

"Oh," he said, startled, then: "Of course. Of course! I mean, who'd be better with these crazy jokes than you guys? Obviously we'd get some ... input ... collaboration ... it makes logical sense..."

While he was lurching conversationally forward, she put a notepad in her lap where he could see it but the LaWLChat posters couldn't, drew a giant dollar sign on it, and stepped on Mitch's foot to get his attention. "...which, obviously, we'd make any contributions worth your while, in terms of money." He smiled. Everyone smiled back. A Mitch Landers smile went a long way towards making an incoherent ramble palatable, especially when combined with a vague promise of cash.

"Oh man, I have lots of ideas!" said Darius.

"Can you imagine if DOCTOR_FERRET sent anything in?" said divalicious. "It'd be, like, 'Kill yourself, Mitch Landers. The movie should end in your violent suicide.'" Everyone laughed, including Mitch.

The meeting broke up not long after that. Everyone shook hands with Kate and Mitch, and everyone effusively told Mitch he was "really cool doing this" and had a "great sense of humor about yourself." He wedged his way into several selfies. "You'd better come through with that money, Magillicuddy!" said Mirthquake-1, and Mitch obligingly put on a scowl and play-strangled him a bit.

Darius was the last to leave. "Hey, Darius!" Kate said. "Sorry I was so surprised when you showed up! I just ... didn't expect to see you all the way up here. Did you take the train?"

He shook his head a little mournfully. "No, too expensive. I took the BoltBus. You get a great view of the rail bridge going across the Susquehanna River, though, and I took some pictures."

"What brought you all the way up here from D.C.?" Mitch asked.

Darius looked at him like he was kind of stupid. "This is where the *Ladies Who Lunch* meeting was. They never have any kind of meetings like that in Washington. I get to talk to train people in person all the time, but not this. It's nice. Is there really going to be a movie?"

"Well," said Kate, "a lot of things could go wrong, but we've got you guys interested, and we have the rights from the company that publishes it, so the chances are good!"

"Oh, yeah," said Mitch, "I meant to tell you. We definitely do not have the movie rights yet."

"OK!" said Kate brightly. *Are you fucking kidding me,* she thought.

"You should get them," said Darius seriously. "They won't let you make the movie without them." Mirthquake-1 shouted something from up the hall, and Darius said, "I have to go with my friends. We're all going to have a drink and talk about the strip. Probably talk about you guys, too." Then he was gone.

8

By the time Kate and Mitch were making out in his hotel room that evening, she had almost forgotten to be mad at him about the film rights, or lack of them. Almost, but not quite, and she worked hard at making sure she didn't lose sight of his mistake. That particle of irritation was all that reminded her that this was still a professional situation.

Earlier, when they had walked through the revolving door into Midtown pedestrian traffic after the focus group, her anger was significantly more accessible. Yes, Mitch was an actor, not a producer; yes, he was still trying to come up with a funny name for his LLC. She still thought that he should be doing things in the *right order,* such as making sure he had the legal right to create a thing before paying her to help generate enthusiasm for it. What was the *point,* otherwise? Why had she bothered investing so much time learning all the inside jokes on the LaWLChat forums?

That's very Maureen, she thought, trying to calm herself. *Very linear and goal-oriented. Wouldn't Carol have enjoyed experiencing something fun?* The three Ladies were very present at that moment; she was still thoroughly in the *LWL* headspace. She thought about the happy band of LaWLChatters, headed to some bar, like the occasional misfits Carol welcomed into her home under her husband's wary eye.

She imagined it would be fun having drinks with them. Also productive. They'd be more open about their thoughts in that context. Maybe she'd ask Darius about it later, if later there was anything to be productive about.

"Hey, *thank you,*" Mitch was saying to a woman who walked by and told him, without slowing down, that she had loved *Low Information Voter,* one of Mitch's recent movies. He had played a veteran congressman with amnesia who was trying to navigate the legislative process without any memory of how it actually worked, all without letting anyone know about his memory loss. "Tell my agent. I want to work with the director again but she won't let me!" By the end of the sentence, he was shouting, as the woman who had complimented him was halfway down the block. She smiled and waved before vanishing around a corner.

"People in New York are cool," he said. "Most places that would have gone on a little *too* long, not that I mind talking to people, but it gets awkward at the end when they're staring at you with those big eyes and you don't know what to say. And in L.A., everyone is super-concerned that *they* won't look cool if they notice that they're surrounded by movie stars. That lady was nice. A-plus-plus interaction. Would interact with again. Where are we going?"

She had, without thinking about it, been shepherding him towards the 51st Street subway station, where they could catch the 6 train downtown to their hotel. But the thought of it suddenly made her tired: the heat trapped underground and the grime and the prospect of barely missing a train and having to stand on the platform with him waiting for another one that was who knows how long off. The *smell*. Mitch had been game to take the Washington Metro for a couple stops, treated it like a fun novelty, but in her head, she suddenly heard something that Christine had told LaMont, when he was trying to wrangle the CEO of a century-old stock brokerage firm onto an Internet talk show where he'd have to wear jeans: *Most of the privileged enjoy displaying their ability to navigate the systems the ordinary have to deal with, most of the time. But they have a floor. They will hit it hard and abruptly, and neither you nor they will know where it is until they reach it.*

There was a corporate Amex in her purse, and today she was putting in zero billable hours for Siemens, even if she had seen Darius. "I was taking you to the subway," she said, "but you know what? Screw the subway. Let's take a cab."

"I'm scandalized, Berkowitz," he said, but was already raising his arm; two cabs swerved across traffic to the curb to compete for his affection. She hadn't seen anything like it and wondered if the drivers recognized him or just sensed the aura of his charisma. He smiled at her in a very specific way as he opened the door for her; he had an arsenal of ways to make you feel more comfortable getting into a car with famous movie star Mitch Landers. *I know! It's ridiculous, right?* said the smile.

"So," he said once they had pulled into traffic, "Darius!"

She sighed. "Darius."

"He didn't know you were you!"

"He knows ... *part* of me."

"But he's part of the group you're spying on, right? For the train company?"

She thought of how Christine would've objected to that formulation: *"Spying" implies the nonconsensual acquisition of knowledge. What we're attempting is the intensification of existing sentiment. Stealth, to be sure...* But she cut that off abruptly and just said, "Yeah."

"That's why you were doing that thing at me."

"What thing?"

"That thing with your face. That was supposed to be 'Play it cool, Mitch,' right? It did not convey that message, I hate to tell you. They didn't notice anything was up," he assured her, "but I know you pretty well."

You do not, she thought, but she smiled, a little.

"So," she said after a moment. "The movie rights."

His shoulders drooped. "Yeah, I, uh, thought those would be easier to come by? I dunno. You'd think the people who own the strip would be *thrilled* to get a little money for a film option. You'd be wrong, though, according to Zach. They're just really evasive. He's working on it. He is definitely ... working on it, he assures me."

They had been sitting in traffic for several minutes. Their driver, a bald man with sad eyes, hadn't spoken since they had gotten into the car and looked like he was putting a superhuman effort into not honking the horn.

"Maybe we should've taken the subway," Mitch said. "Did you know there's a subway in L.A.?" He caught her expression out of the corner of his eye. "OK, fine, obviously you knew that. I don't think anyone rides it, though."

"They do! Thousands of people, every day." *Oh God,* she thought, *shrill pedantry.* One of the unfortunate side effects of enthusiasm. Sometimes, people are *wrong* about the things you care about. It was a problem.

Mitch only laughed. She was starting to see the advantages of hanging out with someone who just assumed that you liked him. "I guess! Nobody I know, though. I did *vote* for them, though. I have no idea why I want you to know that, but I do. We vote on every little thing in California, and I voted for the subways."

Measure R, she thought, a bit of specific data that, at this moment, she considered embarrassing to know, or at least to say. "You're the one paying me, you know. Paying us. You could totally tell me that you voted against the subways and that you park your Hummer illegally at bus stops for kicks. I would still have to help you get your comic strip movie made."

He glanced over to make sure she was smiling. "Yeah, but you wouldn't *like* helping me."

"I probably wouldn't mind it. You're pretty likable." It was true, movie rights or no.

⊥⊥⊥⊥⊥⊥⊥⊥⊥⊥⊥⊥⊥

"That one lady," Mitch said later, once they were at the hotel bar, and he had a certain amount of liquor in him. "She was all convinced that we were going to ruin it. What would 'ruining' *Ladies Who Lunch* even mean at this point?"

The hotel was the New York outpost of a French boutique chain, and the bar was all done up in dark wood, weathered and pockmarked as if it had been an East Village fixture for decades. (It had opened the previous year.) They were the only customers there, in a booth, and the splendidly mustachioed bartender told them, as he unceremoniously dropped Mitch's Old Fashioned and Kate's Diet Coke onto their table, that the kitchen wasn't open yet.

"There's a certain kind of enthusiasm that's so intense it doesn't translate cross-platform," she said. There was a straw in Kate's glass. It was equally difficult to look sophisticated drinking out of a straw and to look sophisticated pulling a straw out of a glass of soda. *Jesus, it's a bendy straw. Just because I'm not drinking booze doesn't mean I'm eight years old, cool guy,* she thought in the direction of their bartender. "They're burrowed down in their experience so comfortably that they don't want it to change. And it will change, if the movie gets made. The existence of other iterations will affect them whether they experience them directly or not. What we have to do is learn how to replicate their enthusiasm journey. Analyze it, mass-produce it, and make it happen more quickly on a subconscious level. Millennials are primed for quick media educations, for real. If we do it right, we can get them in on this iteration even before they travel through the other versions of the strip."

"But if you speed it up, that just seems..." He looked thoughtful, or maybe just confused. "It seems *fake*."

"I know," said Kate. "And what I'm trying to say is that something isn't fake just because it's not the kind of real you've got in your head. Not everyone's going to commit to spending two or three hours a week Photoshopping your face onto dudes in *Ladies Who Lunch*. We cannot create super-enthusiasts out of nothing. But if we can figure out the contours of that enthusiasm, we can activate latent lower-intensity versions of it. And those versions ought to get people to pay $10 for a movie ticket. Or at least $2.99 for an iTunes rental."

"Yeah. I get it. I mean, I guess." Mitch looked sad. It was heartbreaking, like seeing an adorable puppy that had chewed its favorite toy to bits and now didn't understand why it wasn't there to play with anymore.

"I'm just saying." The feeling of power that had flowed through her as she spun her web of Agency jargon ebbed away as quickly as it had risen. "You're trying to convince people to give you money to make this movie, right? Those people have to feel the possibilities. And they have to be *realistic* possibilities. *Probabilities.*"

"Yeah." He looked at his drink. "You know how in movies there's a montage, when something big needs to happen fast? When I found LaWLChat and had the idea that I should make a movie from it, and then I found your agency's website because I Googled 'internet forum marketing' or something like that, I think there was a montage in my head. You know, lots of me typing, making different kinds of faces at the screen"—he did a few for her; happy face, concerned face—"then I'm in a boardroom where a pretty lady in a pantsuit is showing me pie graphs..."

"Do you get the movie rights at some point in there?"

He ignored her. "...Then the two of us are looking at the computer and some other reports, and we're laughing, then eventually some guy at the Weinstein Company hands me a check, and I wink at the camera." He laughed. "I mean, not quite that explicitly, but if you had shown that sequence to me, I would've been like, 'Yeah, that's how that's going to go. Seems logical, one thing follows from another, no gaps in that story.'"

Kate tried to not dwell on the fact that she was wearing a pantsuit at the moment. "I think the Weinstein Company is aiming a little high."

"Probably. But how are we going to win so many Oscars otherwise? They'll call in all their favors. I'll be the first person nominated in multiple categories for the same movie. Best Actor for playing Peter Doyle, the handsome and eligible governor of Illinois, and

Best Supporting Actor for playing Carter Jones, the troubled beat-nik who's dealing dope right out of Eve's high-end scarf boutique."

Kate laughed. "Did you just make that up?"

"Oh, no, Peter Doyle and Carter Jones are all too real, my friend. And I will play them both on the big screen, or my name isn't three-time MTV Movie Award Nicest Smile Winner Mitch Landers." He grinned at her. It was fantastic. Even though he had announced that he was going to demonstrate a facial expression that was a well-monetized part of his professional brand, it didn't look fake. It didn't *feel* fake. It felt like he was having a good time joking around in a bar in the late afternoon, with someone he liked and felt comfortable with. Kate wondered if he really felt that way, or if he had mastered the skill of presenting to the world the affect perfect for any scenario, so perfectly that he didn't even realize he was doing it. Which raised the question of whether there was any practical difference between that and really feeling that way.

"The best thing about the drug storyline"—*His vocal intonation is rising, his eyes are glinting,* she thought, *this is real*—"was that it's never really clear what he's selling. He calls it 'dope' but he also calls it 'rock,' and there are needles but then something that looks like a straw. It's *possible* the people behind the strip are not super familiar with the ins and outs of narcotics use."

She started to ask how familiar *he* was, then decided she didn't want to know, and smiled instead. "You don't want to go past a PG-13 rating, though," she said. "Let's not get all *Trainspotting.*"

He smiled, warily. "How old are you? Wouldn't you have been, like, eight when that movie came out?"

"I'm 28," she blurted very quickly, which was not the case. She was actually 26, but kmac1987 on the railfan boards was 28, and she told herself that was the midbrain source of the abrupt, unpremeditated lie. *Keep your identities in line,* she chided herself. Too late to switch now, so she decided to plow on, this time with some truth: "And, of course, I've seen it. They showed it in my intro to film class in college."

"Intro to film," Mitch said. "Ah, the youth of today." Kate contemplated her persistent refusal to look up how old Mitch was. Under normal circumstances, when wondering about the age of a celebrity while sitting in a bar, you would pull out your phone and look it up. Obviously, that would be rude if the celebrity were sitting right across from you. Kate wondered if that might be slightly less rude than bluntly asking him.

At least a decade older was a safe bet. His line about a "pretty girl in a pantsuit" suddenly made her blush, as she restructured the context in her head. Did she look ridiculous, like a kid playing dress-up? She did mentally refer to this outfit sometimes as her "big-girl clothes."

"I promise," Mitch was saying out of the corner of his mouth, "that this movie's drug scenes will be the squarest ever committed to film. Junkies will kick the habit after seeing it, because they will be embarrassed by my relentlessly uncool portrayal of Carter Jones." The bartender had finally run out of safe directions to point his head, had seen Mitch's raised finger, and was ambling their way, sighing heavily.

"I know it's 5:30," he said, before Mitch or Kate could speak, "but the kitchen's still closed. The afternoon guy didn't show up, and the other afternoon guy quit."

Mitch blinked. "Really?"

"You could order room service from the other kitchen to be

delivered here, but then you'd have to pay the room service price. I could get you a menu if you really want."

"Hey," said Kate, "did you say it was 5:30? Could you turn the TV to Bloomberg News? And bring me another Diet Coke. And bring him whatever it is he wants. Thanks."

"Old Fashioned," Mitch said as the bartender walked away without asking. "Bloomberg News," he said to her. "I take it back, you're not the youth of today at all. You're my *dad*."

The TV was tuned to the Cartoon Network. The bartender gave a longing glance to SpongeBob, then switched over to Bloomberg and shot a sullen glance at Kate, which she ignored. On screen, three dyspeptic-looking middle-aged white men sat around a table, their suits on a spectrum from "well pressed" to "rumpled." Ghostly images representing things that might interest the discerning financial news consumer had been silk-screened onto the blue wall of the set behind them: numbers representing stock prices for fictional ticker symbols at some arbitrary moment in time; plausible-looking currency exchange rates, these in columns; symbols of America of varying levels of abstraction, including the Capitol dome, a bald eagle, and the Masonic pyramid from the back of the dollar bill.

The camera cut to the moderator, a chirpy young woman with blonde hair that, disarmingly, was not sprayed into typical newscaster immobility but tied back into a ponytail. Kate supposed this was meant to convince the viewer that she was young and hip and had a degree of self-awareness about being on television. Kate reached up and half-consciously touched her own hair, which had been pulled back in a similar style.

"... just crumbling," said the best dressed of the three men. "When that bridge in Minneapolis fell into the river, that should've been a wake-up call. Instead, we're still driving our trucks over these ticking time bombs."

"Ooh, it's already started," said Mitch. "When are they going to tell us the score?"

"...partnerships," said the middling dressed man. He had implemented some extreme measures to mask his incipient baldness, including an aggressive comb-over and a spectacularly bushy mustache. "Private investment is the only thing that's ever gotten anything done in this country. The stimulus was supposed to do exactly what you're talking about, but can you point to a single..."

"I'm not going to tell you why we're watching this," Kate said, "because I want to hear what you think afterwards. But you have to pay attention."

"Are you focus-grouping me, Berkowitz?" She decided she liked it when he called her by her last name and also decided not to let on about it. "All right, but let me move to your side of the booth, or I'll get a crick in my pretty, pretty neck."

"...but that's absurd, roads are a public good..."

"...computerized toll systems would've been impossible without public-private partnerships..."

"Gentlemen, please, one at a time." The moderator's smile got bigger, and, incredibly, more sincere. A few strands of hair fell from behind her ear and onto her face, and as she brushed it aside there was only an infinitesimally brief moment when you could see murder in her eyes.

"My report so far is that building roads is good, but also maybe for communists. Did I get that right?" said Mitch, who barely acknowledged the bartender returning with their drinks. "And the guy in the middle needs to talk more and sweat less."

There was a lull in the argument, and while everyone else was busy lovingly imagining stabbing each other in the throat, the sweaty, rumpled man in the middle took in a gulp of air, and then said, in German-accented English, "Yes, and let us not forget that rail is another important mode for freight, and even passengers, even today, even in America."

"Oh, trains," said mustache man. "Tell us more, Mr. Big Government."

"Hey now," said the bridge booster, "Rail has its place, definitely has its place. But it's a zero-sum game out there for funding and we do have to think about modern American lifestyles. Did you know they can build buses now that are basically like trains that run on regular roads? Amazing stuff."

Sigmar looked thoroughly miserable. Kate couldn't see LaMont, but she knew he was there, standing somewhere off-camera on the set or pacing in the green room watching Sigmar on the monitors, and she could feel her friend's anxiety bleeding out from the edges of the screen.

"Yes," Sigmar said, responding to nothing in particular, "and I think that ... that many people, not involved in shipping and transhipment and cargo and related industries, don't appreciate how much cargo is carried by trains today. And it's growing, cargo is growing, even in America. It is as important as trucks. And passenger rail can be as important as airplanes." *Good start,* she thought, somewhat charitably.

"In Europe," he continued, picking up speed. "People say, 'You'll never get Americans on the train! They are all driving their muscle cars or their Hummer-Vees. That's because they don't think about the consequences of what they do about anything. Americans!'"

The atmosphere in the studio got very icy very quickly. "Wow, I take it back," said Mitch. "This guy should not talk more at all."

The other panelists had been holding off on talking over Sigmar, presumably because he looked so fragile, but that truce was at an end. "Typical," said the mustache man, "The *Germans* are going to come over here and tell us how to be more *organized* and better run, marching like good little soldiers."

"No, but—"

"I mean, have you seen America, real America, outside New York?" the third panelist interjected, not waiting for Sigmar's response. "It's big, it's empty, so *maybe* you need to do a little research before you come over here—"

"I was only trying to explain some of the misconceptions! At Siemens, we do not believe this to be the case at all, we are working with localities, with local experts—"

"Oh, I forgot," said the mustache man, "You're here to sell trains, so of course you're going to tell us how great trains are." While watching, Kate had been Googling the names of the panelists and had already found out that this guy was a consultant with IBM, specifically working with equipment used to operate high-tech toll highways. By the rules of the TV panel game, it was gauche if your opponent brought up your job first. But if *you* mention it, it becomes fair game.

If you're building awareness of your personal brand as a thought leader, Christine would say, *never try to sell anything specific. Eschew proper nouns, especially proper nouns to which you have a proprietary connection.* She was going to be angry at LaMont. No, she would be disappointed, which would probably be worse.

"Oh, God," said Kate. She looked at her phone: 5:37. That hadn't taken long at all. "You can turn it off now, if you want," she said to the bartender.

"No way, man, it's just getting good. You tell that Kraut, boys! Fuck his trains! This is America!"

Her phone buzzed to signal an incoming text, and without thinking she jammed it into her pocket. Nothing good could be coming in.

"Hey!" said Mitch. "She said turn it off!"

She felt her phone buzz again against her thigh but ignored it. "I didn't," she said quietly. "I just meant—"

"Fine, whatever," the bartender muttered. Silence descended, and Kate sighed.

"So!" said Mitch. "That was a thing, on TV. Went great for *somebody*."

"Not our guy, though."

"Yeah, I got that. But he's—that's your company's guy, but not your guy, like *your* guy, right? Your guy is Darius?"

"Darius is one of my several guys," she sighed. "Darius has no business being on television, which is why he would have done a *fantastic* job. He would've been grinning and practically jumping out of his chair telling that mustache guy all the ways that trains could actually save money." Probably none of his ideas would hold up to scrutiny, she thought, but you don't get a ton of scrutiny in a five-minute TV debate, especially if you project a sincerely messianic gleam from your eyes. Sigmar projected nothing but mortal terror.

She had a brief, intrusive image: Darius, talking about Carol, and Eve, and Maureen, and Mitch, and the Mitchengängers. Mitch would be there, smiling indulgently, and Kate would be there too, off ... camera? To the side, if this were an in-person play? She filed the thought away. Christine would like it.

Mitch was looking at his drink again. "I think I want food." The bartender could obviously hear them, because he was fifteen feet away and there was nobody else in the room. He stiffened, ready to tell them again that the kitchen was closed.

"Do you want to get actual room service?" said Mitch. "Like, in my room?"

⊞⊞⊞⊞⊞⊞⊞⊞⊞⊞

Twenty minutes later, they were making out. They had picked out what they were going to order from room service but hadn't actually ordered it. Kate was grateful for this, because it meant that she didn't have to anxiously await the knock on the door that would bump them back into a reality in which she did not make out with movie stars, and they did not make out with her. Also, if they had followed through on their plans, the covered plates that the bored, jaded hotel worker would have brought in (she made them bored and jaded in her head, these delivery people who weren't coming, so they'd be all the less likely to feed gossip to *Us*) would be filled with garlic fries. Garlic fries! Who orders something covered in garlic right when she was about to kiss a funny, nice, and (let's be honest) hot guy? Someone who wasn't doing any strategic planning. *It doesn't necessarily pay to fully gameplan out low-probability outcomes in your head*, she thought, *because that can bias you towards unwarranted belief that those outcomes are imminent. But you can avoid actively creating roadblocks. What would Christine say?*

She felt a chill. Christine would probably not recommend hooking up with a client. In fact, Kate imagined she would actively counsel against it. She couldn't remember any specific admonishment against it, but surely—

Whatever, she thought, *this is nice.*

She had kissed him first, in a moment that would surprise her for the rest of her life. It was a typical New York hotel room, with the furniture arranged cunningly to mask how small the place was. Compensation came in the form of sheets with a high thread count (she thought about the sheets, and the bed) and a nice leather sofa facing away from the bed and towards the window with the lovely view. The room service menu was on the couch, so they were both on the couch, and there was only one menu, so they were both looking at it. And they were pointing at items on the menu and sometimes their hands would bump into each other, and *sometimes* it didn't seem all that accidental.

She wanted to kiss him and so she did. She hadn't given it much thought, for once. But she had already half-consciously decided that he wanted her to; while they were in the elevator on the way up to the room, she formed this conclusion without really being aware that she had been trying to figure it out. A person could tell. She could tell. She could usually tell, anyway. It was only when her mouth was far too close to his to back out with dignity that she thought, *Oh, my God, he's an actor, what if he's just acting, what if he's just being nice to me but because he's so good at what he does his "I'm being nice to you" is at the same level of intensity as other guys' "I want to sleep with you"?*

That all flashed through the top of her mind in the split second before their lips met, but once they did she stopped worrying, because he leaned in to her and she could, in between kisses, feel him smiling.

She pushed the room service menu off the couch, heard it hit the floor with a satisfying thump, and moved closer to him. She reached up and touched his hair, which was pleasantly shaggy and, she was mildly surprised to discover, free of product. *This haircut must cost a fortune,* she thought as she ran her fingers deeper into it. Then: *Are you still thinking? Knock it off.* A few seconds. *It didn't work.* Okay, then, a technique her mother had taught her when she was a girl and would get obsessively fixated on something: Make a list of things you're grateful for that apply right to this moment. *Number one: I'm glad I thought about wearing a skirt today, because if I hadn't, I wouldn't have shaved my legs before changing my mind and going with the pantsuit. Number two:* And at that point Mitch moved his hand up her back and rested it on the nape of her neck. *Okay, no more thinking.* This time it worked, for a while.

Not long after, they were on the bed. Mitch's shirt was off (*take responsibility,* she thought, *you took it off*), hers was unbuttoned. Her suit jacket was on the floor back near the sofa. Days later, when she was taking the jacket to the dry cleaner to get the dirt from the heel of Mitch's shoe off of it, she was genuinely pleased with herself for not worrying about it in the moment.

She had taken Mitch's shirt off, and it had been pretty great. It was a sort of Western shirt and had snaps instead of buttons, which made the process much easier than it might have been otherwise. As she was taking it off, she remembered that Mitch didn't take many roles that required baring his torso. He had been in a surfing movie a couple of years ago, but it had gotten mediocre reviews and hadn't stayed in theaters long, so she hadn't seen it. Presumably, she would have seen him shirtless in it if she had. Anyway, he looked good. Most actors, unless not being in shape was specifically their thing, have to stay in shape, even if you don't see them with their clothes off. Staying in shape was part of their *job*. She reached out and touched his chest. Mitch was good at his job.

"Hello," she said. It was the first time either of them had spoken since she kissed him.

"Hi there." He looked happy, maybe with a little hint of smug, but that was OK. She imagined she looked pretty pleased with herself as well. "Hey, can I tell you something?"

She tensed up—not visibly, she hoped, but a bit. She had no plan for the kinds of conversation that might start with that setup. Mitch Landers was a client, a famous person, a person who was, minimum, ten years older than her. She had spent less than twelve hours in his presence, and those were nonconsecutive. Did she *like* him? Yes, obviously. She never kissed someone she didn't like, even if she thought he was hot, and he wanted to kiss her. It was a rule. Did she want to be his *girlfriend?* Before she even mapped out the lifestyle this would entail—possibly bicoastal, or maybe she'd quit her job to manage the weird tabloid nature of what she assumed was his existence—a very clear *no* rang out in her head. *Well, but you barely know him, how do you*—but then *no* came again, louder, stronger.

Did she want to spend the night in his room? *Reply hazy, try again later.*

She thought about telling him to stop talking and then kissing him again, but she didn't think he'd buy it. She had already spent a lot of time talking to him. He knew she liked to talk. "Sure. Of course."

"My real name isn't Mitch Landers."

She laughed, then quickly covered her mouth with her hand. "What?" For some reason, even though she knew the idea was outdated, she assumed he must have an *extremely* Jewish name that the studios forced him to change. She tried not to giggle but couldn't not find the idea hilarious "Oh, my God, I've been fooling around with your secret identity. Are you really ... Shlomo Mayer? Maury Abramowitz-Cohn?"

"What? No!" He actually looked taken aback. "I'm not even ... it's a SAG thing. My real name is Mitchell Lawrence, but there's already a Mitch Lawrence with a SAG card. He's about 75, but every couple of years he gets a small part as a small-time mobster. You can't have two people with the same name, but I tried to change it as little as I could. I don't even remember where I got Landers from."

"Well, thank you for telling me. I feel kind of touched," and she really did.

"Yeah, it's just ... you know, most of the time I don't even think about my real last name. I've been in the business for twenty years now"—*don't do the math,* she said to herself, but she did it anyway—"and half the time I forget. I get a bank statement addressed to Mitchell Lawrence, and I'm like, 'Hey, who's that?'"

"Don't call me Mr. Lawrence, that's my *dad*'s name," she said, trying to do a funny voice and probably failing. "That's the *legal* name on my *Social Security card!*"

"That's the name of the naive young man who went to Hollywood and had his identity erased by the movie industry!" They both laughed. "But you know, whenever I"—he made a clicking noise with his teeth, and pointed quickly back and forth at the two of them in their states of semi-undress—"I have this compulsion to tell, I don't know why."

Christine's voice, in her head: *If people find themselves in recurring situations that require emotional intimacy, the expression of that intimacy can become ritualized. The intimacy is still real, but is safer and less intense.* A tiny, tiny part of her was a little disappointed at the thought of Mitch offering different versions of this reveal to different women over time, over the 20 years that Mitch Landers existed (*20 years ago I was in Mrs. Nieczelak's first grade class* is what occurred to her involuntarily). But that was quickly washed over by a feeling of relief. The pressure was off. Her fear that an attractive celebrity was going to imprint on her like a baby duck, and she'd have to navigate that for months or years, was absurd, and she realized that she had it in her head only now that she had confirmation that it wasn't true.

She said, "I thought you were going to tell me your real name was Dan. Handsome Dan."

"My mom called me Handsome Dan when I was little," he said. He was nuzzling her neck and collarbone. "So what's your real name?"

Was this part of the ritual too? "Kathleen Berkowitz," she said, eyes closed. "Jewish dad, Scottish mom."

"Borrrring."

"Well ... I use fake names when I do my stealth work online, and in person now that I've started doing that, I guess. My username on the railfan boards is kmac1987. Mac is for MacAlaister, my mom's maiden name." *Let's both talk about our mothers,* she thought, *that's super sexy.*

He lifted his head up to look at her. "Wait, so Darius thinks you're Kate MacAlaister?"

"No, that's the best part. I never actually *say* MacAlaister to them. So there are still no holes in my story."

"Wow," he said, kissing her neck again, "you sound like you have this all figured out."

"I do," she said languorously, "Nobody is the wiser." The fear she had felt when Darius walked in, the panic as she tried to remember if she'd ever used a false last name on the railfan boards; all that faded. She liked this version of herself better.

"But," he said, slowly moving downward, "how do I know that Kate Berkowitz is real? Maybe kmac1987 is what you pretend to be for people who don't know you work at the Agency, but Kate Berkowitz is for people who *do* know, to lull them into complacency and distract them from your sinister game, whatever that might be."

"Mmm," she said, "that sounds complicated. Are you lulled?"

"Berkowitz is pretending to be MacAlaister, and someone else is pretending to be Berkowitz. Like those nesting Russian dolls." And then he reached around her and deftly unhooked her bra with two fingers. An awkward road bump that her not particularly extensive experience had taught her to anticipate right about now had suddenly been bypassed. She shrugged out of it and liked the pleased noise that he made.

"If I were going to make up a fake name to trick you," she said, "I think I'd come with something more alluring than 'Berkowitz.'" She was looking up at the ceiling and smiling, not that he could see.

"Wheels within wheels," he murmured. "It's all part of your master plan." They stopped talking after that.

After a while, he moved his face back up to meet hers. "Hey," he said, "Do you know how you can tell this is a French hotel chain?"

She suddenly felt very bold. "Because they put complimentary condoms in the bathroom?"

"Aww, you guessed. I'd been planning that joke for, like, five minutes now."

She put her mouth to his ear and tried on her best erotic whisper.

"I am also staying in this hotel, and I like looking through hotel medicine cabinets." And then she laughed.

He said, "So I should..." and she nodded and he leapt off the bed and trotted into the bathroom. Before he had even turned the corner she was reaching into the pocket of her pants, now on the floor, for her phone, feeling extremely grateful she had put it in her pants pocket rather than her purse, because she had no idea where her purse was. Somewhere in the corner far away from this bed, probably. She was supposed to have met LaMont for dinner half an hour ago and was afraid if she went missing he would call the cops or, worse, Christine. Very quickly she typed:

> something came up tonite see u tomorrow will explain latet

As her thumb moved towards Send, she hoped autocorrect would turn latet into later. It became Kate's before she could stop it from sending. *Damn it.* She retyped:

> *later

and then heard the medicine cabinet closing in the bathroom. She was already holding down the button to power the phone off while scanning for somewhere to stash it. The drawer to the bedside table was slightly open. She slipped the phone into it so it fell quietly onto the Bible, then pushed the drawer shut. *End up on the left side of the bed,* she reminded herself. She looked up to see that Mitch had emerged from the bathroom, was now completely naked, and was holding the square condom wrapper like it was medal he had just won.

▥▥▥▥▥▥▥▥▥▥

Much later, he was the first to fall asleep. She was wide awake, though laying her head on his chest as they watched TV had put her into a sort of Zen state. She didn't have cable at home and only watched things on streaming when she had set aside time for them. "No cable!" Mitch had said. "You're the reason movies are going bankrupt." The idea of lying here and watching him flick through the channels and giving in to the appeal of whatever happened to be on was hypnotic and unfamiliar.

He was still on West Coast time, but had just finished a shoot that had demanded lots of late nights, he said, and surprised her by dozing off before 11. She had caught him with his eyes closed a couple of times—"I'm just resting my eyelids," he said—but by the time the local news came on he was snoring.

She liked having her head on his chest and feeling his hand in her hair, but once his arm flopped off to one side and his breathing got more deep and regular she got antsy. Slowly, quietly, she moved away from him and gently pulled open the drawer. Her heart began to race thinking about how long it had been since she had last checked in with the world. Hours, it had been *hours.* Leaving the TV on as a lullaby for Mitch, she slowly padded her way to the bathroom, still naked, and gently shut the door. The closed toilet lid was cold on the back of her thighs. She watched the phone start up and remember itself. Eleven texts from LaMont, of which she could only see the most recent:

and i am not fucking KIDDING

She had no energy for the personal, though. Let's start with the news feeds. What had happened since the afternoon? Kinkisharyo had finalized a deal to provide commuter railcars to Boston. *Marmaduke 2: The Greatest Dane* had somehow been green-lit despite the first movie's spectacular failure. There was talk of a *Heathcliff* movie from the same producers. She heard Mitch cough, and she held her breath. Then he started snoring again, and she kept on swiping with her thumb and scrolling through the headlines.

9

IN THE WEEK AFTER SHE GOT BACK from NEW YORK, Kate had been
working on being a Carol. Carol was the Lady Who Lunched who
got the least amount of respect on the LaWLChat boards, which is
maybe why Kate felt perversely compelled to stick up for her. Sure,
at her worst—like the plotline where she allowed a con man pretending to be the heir to the throne of Brunei to drain her husband's
bank account—she was passive and dumb. But she was also kind
and warm and didn't think about things too much. She enjoyed
spending time with the people she wanted to spend time with, was
open to their suggestions on activities, and didn't think very much
about where her relationship with them might be going. This was
as true for Bruneian Sultan-in-Waiting Al-Muhtadee Bolkiah (aka
Chet Masterson, a Mitchengänger with a discomfort-inducing
swarthy complexion) as it was for Renee Picard, the Interpol agent
hot on Masterson's tail.

This attitude dovetailed nicely with the aggressively casual
attitude she had decided to take about Mitch. Had she slept with a
client? Yes. Was he also a famous movie star? Absolutely. Would she
be up for it again? Maybe. Was she going to try to make it into an

ongoing, structured thing? Definitely not.

"*Girl,*" LaMont had said, on the train back to D.C., when Sigmar got up to go to the snack bar, and she finally had a chance to tell him.

"Not *bad,*" said Monika in the Agency women's bathroom the next day.

lol she had texted back to Mitch when he sent her a link to a convoluted LaWLChat thread that kept inserting the current *Ladies Who Lunch* Mitchengänger villain, a sinister cravat-wearing jewel thief, into particularly insipid Minion memes from Facebook, and she genuinely didn't feel like she needed to follow up.

It was in this Carol-esque spirit of being relaxed and not over-thinking things that she immediately agreed to Mesut's suggestion that they take the Orange Line to the WMATA public meeting without researching how long it would take to walk from the exurban Metro station through Northern Virginian sprawl to the elementary school where the meeting was being held. "The feel of the current railcars should be fresh in our mind," he said, "so we know what to complain about when we get there. The noises. The smells. Your trains have very strong smells, you know. From the mildew in the carpets." Why not? It stood to reason. It charmed her to see him getting so excited about immersive stealth work. Her main worry when she found out she would be working with a lower-level client-employee was that he would find the project absurd, would think what she did for a living was ridiculous. What she had forgotten was that the Agency was *amazing,* and that their projects were completely outside most people's experience. In practice, client-partners tended to either panic early on or become very, very enthusiastic.

Still, the Agency maxim was true: *Enthusiasm is a prompt to develop expertise. It is not expertise in and of itself, though it can feel that way to the enthusiast.* The train they rode on turned out to be one of the newer models, usually assigned to the Green Line, and was remarkably clean and quiet; the walk from the station to the school was a harrowing trudge up a broad suburban arterial with a sidewalk that tended to appear and disappear, stranding them on the muddy shoulder of a four-lane road that they had to scamper across to safety.

Eventually, they turned left into one of the developments and walked a few hundred yards that were darker and muddier than anything they had encountered before, until they abruptly entered a clearing and saw the school, brilliantly lit up. There were cars and people streaming in and the feeling they had out on the road that they were the only two people left in the world suddenly dissipated. Mesut paused at the entrance to try to wipe the mud off his shoes, tapping them against the doorframe to knock the bigger chunks loose. "This was not," he said, "the best idea I have had in terms of navigation," and perhaps there was value just in hearing him admit it.

The cafeteria was brightly lit, and the walls were adorned with posters of children who looked improbably excited about the salads and vegetable-laden sandwiches on the plates in front of them. The tables—real wood, Kate realized, not the laminate with faux-wood grain that she remembered from her middle school years—were mostly empty. One of them had been moved close to the far wall of the room; various informational displays had been set up on it. The three representatives of WMATA were huddled behind it as if they had barricaded themselves in. A space had been cleared in front of them, and a couple dozen chairs set up in rows, with the meeting's attendees scattered across them. Some people had come by themselves, looking around at everyone else with suspicion or fear. Some were dressed in T-shirts and jeans, and some were a little too dressed up. A few were looking at the WMATA reps with determination or anger, but most were trying not to look at anybody. Almost all of them were white. All of them were men. Kate realized that she and the WMATA employee who seemed to be in charge were the only women there.

In the back, as if being in the back offered any concealment, were Jack and Charlie and Darius and Rajiv, who had their heads together and were trying to be subtle about their chatter. Darius spotted them first and waved them over excitedly. "Hi Kate! Hi Mustafa!" His voice echoed through the room and all the strangers tried hard not to notice.

"Mustafa," Mesut said, audible just to her, then sighed.

"Kate," said Darius as they sat down, "do you think that Orton is going to steal Eve's diamond necklace? I do!" Kate smiled and agreed. She had posted the story in the railfan forums about her accidentally running into Darius even before he had, for this reason exactly: so that nobody would be surprised by this conversation. The explanations, the laughing over the coincidence between her and Darius, had all happened online. Most of the people on the boards, who spent an inordinate amount of time posting pictures of trains, seemed flabbergasted that anyone would waste time talking to anyone about an ancient comic strip.

"Almost missed the fun," said Jack, as Kate and Mesut slid into chairs in front of the trainspotting foursome. Rajiv seemed very intent on the informational brochures the WMATA staffers had been handing out. Charlie leaned back in his chair, looking supremely comfortable and relaxed even though it was built for an eight-year-old rather than someone of his substantial dimensions.

"Sorry," said Mesut, "it took us longer than we thought to walk from the train station."

Charlie looked startled. "You did what from the where now?"

The clock on the wall read 7:58. "Well!" said the WMATA lead brightly. She was a middle-aged African-American woman with her greying hair close-cropped, and her eyes scanned the crowd, not without anxiety. To her left, a skinny white twentysomething guy was tapping a message on his phone; to her right, an older heavy-set bearded white man whose head attached directly to his shoulders stared at the meeting attendees with thinly veiled contempt. "My name is Marlene, and I work in WMATA's Customer Relations Division. Thank you *all* for coming out here tonight!"

There were only about twenty people there. A musician or a stand-up comedian would've been embarrassed by the turnout. But Kate could see that there were far too many people shifting in the tiny chairs for Marlene's comfort. She understood why. When she'd assembled the *Ladies Who Lunch* focus group, she followed the Agency's iron-clad rule: no more than ten, just enough to provide a diversity of opinion. An eleventh would add ten potential new interactions that you don't control. Everyone could've ended up hating the whole idea of the movie by the end of it. You just wouldn't know. Ten was risky enough.

Kate assessed the crowd through Marlene's eyes. Kate's mission tonight was to think like a civilian, but her brain was sliding out of easygoing Carol mode and into her usual trained Agent patterns. Twenty people were too many people. Twenty people who weren't homogeneous were even worse. At least her focus group was drawn from a known population that shared enthusiasm for a specific and immersive experience. What did these people at this overdesigned exurban elementary school have in common? They rode the Metro, presumably. They were observant enough or bored enough to read the chipper signs WMATA put up in stations and inside trains, touting the NextGen Railcar Project and encouraging the public to help "shape the process." They were willing to come to a meeting on a Tuesday night. Beyond that, who knew? Riding the Metro was a specific and immersive experience, she supposed. The smell alone was immersive. And very specific. There was a lot more potential for these people to be pissed off than if they were here just to make dick jokes about comic strips.

If she were Marlene, she'd be most worried about the group of six people all sitting together in the back, the group of which she was currently a member. Would they cow everyone else and dominate the discussion, or would they inspire an opposing bloc to coalesce? When you're running a meeting, you want a direct relationship between you and the group members. Once a hierarchy starts forming, it's trouble.

"Remember," she had told Mesut as they tramped through the dark towards the school, "we should be a perceived source of strength and solidarity for the other trainspotters. But that doesn't mean we need to actively participate. Really, we probably shouldn't."

"Is that something your Christine said to you?"

It was, and there wasn't any shame in it, but she still resented the question.

"Yeah. She does this sort of thing a lot. Direct client work. Sometimes even stealth stuff. She knows what she's doing."

"Oh, I'm sure. She just has a distinct way of talking. 'Perceived source of strength and solidarity.' And so on."

"*You* have a distinct way of talking." *What? Did I just say that?*

Am I twelve?

Mesut only smiled. "It is true. But of course I only learned English as an adult. Maybe if I am here long enough I will learn to talk in English in a distinct way on purpose."

"Maybe you have a distinct way of speaking German, too, though," she said. "How would I know?"

"That is what the people who speak German tell me! I often do not believe them, but I am maybe not the best judge."

Now Marlene was launching into her spiel two minutes early, a move based on the hope that everyone who was showing up had already arrived. "User-experience engineers have been assessing the current Metro experience in light of what we know the needs are for twenty-first-century commuters. All that information will help shape our procurement process as we decide on a manufacturer and design for the next series of cars."

"Air conditioning!" said Jack. "Very twenty-first century."

Charlie let long sigh slip through his teeth. There was scattered laughter. Marlene let her smile droop a notch, then ratcheted it up two more. "Yes, sir! All of our user surveys have let us know that's a top priority for customers. We know the equipment on the Orange Line is a particular challenge in that department."

"The Adtranz junk," Jack said.

"Well," said Marlene. No-Neck sat up slightly straighter as Jack dropped the name of the long-defunct transit manufacturer. Phone Kid looked up from his phone for a moment, then looked back down and started tapping out a message. "Our maintenance staff does an excellent job with the hand they've been dealt, but there are always limitations. Our goal tonight is to look to the future."

"She doesn't want to hear what any of us have to say, man," said

Rajiv, not looking up from his brochures, just loud enough for the six of them to hear. Kate did a double take. This was probably the most words she had ever heard him string together in person. Jack opened his mouth again, to say something to Rajiv or Marlene or the whole room, but Charlie put his hand on Jack's elbow. "There'll be time," he growled.

No-Neck was now propping up set of large matted drawings. He peeked out from behind them occasionally, looking resentful that he, a presumably well-compensated employee of an important public agency, had been reduced to serving as a human easel for the evening. The picture he was displaying looked nothing like the S360. If you were being uncharitable, you could say it looked like someone told an artist to draw a present-day Metrorail car and then future it up by about 15 years. The angles had been softened into curves, but it still had the same paneling along the side, still had the same six-sided cross section. "Hexagon," Rajiv muttered under his breath. He was holding up a brochure that had the same art that would be part of tonight's presentation and showing it to Jack.

No-Neck flipped through the drawings as Marlene narrated. "We're planning on using new, eco-green synthetics on all interior surfaces. The floors will be a laminate made from recycled plastics and will have a rubber-style gripping profile. The seats will also be synthetic, but a microfiber that mimics the feel of the current upholstery."

"Well, it seems that is one less place for the mildew to grow," Mesut said, loud enough to get a chuckle out of Charlie and Jack. Kate glared at the three of them, but mostly at Mesut.

Marlene had caught her stride, and was describing WMATA's plans for the railcar bodies. "The NextGen car will take advantage

NextGen Car Program

of a number of advances in safety technology. Thinner frames with innovative reinforcement at key points produce railcars that weigh less and use less energy for acceleration but still score better on crash tests."

Mesut suddenly put his mouth near her ear. "That's us," he said, very quietly. When she looked puzzled, he leaned over again. "Siemens. My group." He looked so proud that Kate couldn't be mad at him for breaking stealth.

"I don't know what you two lovebirds are chattering about up there," said Jack—it wasn't unkind, but it was enough to get Kate to move her leg abruptly away from Mesut anyway—"but you're missing the important part."

"Wait, is crash safety the important part now?" said Charlie. "I thought it was air conditioning. Or the shape of the cross section? What's it this week?"

"You're missing the point. What she's going on about"—there was a new poster Marlene was pointing at now, a stylized depiction of a two-train collision, with smiling passengers cheerfully lounging in the interior "zone of safety" while the exterior car shell crumpled harmlessly—"there's only one vendor that builds them that way, and we know which one it is, don't we, BerlinZug?" He punched Mesut lightly in the shoulder. It was, Kate supposed, intended as a friendly gesture.

"We ... do?" Mesut said. He sat immobile, almost but not quite making eye contact with Jack.

"Siemens," said Rajiv, sharply. "But there's supposed to be a ... a bidding process!"

The six of them had put their heads close and were talking in low tones, and so Kate didn't notice at first that Marlene was taking a question from a man with wire-rimmed glasses and a ponytail in the front row. Actually, it wasn't so much a question as the guy talking and Marlene smiling like she wasn't being paid enough.

"I'm really glad to see from your drawings that you've chosen to honor the essential unity of the Metro's timeless design language," he said.

"Well," Marlene said, "these are really more conceptual, trying to demonstrate the crashworthin—"

"Yes, yes, safety is important, obviously," Ponytail said. "But isn't it *interesting* that when you blocked out the outlines of the cars for these drawings, your minds immediately went to that stout six-sided form factor, even though aesthetics weren't intended to factor into this *particular* depiction?"

"I wish all these people cared about train collisions as much as they care about how many *sides* the train has," Mesut said. Kate was glad that everyone seemed to ignore him.

"Who is this guy?" said Charlie. "We must know this guy."

An enthusiast community can feel like a complete and self-contained universe, Christine had told Kate before one of her first forays into online forum work. *There may be functionally identical universes nearby in conceptual space, with different inhabitants, all coexisting and mutually unaware.*

"Obviously, we want our customers to enjoy their Metro experience," Marlene was saying, "and the way the trains look impacts that. A modern look—"

"Yes, exactly! The Metro system is a *classic* of modernism." Ponytail was glad she was finally seeing sense. "And it instantly locates you in a specific geography. When that train pulls into the station"—he gestured to the crash diagram, to him alive with 40

173

years of industrial design glory—"you know you're in our nation's capital. I mean, did any of you see that German train they had running on the Orange Line this month?" He half-turned in his seat to take in the rest of the people, who were looking at him with varying degrees of trepidation. "When I saw that, I thought, where am I? I could have been *anywhere*."

"You're right," said Jack.

Ponytail seemed oblivious to Jack's undertones of hostility. "I know! I mean, I was like, am I in *Spain*?"

"Yeah," said Jack. "In *Spain*, the air conditioning doesn't go on the fritz every time it gets hotter than 75 degrees. In *France*, they don't think having ten percent of your rolling stock in the shop on a given day is OK."

There was total silence in the room. Marlene was clenching her jaw, and Kate could see that she was feeling the meeting slipping away from her. Kate was feeling it, too. It wasn't her meeting, except that it kind of was. She and Marlene were working together, even if Marlene didn't know it. It was too unwieldy. Too many layers. Would this have happened without her? She was convinced it wouldn't have, though she knew that wasn't rational. Maybe it was the observer paradox. She didn't want to be here. Just being here watching it unfold made it more awful. Maybe if she had read about it on the boards tomorrow morning, it would have seemed funny. Or, at least, the fallout could have been managed. She could have sat at her desk, drinking coffee, filing her nails, with the luxury of typing a sentence, a whole paragraph into the board's text box, then thinking about it, then deleting it, then rewriting it. Live-sites happened in real time, she thought with sudden awful clarity, because they were *real*.

Kate wanted to lock eyes with Marlene, to let her know that she understood what she was going through, though she simultaneously felt silly for thinking that would help and nervous about blowing her cover. Instead, she turned her head a fraction to look at No-Neck. He had a small, hard smile.

Jack was on a roll. "When Adtranz delivered those garbage cars in the '90s, WMATA sent them a phone book about how they were supposed to look, how the rugs were supposed to feel, the seats, the 'branding'"—he bracketed the word with aggressively contemptuous air quotes—"all that jive. So they sold us these things that weren't like anything else anywhere."

"You could save a few bucks with a generic cookie-cutter train, I guess," said Ponytail, "if you're worried that your tax dollars might pay for something beautiful."

"If it were cookie-cutter, it'd be easy to find parts for it. If it were cookie-cutter, we could call up guys in Los Angeles or New York or, God forbid, Spain, and be like, 'Hey, our brake shoes seem to get less sensitive over time, you ever have that problem? What'd you do about it?'"

This is it, Kate thought. *I have to take charge of this.* But nothing came. Christine's voice was in her head all the time. Most of the time. So often that she didn't notice it. She noticed moments like this, when it was silent.

She looked at No-Neck's smile again and thought about how differently he was reacting to this than Marlene. Was he glad to see someone speaking up for the purchase of a less-customized order of rolling stock? Would Jack's passion be quantified somehow and put into a matrix and shared at a meeting of an internal working group, used as a weapon in a byzantine internal bureaucratic struggle?

From somewhere deep inside her head, a sentence bubbled to the surface: *Don't fear constructive conflict.* It came from so far away that she wasn't sure if it was something Christine had said or the *sort* of thing she would say or just an excuse to not intervene in the silent, glaring standoff between Jack and Ponytail, which had lasted only seconds but seemed like it would never end. Kate's parents had never fought in front of her, and she had a hard time imagining a fight that wasn't bad. But maybe this one was OK.

Ponytail was, literally, the first to blink. He turned back around in his seat and looked at the WMATA staffers and said, with a showy intimacy, "I'm sorry about this. It must be hard trying to run these open houses when all the foamers come out of the woodwork."

There was a pause. Kate thought that everyone was going to let it pass and Marlene would get her presentation back in gear, but then Rajiv, of all people, said, "Oh, no, he *didn't,*" not loudly but loud enough for everyone to hear. The incongruity of the phrase and the setting and the pure unexpected amount of *sass* he put into it made Kate want to giggle. She had to clamp her jaw tight to stay quiet.

Jack's chair screeched on the floor laminate as he stood up. "That's an ugly word, asshole."

"Sir. Sir! Have some respect for your fellow Metro customers, and for us. And for *yourself.*" It took Kate a moment to recognize the expression on Marlene's face: it was *relief.* She had just been handed a spanner she could jam violently into the works and put a stop to all this. "That language is inappropriate."

"Oh, fuck appropriate," said Jack. He turned to Ponytail. "And fuck unity of industrial design. And fuck you for thinking people who care about this shit are stupid."

Ponytail was smirking unconvincingly. "Oh, please. Don't ...

think ... of course I care. Why else would I be here?"

"Well then, fuck you for not caring about the right things, numbnuts."

"Sir!" Marlene said again. No-Neck let out a heavy sigh and started to stand up, but Jack just waved his hand at him. "Yeah, yeah, I know the way out." Mesut and Kate looked at one another as he stalked away, each hoping the other would know whether they were supposed to follow him. Rajiv looked anxious, too. But Charlie and Darius just sat calmly in their chairs.

"I want to apologize to everyone for that," Marlene said. She was shuffling her notes in front of her, trying to find her place. "If we can ... if we can come back to the, uh, the safety features..."

Charlie looked up at the clock on the wall behind the WMATA staffers. It read 8:21. "That's a new fucking record," he said under his breath.

"No swears," said Darius.

"What kind of record is this?" asked Mesut, and at the same time, talking over him, Kate said, "Is that the fastest Jack blew up at a meeting?"

Charlie laughed softly. "No, that's the longest he's ever lasted."

Charlie drove Kate and Mesut back to the Metro station. "It's not built for walking out here. I admire your dedication, but you could've been sideswiped and left dead in a ditch." He chuckled. "I sound like my fucking mother."

Charlie and Darius were in the front seat of Charlie's creaky old sedan; Mesut and Kate were in the back, with the newspapers that had been spread out all over the seat hastily pushed together to form a pile between them. There was an unplaceable odor in the air. The smells of public transit tended to be consistent. Put enough people in an enclosed space, and you get a statistical average of the odor of the human body. People's smells varied in character and intensity, but *en masse* they smell like people. Like the way you get a muddy brown if you rub enough crayons over the same spot, no matter which colors you start with. Overlay that with industrial cleaning chemicals and, on the Washington Metro and its ill-advised carpeting, mildew. It's not pleasant, necessarily, but at least it's predictable and tolerable, with the occasional horrifying exception.

But the car was your private kingdom, and it was filled with the specific Crayola colors of your particular odors. Charlie ate take-out food in his car on a regular basis. Kate could tell that much. *Maybe there's a layer of dog, too?* she thought.

"I don't mind that the man said 'foamer' at the meeting," said Darius. "It didn't bother me. I say I'm foamerguy online, on the transit boards."

"Yes, what is this 'foamer' in English?" said Mesut. Kate suddenly realized that she hadn't explained to him the emotional engine of tonight's drama.

"It's what railroad workers call trainspotters," said Charlie. "You know, they're so jazzed up about seeing some new train that they're foaming at the mouth. And, more to the point, are trespassing on railroad property, which pisses the railroad guys off. And it's not nice," he said to Darius, "at least the way that guy said it."

"I say it," said Darius. "I don't mind saying it. It means I'm really excited about Metro trains, which I am."

"Yeah, well, you're saying it about yourself," said Charlie. "That jerk was saying it about us, not him. That's the difference."

They reached the end of the short street leading from the school and turned onto the main road. "Do you think Jack is correct about what he is saying?" asked Mesut. "That they are already deciding on Siemens trains?"

"Don't tell him I said this, but Jack actually knows what he's talking about a lot of the time," said Charlie. "So, circumstantially, he's not wrong about the signals. But nobody knows everything about anything. The WMATA people there probably didn't know everything."

"So why did we even need to go?" said Kate. Her gut was still in knots. She felt like the director of play that had just bombed in previews.

"Didn't you want to see the pretty pictures? They don't put those up on the website. Probably don't have anyone who knows how. Plus, you don't get to see a classic in-person Jacksplosion every day of the week."

Organic enthusiasm is not goal-focused, she thought. The other trainspotters didn't go to the meeting to ensure that money was funneled from WMATA's bank account into Siemens' bank account. They did it because it was *fun.* Jack had suddenly decided that WMATA ought to buy Siemens railcars because that dovetailed with his opinions about the agency's poor decisions in the past. It was fun for him to have these opinions, but his stake in them was different from Kate's.

"Do you think Jack picked that fight on purpose?" Kate said.

Charlie laughed. "You got a phone with Internet, right? Bring up the forums and see if anyone's posted anything in the last half hour."

DCRailTalk's forum software was old enough that it didn't have a view for mobile devices, but after a few awkward taps and zooms, she was able to see the latest thread atop the list of discussions. Kate read the headline aloud: "WMATA clowns prove they can't run a meeting, ignorant public proves pointlessness of holding meetings." The post was five paragraphs long. There were no replies yet.

"I don't think he did it on purpose, if you mean he *planned* it," said Charlie. "But you don't do a whole write-up about something you're *ashamed* of."

They got out of the car at the Kiss and Ride drop-off point; Darius started to get out with them, but Charlie told him he'd drive him back to the District. Kate and Mesut made their way up to the platform and waited without talking. The station was elevated, open to the chilly air, the occasional shelters offering protection from rain but not from the mist that hung around them. The illumination from the station lights scattered up and out over the exurban landscape.

Kate closed her eyes and tried to pick up what joy she could from the station, even though it was empty. She had to love it convincingly. She had to pick up the vibrations from somewhere. Eventually, the train pulled in, and the familiar recorded sound played, the four-note cycle followed by a stern, artificial woman's voice. *DEE-do-DEE-do. Step back. Doors opening. Step back. Doors closing. DEE-do-DEE-do.* The voice stirred something in her—affection, if not enthusiasm. It sounded like home, even though she hadn't grown up here. In New York, the subway had a man's voice. It didn't seem right.

It was late, and they were almost alone in the car. A few passengers here and there read or slouched down in their seats as music leaked out of their headphones into the air. "This is Breda," Mesut said suddenly. "Breda made this car. The Italian company, I mean. I think so, anyway."

"How can you tell?"

"Something about the engine noise," he said. "It's hard to describe. I could say it has an Italian accent," and then he laughed in a half-embarrassed way before looking serious, "but, of course, U.S. laws mean they have to build the cars here even if it is a foreign company."

"Can you do that for any subway car? Anywhere?"

"I don't know. I didn't know I could identify this one until I did it. Maybe it is a trick I will learn, to impress girls. Are you impressed?" She didn't look impressed, and he sighed. "So, did you enjoy that meeting?"

"No."

"You could have not stopped Jack from fighting, of course. And, if what they say is right, maybe this is a game that we are winning, yes?"

"I guess. I just don't know how helpful that whole blow-up was. We're supposed to be … subtle."

"Did you pick Jack for this job to be *subtle*? Because that seems like it would be not the right approach."

He was being funny on purpose, she knew, but she didn't laugh. She was about to say that she hadn't picked Jack for this job at all, but that wasn't true. There hadn't been a moment where she looked at Jack's posts and thought *This is the guy,* but she was definitely drawn to certain posters. It was like being at a party. There are lots of people there, and almost all of them are perfectly nice, but you only talk to some. There were a lot of railfans on the boards whom she had never private messaged, never bantered with, never pressed for ideas. The little group at the meeting tonight was made up of the ones she had picked for the job. For *her* job.

The train howled as the elevated tracks dropped to the ground

181

and plunged into the tunnel. "Anyway," Mesut went on, "Jack and Charlie like our train. They should like it, because it is the best one."

This time she did laugh. "If people always picked the best thing to buy, I wouldn't have a job. And there'd only be one company for everything that existed."

"So that is your job? Making sure that things get sold that are not the best?"

"No," she said, and it came so quickly that she knew she believed it. "My job is figuring out what reasons people have for thinking something's the best. And then you show them where those reasons match up with what your client has to offer. The client is paying, but the reasons are real." She was starting to puff herself up a little bit. "Jack got into a *fight* tonight for the S360. Would you have done that?"

"It was not a fight because nobody punched anybody. But no, I would not punch anybody for the S360. I would not yell at them, either. I don't enjoy yelling or punching."

"Well," she said, "That's why I picked him for the job, I guess."

The train pulled into Kate's stop; Mesut would ride on, under the Potomac and into the District. *DEE-do-DEE-do. Step back. Doors opening.* "Also," said Mesut, "if I did yell at someone or punch them because of my job, I would probably be fired."

"You can't fire someone who isn't working for you," she said stepping out of the train. *Step back. Doors closing. DEE-do-DEE-do.*

10

AN HOUR AFTER THE FOCUS GROUP had broken up, a new thread called LANDERPALOOZA IRL was live on the LaWLChat forums. It had been started by Mirthquake-1 from his phone, and his first post was a murky but exuberant group selfie of everyone who had attended sitting at a bar. There was no caption. The second post, entitled "landers creepshot," was from divalicious and was a blurry, surreptitious picture of Mitch smiling and shaking hands with Stockyard_Channing.

real mitch is 60% hotter and 400% nicer as any of his 'gangers, she wrote in the caption, and maybe 95% as smart.

Kate felt her cheeks get a little warmer when she read it.

Kate had started scrolling through the thread the afternoon after the focus group, on the train back to D.C. None of the people who had been there provided any explanation for nearly three hours, and in that time, the board went *nuts*.

Posted by
barbieworld
Sep 26 05:55 pm

What is this?

Posted by **Divinity Incarnate** *Sep 26 05:57 pm*	what is happening???? i feel funny
Posted by **laim** *Sep 26 05:58 pm*	YOU MET MITCH. Is this real. ahve we passed through into the dream world
Posted by **DOCTOR_FERRET** *Sep 26 05:59 pm*	christ not this clown
Posted by **DemonDog** *Sep 26 06:01 pm*	Did any of you tell him about Ladies Who Lunch and his role in it?
Posted by **barbieworld** *Sep 26 06:05 pm*	I feel like I am missing vital context and if someone here doesn't supply it soon I will do some real violence, I swear to god

But a couple hours dragged by and nobody provided any context, which whipped people into a further frenzy. One forum member posted divalicious's blurry photo of Mitch to Twitter—not just the image, but a screenshot of the image embedded on the LaWL-Chat forum site, complete with divalicious's caption. He added his own commentary:

guys i can't even explain this but it seems great?

Within minutes, a screenshot of that tweet was uploaded by one of *his* followers to Tumblr, and, properly tagged to #mitchlanders and #sexylanders, was reblogged prolifically by Mitch aficionados everywhere, firing out of the insular world of *Ladies Who Lunch* fandom and into the expansive galaxy of Landers lovers. Nobody there understood either of the captions. Most didn't really care, though several hardcore fans felt the need to add that of *course* he was nicer and cuter than the 'gangers, whoever those were.

Nobody stood up for his intellectual prowess. Kate felt bad about that, until she thought about the film rights.

Finally, around nine o'clock that night, while Kate and Mitch were otherwise occupied back at the hotel, Darius had posted a long and extremely detailed description of the focus group and the get-together afterwards, and everyone went nuts again. People started nominating their favorite storylines of the past few years for screen adaptations. *The time the drug gang hid heroin in the girls' suitcases when they flew back from Amsterdam. When Carol saved the homeless man's life who secretly turned out to be a millionaire who secretly turned out to be a con artist. Eve's false pregnancy!*

Within a week, a few posters had begun uploading scripts—not full-length screenplays, just scenes, but it made Kate nervous. She wanted to text Mitch about it, but the problem was that she didn't want to text Mitch at all about anything. And once she had to sit through the meeting where Jack exploded, her Carol-style go-with-the-flow attitude was blown to bits. It would've been better if she had landed in Eve-ian directness or Maureen-ish calculation, but she had fallen back into endless obsessive rumination, which was pure Kate.

Here was the thing about having sex with handsome, famous people, she was discovering: it was, if she thought about it in a broader context, thrilling as a capital-e Experience, and it had also been, in this specific case, really thrilling while it was happening. Mitch was good, or she was good, or they were a good match, or whatever you want to say about sex when you think the other person is charming and buff and it goes on as long as you want but not *too* long and you both come at least once. It didn't have to mean anything. It didn't necessarily have to happen again, or at least there didn't have to be a limitless vista ahead of times where normal Kate Berkowitz slept with handsome famous Mitch Landers.

Of course, there was a tug; she'd be a robot if there wasn't a tug. But as she took the Metro to work and checked the train news and LaWLChat and went to the office and took LaMont to Pickles and regaled him with the details and listened to him laugh, and went home and binge-watched Netflix and checked her Twitter lists and RSS feeds and made herself Greek salad, she realized how much she would rather do all that than whatever a person who slept with Mitch Landers on the regular did. Move to L.A., probably. Maybe if it were February there'd be more appeal, but it was October, and it was glorious.

Here was the thing about having sex with a client, she was discovering: it makes business communication with them difficult. This was why you don't do it, of course. A week before, Kate probably could have come up with several abstract ideas about why you shouldn't have sexual relationships with business partners. Abstract ideas are easy to ignore, clearly. If someone had told her *You're going to need to text him with a short, easy-to-answer work question but you're not sure if you can now because the last thing he texted you was* thinkin of u *and then a series of narratively incoherent emojis and you never texted him back,* which was her current dilemma—well, she couldn't say that she would have *not* slept with him, but she might have weighed the pros against the cons more.

She did, eventually, text Mitch her question. She was happy that texting was his main mode of communication. It would've made it easier to separate business from ambivalent feelings in the aftermath of pleasure if he split up his messages by topic and platform: questions and answers about the marketing campaign via email, mild endearments via text, invitations to ski weekends by phone call, pictures of his junk via Instagram private message. (Nothing like the last two ever happened: one advantage of being involved with a fortysomething man who was very aware of his fame was that the chances of receiving a penis picture, and having to politely decline further pictures, were really low.) But it did make it easier for her that the only object in her life that she had to associate with Mitch and his problems was her phone.

She could put the phone down and keep him out of mind altogether. Not that she would, of course. But she could.

> Any progress on the movie rights?

She wasn't even sure why she was so focused on this. It wasn't her job. Mitch was paying the Agency to elicit enthusiasm for whatever he wanted enthusiasm elicited for. She supposed if he never got the rights, he'd eventually run out of money and interest and never be able to raise more money or interest, so he'd have to stop paying them, which would be bad.

The lack of a legal agreement between Currently Unnamed Mitch Landers Production Company LLC and Monarch Features (a division of The Hearst Corporation) granting the former permission to develop a film version of certain intellectual property held by the latter also gave the assignment a certain feeling of unreality. With a signature on paper, she'd be doing her part to bring a very different kind of movie to fruition by generating creative demand within pre-receptive communities. Without it, she might as well be drumming up interest in a Mitch Landers fan fiction blog.

zachs still tryin to
track them dwon.
nobody at monarch
seems to want to get
back to us???

She sighed. Should she try to get someone from the Agency's
legal department involved? *Not our job, not our job. Not my job.*

This was her job: obsessively checking Variety.com and Dead-
line.com and other industry sites to see when the news would filter
out of the LaWLChat bubble. It would not come from an official
press release. You don't hire the Agency if you want a *press release.* It
finally happened about three days after the focus group: Defamer's
weekend writer, bored and needing to shovel more content into
web publishing's bottomless maw, saw those out-of-context Tumblr
screenshots and got curious enough about what "gangers" could
mean that she Googled them, stumbling onto the thread in question. "Mitch Landers Will Be Playing Multiple Roles In A Movie
Based On A Sixty-Year-Old Comic Strip, Because Why Not" was
the headline, and the scooplet rippled outward through the insular
Hollywood press.

It was the moment Kate prepared for. She had curated a list
of links to the best of the LaWLChat forum threads, "best" here
meaning as funny as possible without being incomprehensible to
people who hadn't put in the work necessary to be in on the joke.
They had been waiting in a text document, this list of URLs, and
now she carefully dropped them, little bombs of information, tiny
windows into enthusiasm, across blog comment sections and in
wannabe insider Facebook groups. There were a few different poses
she could assume: the intrigued outsider ("Did you guys actually

look at the message board? Jesus these guys are obsessed. Pretty hilarious, though."), the casually smug insider ("I used to post there a few years ago and was always amazed how funny everyone is— those Photoshop contests were epic. Not sure if it's going to work as a movie but who would've thought it would work as a Photoshop contest, honestly.") Always link, link, link back to LaWLChat, hope people would spread it around, hope the germ of what made Mitch laugh would start making other people laugh as well, people with producer jobs, people who worked at studios who had to pitch ideas to their bosses for a living.

"He doesn't have the *rights?*" said LaMont in the break room one day as he and Kate and Mesut ate lunch. "Oh, my God, that's classic. Classic Mitch."

"There's no such thing as classic Mitch," Kate said. "I don't know what that even is. *You* wouldn't know what that even is, definitely."

"Um, I've watched *Oops, I Did It Again* three times in the last month alone, so I think I know what constitutes classic Mitch." This was a moderately successful movie from four years ago, in which Mitch's character had retrograde amnesia and his family had to create new challenges for him that he could solve in a day so that he didn't lose his sense of purpose. It was, despite that description, a comedy.

"So ... there will be no movie?" said Mesut. "It seems like you are doing a lot of work for a thing that does not exist and maybe will never exist. Even if we do not sell the S360 to WMATA, the train still exists." He held his coffee cup in both hands, which he could do because his phone was in his pocket. His phone was always in his pocket and turned off when he was in the break room. "What is the point of taking a break if you are looking at your phone? Work happens on your phone," he had said. She tried to do it herself when he was there, out of some combination of embarrassment and a desire for self-improvement. It made her incredibly antsy.

"There's going to be a movie," she said with confidence. Then: "Or not. I don't know. But he'll get the rights eventually. That's like the least of the barriers to this project happening, honestly." Her phone buzzed in her pocket, three times in rapid succession. *Doesn't count if someone's trying to text me,* she thought, and pulled it out.

"Mitch," she said, and didn't read the text out loud, because it started hey cutie . She quickly flipped to the next message, hoping her face didn't flush.

"Did he get the rights?" asked LaMont. He was looking at his phone. He had been looking at his phone for the entire conversation.

"No," she said. "Also, he spelled 'rights' r-i-t-e-s."

"Classic Mitch."

She had hoped Monarch would do a deal once word about Mitch's imaginary movie had filtered out into the world. She hadn't and wouldn't have planned the play this way, but it didn't hurt to have an optimistic scenario in mind. It's one thing for an anonymous low-level executive from some production company you've never heard of to call an anonymous low-level executive at a slowly contracting media conglomerate and talk about potential movie franchises in the abstract; it's another for a syndicate bigwig to see a property they hadn't thought of in years suddenly be the subject of press buzz about something new and weird and interesting. Of course, in the *pessimistic* scenario, this just leads them to strike a harder bargain, to add a zero or two to the initially proposed price.

But as near as she could tell, as filtered from Zach via Mitch's terrible texting orthography, that wasn't what was happening either.

There were no attempts at negotiations, not even starting from insanely elevated offers.

> they keep telling zach their interested but never call him back.

> every time he calls they foreward him to someone new. its pretty weird???

Something else was going on. It wasn't her job, but she still wanted to shake it loose.

There was less chatter about the movie on LaWLChat than Kate would've liked. After a flurry of interest in the days after the focus group, the discussion there had gone back to its usual patterns. It didn't help that the strip's current plot was particularly juicy: Carol's husband had to go to Australia for work and the other girls tagged along, leading Maureen and Eve into romances with a 22-year-old surfer and an Aborigine mystic, respectively. The active Landerpalooza thread was all Aussie-themed. do you like what you see lady? lol Mitch texted her, along with a link to a Photoshop featuring his face superimposed onto a shirtless Paul-Hogan-as-Crocodile-Dundee, looming menacingly over the ladies as they lay out on the beach.

What does this even mean? Kate wondered. Much later, she realized that this would be the closest he ever came to sexting her.

But there was only one thread dedicated to the movie, and it was fairly low-traffic, just a few posts a day, mostly plot ideas or a few pages of screenplay. Darius was the most active poster, and a lot of his concepts were thuddingly literal.

| Posted by
Darayavahus
Oct 03 12:33 pm | All three girls date men at the same time who look like Mitch Landers. They go horseback riding. There is a ghost cowboy. The ghost also looks like Mitch Landers. |

When the movie came up in other discussion threads, there was less enthusiasm than Kate would've liked. Once the initial glow of excitement had worn off, people had practical questions.

| Posted by
Mirthquake-1
Oct 04 02:09 pm | i'm telling you this is going to be funny as hell |

| Posted by
SlamDunk
Oct 04 02:09 pm | Emma Stone for Maureen BTW |

| Posted by
divalicious
Oct 04 02:11 pm | I know we love this strip but the whole point of why we love it is that it sucks. Like we make fun of it because it sucks. |

| Posted by
Mirthquake-1
Oct 04 02:15 pm | i guess but the movie will suck too. in a good way? |

| Posted by
divalicious
Oct 04 02:29 pm | It only takes 15 seconds to read the strip and jump to the part where we make fun of it tho. I don't know if I can last 2 hours. |

| Posted by
Darayavahus
Oct 04 02:33 pm | Mitch Landers said that we could get paid if we help on the movie. How do you think that will happen??? Lets talk about it on facetime! |

| Posted by
Mirthquake-1
Oct 04 02:36 pm | @divalicious: i guess it depends on how they approach it. maybe they'll fuck it up, i dunno. @Darayavahus: not quickly and not very much, is my guess |

She texted Mitch about the payment question, eventually. How would any contributions the LaWLChatters make be structured? Would they get story credit, maybe?

> we can do another round table discuss/focus group like in nyc.

> have em all sign releases

> associate producer credit, doesnt come with writers guild scale money or rights or anyting

> u wanna run teh group again?

Little nominal checks for everyone, she thought, staring at the phone. There was a knot in her gut.

> Honestly when it gets to that point that'll be more the creative phase of the project, don't you think? Not really the Agency's core competence.

> oh come on kate u know that once it comes out the LaWLChat guys are gonna be part of the publicity for this movie

Cheap story ideas and free advertising. *Much smarter than a*

Mitchengänger, she thought.

> plus itd be fun to hang
> out together while were
> working. cmmooonnnn

She stood up in her cube and looked around the office. There was so much exposed guts and history to the building: the floor underfoot was the warehouse's original wooden floor, its scuffs now safely slathered in polyurethane so you could even walk on it in socks. The exposed metal structural beams and HVAC infrastructure. And yet also: fluorescent lights humming just at the threshold of human hearing, the omnipresent workplace mosquito. Her cube walls, that grey-beige fabric stretched taut over a plastic frame. The laptop sitting on whatever mysterious synthetic composite material made up the desktop. For a long way in any direction, heads bowed over desks just visible over the cube walls and keys clacking and occasionally someone talking softly on the phone to someone else who still talked on the phone. She tapped out:

> Maybe

She paused, and wondered where he was texting her from. Some San Fernando Valley office or studio space, maybe? His trailer on whatever movie he was filming now? The beach? She tried and failed to visualize him. She didn't really know where to put him. She knew what his hipbone felt like under her thumb but that was about it. She added:

> Why didn't you tell them
> you were handsome_dan?

He replied:

> it just seemed like itd be weird. theyd think i was spying on them more than they already think

She thought for a minute.

> When we have some news for the LaWLChatters, will you post it as handsome_ dan? Maybe as "something you heard"? I want it to seem organic.

There was a long pause. She almost put her phone down and took a walk to get coffee, but then he replied:

> doing things in disguise is more your jam, isn't it? lol

She sighed. *Figures.* That left one entry vector into LaWLChat: someone who knew her organically, or thought he did, someone who was already showing elevated enthusiasm for the project.

Posted by
Darayavahus
Oct 06 05:45 am

Am I the first one to post about today's strip? I hope the surfing shark attack is in the movie!!!

Darius, she thought, *keep it up.*

11

"This is definitely what I expected when I came to the United States in terms of what is ... I think the word in English is 'seedy,' yes?" Kate and Mesut had just left the Metro. New York Avenue was a relatively new infill station on the Red Line, all gleaming bright surfaces and clean glass, but then you went down to the street: there was trash on the ground, and long warehouse walls with graffiti and broken windows, and streetlights that flickered or didn't work at all. She felt OK walking down this street in the dark, just the two of them. She was an American and this was her squalorous element, she supposed.

"Define 'seedy,'" she said.

"You know, like, this area, which is in the middle of the city but seems to have been abandoned. There is nobody in any of these buildings. The road is of poor quality. There is a new Metro station, but it doesn't seem to be serving anything."

"All the new development is on the other side of the tracks." The elevated Metro line and the Northeast Corridor tracks coming into Union Station formed a physical barrier, cutting them off from a more vibrant neighborhood and leaving them in this dead zone.

"Anyway, what do you mean you *expected* seedy?"

"The mayor of this city smoked a pipe of cocaine in a video, if you are aware of that."

"Twenty-five years ago! And he did it in a nice hotel, not on the *street.*"

He didn't say anything. "If we were going to an EDM show in Berlin," she said, "where would we be walking? They don't have them at the opera house, do they?" It came out more combative than she intended.

"No, no, we would get off the S-Bahn in a part of the city with lots of warehouses, many no longer used. The former East, probably. And there would be graffiti. Of course, Berlin has graffiti, every large city does. But there it seems better curated, in my opinion. No offense."

She laughed. "I live in *Arlington.* Trash-talk D.C.'s graffiti all you want, I don't care."

The street was starting to feel less abandoned: there was noise coming from far up ahead, people talking and laughing and shouting over each other to be heard, and light spilling out of one of the warehouses. She could hear music coming from inside, a throbbing, driving electronic beat, very, very fast. A man said something with a deep voice and a woman laughed. People were emerging from parked cars and side streets, joining them on the sidewalk, wearing an eclectic array of outfits: ironic T-shirts with ringer collars and inscrutable logos; faux-working-class jackets that might be actual working-class jackets; gold and silvery booty shorts and body paint. One guy wore all black, like a puppeteer. There were more men than women and more beards than not. Kate was wearing business casual—black dress pants that were cut sort of cool, but sort of cool for *work,* and a polka-dot Ann Taylor blouse. She wished she'd had time to go back to Arlington, free of graffiti as it was, because somewhere in the back of her closet were clothes that were, if not actively hip, then at least less conspicuous.

There was a guy across the street in a suit and tie, heading in the same direction they were, who looked about as wary as she felt. He was too old to be wearing it ironically, she decided. Mesut, with his jacket that was a little too big and his pants that were a little too short, looked simultaneously very ordinary and as if he were visiting from a strange planet, and frankly stood out less than she did.

At that moment, Kate was finding it harder and harder to avoid thinking about the biggest downside to coming here tonight: she didn't like electronic dance music, at all. She had largely been able to put that out of her mind so far. When she'd said she would come, in fact, it actually felt like something of a triumph. "Hey, nerds!" Monika had said brightly as Kate and Mesut huddled in her cube, talking about Jack. Both swung awkwardly around in their office chairs, half-crashing into each other in the process. Kate pushed away from Mesut, viscerally feeling a vague panic like she'd been caught doing something she shouldn't, though she wasn't sure what. Monika was standing in the cube entrance. "I don't suppose you guys know anything about Sons of UNIVAC, do you?"

"No," said Kate. "Yes," said Mesut, and both women looked at him in surprise. Then Monika smiled. "Of course you do," she said, and Mesut sat up straighter and brushed nonexistent lint off his dorky European jacket, and they talked about Sons of UNIVAC, with whom Mesut was very well acquainted. They were an experimental electronic music collective who used reproductions of early computing hardware to make experimental electronic music of the sort that, had she thought about it at the time, Kate could've predicted pretty easily that she would hate. "They are legendary, of course. Everyone in the German scene knows of them. Also obviously they cannot bring their equipment to Europe because it would be too delicate. There are vacuum tubes and such. So I have only heard recordings, which is too bad."

Kate knew how it would sound before she said it, but she still said it. "But, I mean, it's just electronic? Like, the equipment goes right to a digital file? So..."

Mesut looked at her in frank horror. "The components are analog, not digital. UNIV-*AC*. Analog computer. So, the sounds are different every time, like a real instrument. An ordinary instrument," he corrected himself, and she could feel the brief hint of shame when he realized he had fallen into the language of the haters.

"Plus: acoustics," said Monika. "Everything is different in a live space. And all the people. The energy!" There was literally nothing that made Kate feel older than going to see live music: the concrete floors were agony on her feet, no matter how sensible her shoes, everyone was taller than she was, people spilled drinks on her, and it was all so fucking loud.

"OK, so, Sons of UNIVAC are doing a secret show at a warehouse in NoMa tonight," said Monika. She lowered her voice and looked around conspiratorially, as if the secret show were a secret even from everyone at the Agency and not (as it was immediately clear to Kate) an Agency project. It was a transparent move to spark Mesut's interest and enthusiasm via a shared secret bubble, and Kate resented Monika for doing it and Mesut because it worked. Monika was double-booked on two project events tonight. Would Kate go to do an enthusiasm census? Mesut was welcome to tag along, of course. Kate agreed, even though the enthusiasm census was not an Agency tool that Kate had a lot of respect or use for. It was qualitative, not quantitative. What was the turnout like, compared to similar events? What was the vibe like? Were people having fun? Did they look confused? Did it seem like they had been tricked into going to a show full of "music" that was just electronic bloops and squawks with no discernible melody? Kate was getting ahead of herself.

"Wait, but Sons of UNIVAC paid you to secretly promote this show?" Mesut said. He looked concerned. "That is ... surprising to me. They have a very long essay on their web site that discusses capitalism and their many disagreements with it."

"They're not the client," Monika said. "Sons of UNIVAC doesn't know about any of the under-the-radar promotion we've done for this. Sony is launching a new euro/experimental label and is thinking of trying to sign the band, but they want to get a sense of their potential first."

"So ... Sony is paying you to promote a music collective that they haven't even spoken to yet?"

"Sony *paid* us to do enthusiasm censuses for a few of their shows over the past year and that's it. Boring boring. We finished that months ago. But we decided to do sub rosa promotional work on this last one—not on Sony's dime, obviously. Then we'll measure the difference, and when it works"—Monika smiled a hard smile; there was no doubt in her mind it would work—"we'll have a whole presentation ready to go about how this is the kind of band that resists conventional marketing. If they want to monetize them, they have to go through us."

Mesut looked at Monika for a long moment. Whatever nascent attraction he had felt earlier had been overlaid—though not necessarily replaced—by a healthy dose of respect, bordering on fear. He

leaned away from her, less subtly than he probably imagined, then looked at Kate and said, "This is even much more devious than what we are doing, I think."

"There's a whole extra layer to this play," said Kate that night as they got closer to the warehouse and heard the murmuring (from people) and the squealing (from machines). "It's weird that this is the climax of the project that Monika's been working on for months, but she's not here to assess it, right?"

Mesut shrugged. "Well, but Christine told her that she had to be at an event for some other client. You do not want to anger Christine, after all. She might say something to you that is difficult to understand but very terrifying."

"Stop it," Kate said, and then said, "You haven't even spoken more than five minutes with her," and then said, "Anyway, she really does know what she's doing." When Monika had asked if Kate would go to see the Sons of UNIVAC show, she'd looked a little smug: she'd love do the census herself, but she had to go see a different band (the kind of band normals might have heard of, not an oddball "collective") who were opening for *another* band (one normals *definitely* would've heard of), and Monika was supposed to talk to the promoters about how the two audiences would mesh. "Christine asked me to do it personally," she said, "and she suggested that you might be available to cover for me?" And that's when Kate knew she had won, knew it at the same moment that she also knew that yes, it *was* a competition.

"It was already a double-blind sort of thing, right?" she explained to Mesut. They were less than a block away from the warehouse, and she knew that their ability to have a coherent conversation was about to be wiped away in a blast of electronica. "Sons of UNIVAC don't know Sony is paying to have their marketability assessed. Sony doesn't know we're already testing out enthusiasm-generation techniques that we'll try to sell them on."

"I have done science, you know, in school, and this is not what 'double-blind' actually means, if you are interested."

Kate ignored him. "Monika didn't know that she wouldn't be the one conducting the final enthusiasm census. But that was always the plan. She's gotten too enthusiastic about the collective and their potential. It happens. You can't get around it. But Christine wants another set of eyes to see how things worked out. I won't have the same problems with countertransference."

"This is also not what countertransference means. Talking with you makes me more impressed with my own English, sometimes."

"So it's like a triple-blind," she said. Mesut looked like he wanted to object, but didn't. The sidewalk was now fully packed with people going to the concert. "And I got picked for the last part. She picked me. Christine did." Everyone was eyeing each other warily, the club kids and the hipsters and the hip-normals and the guy in the suit, thinking, *So this is what people who'd go to a Sons of UNIVAC show look like. This is the sort of person I am.* Nobody was sure yet whether they approved. Kate had looked over Monika's notes: for an all-electronic music collective, they were relatively aloof from the Internet. ("Well, you couldn't connect a computer from the 1950s to *Twitter,*" Mesut had said, as if that explained it.) Their music ("compositions," never songs) could be downloaded on a pay-what-you-will pricing plan from their website, but there was no discussion area, no social media front door. In the months after their last, un-Agencied concert, Monika had created a series of sideforums on various EDM fan sites and modernist composer discussion forums, and even an unofficial Facebook fan page, and she scoured the comment areas of other music sites looking for fans she could lure. She had created a community out of nothing despite the band's aloofness. But it was a community that hadn't met in person. It wasn't sure what to make of itself. Kate pulled out her phone and tapped in a few notes.

"Well, I am glad she chose you, because now I get to come see this. I actually had heard about this show, you know. Monika seemed very pleased about how secret it was, so I did not want to say anything, in case it would make her upset. Sons of UNIVAC ran a Kickstarter around ... three months ago? ... to fund it, but they didn't say where it would be, except 'America,' and I didn't think I'd be in America, so I didn't contribute. But it was very exciting to a lot of people in the scene, in the US and in Europe. The crowdfunding. The success. They raised tens of thousands of dollars."

"Yeah, Monika did parabuzz for that, you know. The Kickstarter. She pulled a lot of strings in the community pools she'd created to get it over the top, get the funding amount to their goal. I think she might have used some company credit cards to throw in some cash. That's how we got these." Kate waved the printed-out QR codes at Mesut. They were queuing in line now to enter the warehouse; a man with a variety of facial tattoos and no shirt was wielding a gun-shaped barcode scanner, nodding people inside. Occasionally, the scanner would make an angry buzz, and he would puff himself up to full menacing size, and the attempted fraudsters would slink off shame-faced without incident.

Mesut was clearly unsettled to hear that the Agency had been involved in the Kickstarter. "There are far too many layers involved in all your schemes," he said. "I sometimes worry that the job you and I are doing together with the S360 is some kind of confusing trick at Siemens' expense."

"It's not, I promise."

Mesut looked at her and said, "How would you know?" and she couldn't decide if he were teasing her or not. Then No-Shirt scanned their tickets, and they passed through the doorway, and they couldn't hear each other anymore, because there was a huge open space where people were milling around in various dance-ish patterns, and then a stage on which there were seven serious-looking young white men in jeans and dress shirts, and a collection of cabinet-sized computer equipment with knobs and dials that the men were fiddling with, and then behind all *that* was a set of very modern, very large speakers, and loud, loud noises were coming out of them.

The music was not to Kate's liking. The music was not Kate's cup of tea. It wasn't her scene. It wasn't the sort of thing she would've listened to, had she been in charge of the radio dial, the iTunes playlist, the Spotify channel. She would've picked something else. NPR, maybe. Or that station that plays Taylor Swift non-stop. Or silence. But *other people*—well, other people loved it. They loved the music. She was surrounded by people who loved it. And they weren't *wrong*. This is the sort of self-talk the Agency trains you to engage in when confronted with enthusiasm for a subject that is completely foreign to you. It was a mantra that helped Kate power through three months of pushing PartySweat. By the end, the joy she felt for entrepreneur-bros doubling revenues from their sales downlines was entirely genuine. If she could do *that,* she thought, getting through a couple hours of experimental noise electronica would be—not *easy,* exactly, but she could get through it. Observe, report back. Help Monika finish her project (and Christine would know that this final step, this final assessment, had been Kate's work).

Kate popped in her earplugs—they were standard issue from the Agency for concert assignments, there was a bowl of them next to the laser printer in the Musical Enthusiasm pod, looking like candy until you got close—and saw more than a few others doing the same thing as they filed into the vast interior of the warehouse and were met by the wave of noise, or music, or whatever you'd call what Sons of UNIVAC was putting out. It sounded like a thousand quavering theremins soloing at once, more or less coordinated, with bursts of static coming in to form the bass line, the rhythm, though that rhythm was doing nothing as cloying or obvious as creating an easy 2/4 or 4/4 structure that would let you know where the song was going or what was happening, exactly. Identifiable melodies, danceable rhythms: these bourgeois affectations did not interest the men on stage. Mesut had seen her put in the earplugs and gave her a nod that she interpreted as *Smart move,* though he didn't follow suit. He pointed to himself, then to the stage, and smiled and waved goodbye.

Even if she wasn't going to enjoy the music—and she wasn't—she was here to enjoy the crowd, professionally, or at least to assess their levels of enjoyment. The former was a technique for achieving the latter. The audience had not and would not come close to filling the warehouse's vast open space, and had separated into three distinct layers. There was a dense mass against the stage, four or five people thick, almost entirely male. She could see only the backs of their heads as they gazed up at the Sons, but she was willing to bet their faces were in various configurations of awe. This was where Mesut was heading, and she watched him wedge himself into the frontmost clot of Sons fans. He wasn't aggressive about it. He just sort of leaned into the back of the crowd, and when a little bit of space opened up, he shifted to occupy it, until he was engulfed. She liked watching his body make these little feints and strategic moves, probably unconsciously, all the while swaying to a beat that she was unable to make out, but that grabbed hold of him as he sank into the mass. His usual awkward, vaguely twitchy energy was gone. She watched his weird jacket with the too-short sleeves vanish, until all she could see was the black, slightly shaggy mass of his hair, his head keeping time so she didn't have to.

He was happy. Kate had known, would've been able to tell anyone who had asked, that this sort of thing, with the noise and the computers and the intense-looking boys fiddling with knobs and not making eye contact with anybody, was his sort of thing. But she still was surprised, pleasantly, by his happiness. There was a layer of sardonic detachment that she always felt when talking to him—maybe because of the language barrier, or the cultural gap, but probably just his personality. Even among the railfans he had a slightly different energy, a lack of letting go on his part. He wasn't a fan as much as he was playing a part. That was his job. Here, he was off the clock.

She wasn't. But as she saw his happiness, and then saw all the people standing around him moved by the same sort of love for what was happening on stage in front of them, saw their joy like a light in their brain and the lights connected by joy tendrils between their heads that tied them together into a larger structure, reinforcing, boosting their happiness in a virtuous cycle—as she saw all that happen, she felt herself taking deeper gulps of air and her fingertips tingle, and she knew she was getting something out of it. It was second-order joy, a moon glow reflecting the sun of the Sons' true fans, but it was enough to make her glad she came. Second-order joy is still real joy. And she knew—knew from observation, knew because it was part of the understanding of how people work that made the Agency possible—she knew that sometimes second-order joy became genuine affection for the enthusiasm-object.

Not this time, though. Not for her. *God,* Kate thought as she futilely pushed the earplugs into her skull, *this really is terrible.*

The first layer of people in front of the stage was, Kate assumed, made up of people who'd have been here even if Monika hadn't secretly created Sons of UNIVAC's best-attended show. The people in the back would've come too, probably. She had now turned away from the stage, reluctantly leaving the happy little back of Mesut's head behind, and let her field of vision sweep to the rear of the warehouse. She was facing the opposite direction from everyone else in the crowd, and by turning around she wrenched herself out of whatever integration she'd had with the community around her. The room was oddly well lit for a concert: not the normal ambient lighting you'd see in a grocery store or a dentist's office, but not the usual live music murk, either. She could see the people in the back of the room, standing motionless for the most part. She walked backwards, from their perspective, towards them. More women were in this part of the crowd, though still not that many. No uniform—there was an impressive lack of uniformity in hair and dress—but this bunch tended to be less exuberant than those up front. The older black guy with horn-rimmed glasses and a T-shirt with the cover of *Unknown Pleasures* on it. The young white woman with a pixie haircut and a dress shirt with cute little bicycles on it, and yet: her jaw set solidly, her eyes intense, daring you to call her whimsical or adorable. As you got closer, you could see some heads nodding, subtly but with impeccable timing. These people could find the beat just like the people up front; they just weren't as showy about it.

Then there were the people in the middle, the ones Kate was surrounded by. They were, she recognized, the most interesting, the most important for her current task. This is where there was the broadest range of affect and cultural presentation, which is to say that there were serious weirdos and also extremely normal people and they both seemed out of place. They lacked the coherence, the sense of purpose of the front and back crowds; they were disparate molecules, bouncing back and forth, unsure of themselves, not sure why they were here. Several of them, she could tell, hated Sons of UNIVAC almost as much as she did.

"How did you hear about this show?" she asked a bearded white man in a shirt and tie, who was grimacing. She had to ask him a couple times before he could understand her.

"I came with a guy I work with?" he said, gesturing vaguely in the direction of the stage. "He's been talking about it for weeks. Like three people on Twitter he follows posted about it simultaneously, and he said it was a sign. Been listening on his headphones non-stop." He shook his head in a way that indicated his rueful disbelief about how the evening was unfolding for him.

Kate moved through the middle, uncertain section of the crowd. Anyone who looked like they were willing to talk, she talked to; there were a surprising number of them, for a concert. But a Agencied concert would have a lot of people who weren't committed to enthusiasm yet. She got some rueful variations on "I heard it from a friend" or "Someone on Facebook kept saying it would be fun" or "My buddy emailed me a link to the Kickstarter, and I thought it'd be cool to get it over the top." And: "It's not what I expected" or "A little of this goes a long way, you know?" But also: "It's ... different, right? But I kind of dig it" and "I see what they're going for, here, I really do" and "Do think that's really antique computer equipment? I love that dieselpunk aesthetic."

Conversations can help reinforce emergent enthusiasm, Christine told Kate, the first time Kate read the endless pep-talking on the PartySweat multi-level marketing boards. *We talk each other into liking things all the time.* So when all the middle-crowd waverers asked her what she thought of Sons of UNIVAC, she always smiled and answered on the positive side of noncommittal. "They seem cool!" "Yeah, it's amazing how many people came out for this." "Do you know if they have CDs for sale?" She couldn't bring herself to down-talk a client, even though there was no client. Sons of UNIVAC were not a client. Sony wasn't a client, not like this, not yet.

Enthusiasm was the client. She could see it under the skin and behind the eyes of a lot of these people. Why smother it, just because she didn't share it?

"How did *you* hear about the show?" the dieselpunk aficionado asked her. She was short, shorter than Kate, and her hair was done up in an elaborate 'do that would've worked on a film noir temptress; her outfit was sort of twee and retro, though not so much as to verge into World War II home front cosplay. She was the first person who had asked Kate anything about herself, and she appreciated the sudden bubble of intimacy that seemed to surround them. Kate was ready to answer the question: you don't go into a stealth scenario without at least a basic backstory. Fudging logistical details made for less of a lie than pretending she liked experimental noise music, so nothing about her answer was actually untrue. "Oh, I came with a guy, he's really into this stuff, more than I am," she said, nodding towards the stage; as she looked in that direction (completely by coincidence: Kate didn't believe things like this happened non-coincidentally) she realized that Mesut was scanning the crowd looking for her. When he spotted her, he flashed a smile, one uncut by any self-protective layer of wry sarcasm. He was a little sweaty. Then he turned around and put his hands in the air, literally as if he didn't care. Nobody around him was doing anything remotely like it. It was honestly adorable.

"A guy, or, like, a *guy* guy?" Dieselpunk asked.

"I'm not really sure," she answered, and that didn't seem like a lie, either.

Forty-five minutes later, Kate was in a stall in the ladies' room with the door closed, sitting on a toilet with the lid down, tapping notes into her phone. "In stealth scenarios, you'll be in situations where it would be unnatural to take notes," Christine had once told her, "so make sure to scope out potential places of privacy in advance." A bathroom was always a safe bet.

She had polled enough people to feel like she was done and could get away from the music and never listen to it again. Probably someone whose personal enthusiasm was generated more internally would have, *could* have, stayed longer, but she had gotten the gist of the scene. *Significant attendance generated by messaging perceived as organic,* she wrote. *If enthusiasm survived contact with actual music, messaging made attendees more open to further enthusiasm.* "I mean, I'm big into swing; this isn't my scene at *all,*" Dieselpunk had said. "I saw the link to this show when a Captain America fan Tumblr I follow reblogged it, and ... I dunno, something about the past and the future together really got to me. I can see where they're coming from."

Christine would give Monika a lot of praise for the campaign, and Kate didn't begrudge it. She thought about how much vacuum tube squealing Monika must've endured to get to this point. *She*

211

deserves a bonus check just for that.

She bumped into Mesut on her way out of the bathroom. "Oh good, I thought you left," he said. "I thought I had missed you."

"You almost did," she said. "I've got my data, and I've had about enough of..." she trailed off and spun her finger in the air around their heads, as if to say *enough of this, whatever this is, I don't even have a word for what this is.*

Mesut grinned. "So you are not a dance floor convert?"

"I didn't really do any *dancing*." She grinned, too. She wasn't being unkind.

She didn't expect him to leave the concert with her—she would have felt bad if he had, actually—but he did offer to walk her back to the Metro. "Sons of UNIVAC are notorious for shows that are many hours long," he said, as they walked into the street. It was fall and cool, and Kate didn't realize how hot it had been in the warehouse, the air all full of sweat and excitement, until she was outside. It must have drizzled while they were inside, but the moon was out, and you could see a little bit of sheen on the street, rainwater mixed with the city's omnipresent layer of oil. "A small break will be good for my hearing. Then I will go back and stay until they are done." He looked fondly down at the stamp on his hand that would get him readmitted. "They typically end in an extended dissonant crescendo that is supposed to be incredible."

Kate laughed at that, and it was a *little* unkind. "I'm sorry," she said, and she wasn't usually in the habit of apologizing to boys about not sharing their music choices, but still. "I mean, I'm sure it is incredible. Incredible is probably a word I would use to describe it."

"Not everyone has to *like* the things I *like*," Mesut said. "I know you like things for a living, but you don't have to *really* like it. You are no longer working." They had reached the entrance to the Metro station, looming above them, the light filtering down from above onto the dark and empty sidewalks.

"Oh, am I?" she said. "I don't think you're in charge of telling me when I'm on the clock or not. Are you my boss now?"

"Yes," he said. He still had that same grin he flashed her from in front of the stage, and they could hear squealing electronica in the distance. "I wasn't going to tell you, but you figured it out. There is no such company as Siemens; that is just a front. I have been hired by Christine to keep an eye on you and Monika for her. It is what you would call a quadruple-blind. I don't even like electronic music. I am only going back to the show to maintain the integrity of the experiment."

"No, you love it. You're really excited to go back. I can tell."

He laughed a little bit, and shook his head, puzzled. "Yes, I ... of course I am." Then she kissed him, despite the thought, right as she leaned in, that it was probably a medium-bad idea, not that it wasn't nice. She pulled away, and they sized each other up.

"Tell me about it later. Why you like it so much. The music. When I'm off the clock." She was just kind of saying things now; she wasn't even sure what she was getting at.

Mesut looked amused. "I don't think I will convince you."

"It's not about convincing me," she said, then turned towards the Metro station, suddenly feeling awkward. "I'll see you tomorrow," she said over her shoulder.

"I might be late," he shouted after her. "This show ... it will last a long time," then, more quietly, though she could still hear it, "which I said already."

"I promise not to tell on you," she said. She reached the fare gates and took out her SmarTrip card and had a sudden panicked thought that she might not have enough money on it, that she'd have to turn around and walk over to the fare machine to add more while he watched. But she tapped it against the sensor, and the gates parted with a mechanical *whirr,* and she was through, and she was gone.

12

"You look pleased with yourself," Monika said to Kate, and she was right. Kate was sitting in the break room, staring intently at her phone and chewing on a microwaved burrito without really tasting it. She had abruptly terminated the experiment of not looking at her phone in the break room earlier that week, though she was holding firm on not eating her lunch in front of her computer in her cube. The break room was more an alcove, really, just three walls open to the sea of cubicles. The barriers between work and lunch were not firm, which meant that your cube might smell like food, but also that your lunch might smell like work.

Monika was carrying a bowl of salad and an actual book as she sat down at the table with Kate. She seemed relaxed. Christine had been happy with the Sons of UNIVAC reports they had both filed that morning, and Monika had been (appropriately) generous with the credit.

"I'm pretty sure I figured out who it is," said Kate. She was using her chewed-down pinky fingernail to swipe her phone so as to avoid getting grease on the screen. "This guy who's been driving me crazy. Actually, I figured out who two different people who've been driving me crazy are. The best part is"—and here she took a big bite, savoring the maxed-out food-science chemicals, then finished the sentence through a mouthful of burrito—"that I'm pretty sure they're the same guy."

"Sockpuppets? Some dude coming at you with two different accounts?"

She shook her head. "One account attached to one dude. But I think he's causing two different problems that I didn't think were related. Now I'm going to make him fix them."

"Damn, girl, you're scaring me a little," said Monika, turning back to her book. But she was smiling, and Kate was satisfied. *What would Maureen do?* thought Kate. There were reasons that women who posted to LaWLChat had created an entire discussion thread full of only semi-ironic Maureen inspirational posters.

Maureen once got irritated that one of her neighbors always double-parked in front of her apartment building and single-handedly infiltrated the man's sweatshop operation and sent the photos to the *Chicago Tribune*. If she were Maureen, Maureen would get her man, and the problems would be *fixed*.

DOCTOR_FERRET had unsettled Kate from the first time she had dipped into the LaWLChat forums. Not because he was rude or aggressive, though he definitely was. There was a rawness to his posts that clashed with everyone else's playfulness. Even when the forum posters were sour or aggrieved—and they often were! they had, after all, dedicated themselves to spending hours a day slagging on a newspaper comic strip—there was a sense of playfulness as they tried to get a laugh out of their fellow posters.

Posted by **prettypug** *Jun 05 09:01 am*	carol. raccoons are not pets. they are NOT PETS. why are you letting this one live in your house. they have clever grasping hands and will murder you while you sleep.
Posted by **hitormiss** *Jun 05 09:08 am*	Are we even sure that's a raccoon? We only have her word on this, and let's be real she's not the brightest. Usually it's hidden below the bottom of the frame. The couple times we saw it, it was just a grayish small-animal-shaped blob.
Posted by **MyBootsOn** *Jun 05 09:12 am*	We saw it's face that one time. Looked like a shrew to me. Or a rat. Or Rick Santorum.
Posted by **Darayavahus** *Jun 05 09:14 am*	Guys no politics remember we promised no politics??? They make everbody fight
Posted by **prettypug** *Jun 05 09:18 am*	my fellow americans, i announce today my candidacy for mayor of the unnamed suburb of chicago where one or possibly two of the ladies who lunch live. the centerpiece of my platform shall be the extermination of all raccoons, shrews, and other animal blobs. i am neutral on the subject of real-life animal blob rick santorum.
Posted by **DOCTOR_FERRET** *Jun 05 09:21 am*	oh look a bunch of babies afraid of a wild animal. of course it's a raccoon
Posted by **MyBootsOn** *Jun 05 09:22 am*	And ferrets. Can you ban ferrets too puggsly? Got my vote if you do.

Kate had tracked down DOCTOR_FERRET's earlier posts. She'd imagined that his implacable hostility towards the entire LaWLChat universe had an origin story: bruised feelings from some harsh reaction to his unwitting violation of social norms when he first stumbled upon the group, maybe. He only commented once a week or so, but he did it regularly enough that it was driven by some underlying enthusiasm twisted in a negative direction. Anger at being rejected from a clique might explain the intensity if not the duration. But no: the very first thing he had to say to the LaWL-Chatters, posted eighteen months ago, was:

| Posted by **DOCTOR_FERRET** Mar 01 04:15 pm | wow ive never seen so much shit piled up in one place by people with no jobs or hobbies. |

Enthusiast communities have all sorts of ways to react to outsider hostility, including arch self-deprecation:

| Posted by **Mirthquake-1** Mar 01 04:18 pm | Sir! Or ma'am! Good doctor! You wound us. This *is* our hobby. We're working on the jobs part. |

Pleas for civility:

| Posted by **Darayavahus** Mar 01 10:10 pm | Hi dr ferret, this group has some commenting guidelines we worked out to make sure everyone has a good time. They are up at http://moviespace.com/forums/viewtopic.php?f=675&t=1494875 and you should read them! |

Or even outright counter-hostility:

Posted by **hitormiss** *Mar 09 07:19 am*	Jesus Christ, you again, shithead. Why don't you stop pissing on everyone's fun and go pick on someone your own IQ.

All of them failed for the simple reason that DOCTOR_FER-RET didn't acknowledge anybody's responses. His insults were sometimes replies to specific comments but often just shot out into the void. The other commenters began to follow his lead: his posts were ignored, his name anathema, his existence acknowledged only obliquely.

It was an odd detente, and Kate had spent most of the morning trying to understand it. She had been expecting him to come for her, especially about the movie; he'd issued snide, glancing blows when it was announced, but she was ready for it to become more personal. She had been surfing across his insults for a solid 15 minutes when her THEY'VE FOUND YOU alert popped up. Cold fear washed over her as she tabbed over to Outlook, then relief: it was just *Jack.* Jack's outburst at the public meeting seemed positively charming at the moment. Jack could wait. She had waded back into LaWLChat when Mesut knocked gently at the entrance to her cube.

"Er, hello," he said, more hesitant than she was used to, and smiled sheepishly. It was the first time she had seen him since the Sons of UNIVAC show the previous night. "Sorry to interrupt, and to ... to not have interrupted you earlier ... and to ... interrupt you for something irritating, but load up the DCRailTalk forums. There is something you should ... well, just look."

"Hello to you too," she said. "I'm about to see something terrible, right?" *I'm about to see something Jack-related.*

"Terrible is a strong word. But Jack has made a series of posts

219

that seem ... important."

Kate loaded the familiar list of forums, an animated GIF of one of the old New York City Redbird subway cars rolling in an endless loop at the top of the page. She clicked on "Today's Rail News," to see the latest threads, and there, under the Metra rolling stock announcement (*they went with Bombardier,* she thought, *boring*), there were three threads started by The_Real_Jack:

TOPIC	REPLIES	VIEWS	LAST POST
WE ARE BEING USED by The_Real_Jack	0	293	10:46 am
not as they seem by The_Real_Jack	0	417	10:22 am
infiltration???? by The_Real_Jack	2	853	10:04 am

"Uh oh."

"Yes, but also maybe not what you think."

Kate sighed and clicked on the oldest of the three threads.

The_Real_Jack 2 hours ago

Been reflecting on events at a WMATA informational meeting in Virginia last week.

In the days since the Orange Line meeting, Jack had returned to his usual posting schedule and topic choices—mostly complaints about inept North American transit planning and praise for the metros of the former Soviet Union. He hadn't revisited his public blow-up, but he had also been conspicuously silent on Washington-area transit discussions. There had been a thread on how far the new DC Streetcar stop at Union Station was going to be from the Metro entrance there, one of Jack's favorite things to complain about, but he hadn't taken the bait. Kate and Mesut had discussed whether he would even acknowledge the incident. Both suspected he wouldn't, but for different reasons: Mesut thought he might feel some shame about the whole thing, whereas Kate was convinced that for Jack the evening had been nothing out of the norm, so why bother bringing it up?

> Some of you know because you were there that things got a little heated. There was an attendee that I did not recognize who said some pretty asinine things about form vs. function when it comes to rolling stock and I tried to set him straight in a manner that he and others did not appreciate. I now believe that this entire incident was orchestrated by outside forces with their own agendas.

"Oh, my God," said Kate.

"So the man with a ponytail—he is a professional actor, or someone who works here?" Mesut looked theatrically around the cube farm. "I do not see him, but perhaps he was wearing a false ponytail."

> It is currently not clear to me what the purpose might be behind this false flag incident. I suspect someone has become aware of my passions from reading this message board and is using them to attack the principles I stand for. We all need to proceed with caution when posting from here on in.

Rajiv 2 hours ago

> lol jack why are you posting this in the open, how can you be sure they aren't watching you right now #blackhelicopters

The_Real_Jack 1 hour ago

> Laugh all you want, son. I for one plan to stay vigilant.

"So I am thinking this is maybe not the worst thing?" said Mesut. "If he is aware of something, he is not aware of us, it seems."

Kate held the bridge of her nose between her thumb and forefinger, very gently. "Ugh, but if he starts looking for webs of manipulation, he'll point himself our way eventually. Plus, he won't act normal if he thinks he's being watched."

"Jack acted normally before?" Before she could respond, Mesut pointed at the top left of the forum page, at the bright red NEW MAIL message indicating that someone had sent a private note through the forums software. This was what had triggered her THEY'VE FOUND YOU alert. "I will wager that I know who this note is from," said Mesut.

"Did you get one?"

"Well, you need to be suspicious about the swarthy foreigner, obviously. Who knows what he is capable of. The pretty redhead is the safer confidant."

She smiled a little to herself and clicked the envelope.

The_Real_Jack Private message sent 1 hour ago

Imagine you've seen my posts by now. You seem like you've got a good head on your shoulders. Would like to meet in person to discuss. Call or text, 202-555-0130.

"See, you are a very trustworthy person," said Mesut, "which is why you are so good at being a corporate spy." He looked serious. "If you want me to come with you, I will. For safety."

Kate tried to imagine a tussle between Jack, middle-aged and prematurely stooped, and Mesut, all skinny limbs and slightly too-short pants. "Don't worry, I think I can handle it. I promise not to go back to his secret lair with him or anything." She frowned, then started typing. Potential exposure was always a danger when working stealth. It would be great if she could convince Jack he was nuts. But curiosity about the secret workings of the world is a kind of enthusiasm, and the first rule of the Agency is that you never try to kill enthusiasm. You redirect it.

> **kmac1987** Private message sent 1 minute ago
>
> Yeah, I saw them. That's a spooky thought. Any idea who might be behind it? Not sure what I can do to help, but I would like to try. Busy this weekend but can maybe meet early next week? Best way to reach me is by email: kmacal1987@gmail.com.

That bought her a few days. She wasn't aware of the knot of tension at the back of her neck until it unwound. It tightened up again as a new message appeared immediately in her private inbox.

> **The_Real_Jack** Private message sent 1 minute ago
>
> Appreciate it. Looking forward to it.

"Well, I am glad to have shared this excitement with you, before I go read some more of your transit regulations. May I have a donut?"

We didn't make any weekend plans, she realized after he left, a donut from her Friday stash in hand, then felt silly about it. One outing did not establish a standing date, even if you did kiss someone at the end of it. It was her job to keep him entertained, sort of, but she was no longer worried about him spending Saturday night alone in his hotel room watching cable, and was more worried that she wasn't cool enough to go to whatever Saturday night warehouse party or performance art piece he had discovered. He had seen her tell Jack that she was busy all weekend, but she thought that was a fairly transparent stalling tactic.

Back to DOCTOR_FERRET. Speaking of stalling. This wasn't part of the job. The other LaWLChatters had managed to shun him so completely that he wasn't noticeably dampening any enthusiasm for the movie, or anything else for that matter. But it still nagged at her. It seemed like there was something important that she was missing. She brought up a chronological list of his posts to find the ones from just after the focus group, when everyone had been so excited.

Posted by **DOCTOR_FERRET** *Sep 28 08:59 pm*	this ain't news, dumb dumbs, where ya been
Posted by **DOCTOR_FERRET** *Sep 28 09:02 pm*	and it's not gonna happen either
Posted by **DOCTOR_FERRET** *Sep 28 09:08 pm*	100% gauranteed it's not. you're in a fool's paradise
Posted by **Darayavahus** *Sep 28 09:12 pm*	@DOCTOR_FERRET but my friend was there with Mitch Landers and they said it would!!! do you know something else? i'm excited!!!!!
Posted by **DOCTOR_FERRET** *Sep 28 09:15 pm*	@Darayavahus your friend is missing a big piece of the picture. is landers as dopey in person as he seems?

Your friend is missing a big piece of the picture. That was not his usual style. It wasn't just aggression. It was *implying* something.

Kate started jumping through his posts at random, looking for anything that didn't fit the usual pattern—or, perhaps, looking for the pattern she had missed.

Posted by **DOCTOR_FERRET** *Apr 12 07:29 pm*	@mirthquake-1 so you think you can do better huh
Posted by **DOCTOR_FERRET** *May 15 08:02 pm*	landers is a clown and you should be embarrassed by all this
Posted by **DOCTOR_FERRET** *Feb 17 05:08 pm*	@divalicious the man's on a date and he's wearing clothes that people with jobs wear to be respectable. don't know what you wear out of the house. i'm sure it's trash

It was noon and Kate was hungry and even though a thought was trembling at the edge of her verbalizing it, she still got up, walked to the break room, got her burrito out of the freezer, and put it into the microwave. *It couldn't be,* she thought. *That'd be absurd. It would explain a lot, but not everything.*

She was sitting at the table as Monika walked up, chewing on her burrito, when she finally tapped his name into the Wikipedia app on her phone. She half-expected him to not even have a page. He did. And when she tapped on his picture and zoomed in—well, yeah, she looked pretty pleased with herself at that point. She had every right to.

‡‡‡‡‡‡‡‡‡‡‡‡

Kate never considered going alone. She did, just for a second, think about asking Monika, partly because she was sitting there when it all became clear. *You're always thinking you should do things with Monika outside of work,* she told herself, then laughed, first because what she had in mind, technically, was still work, and second because it would be a profoundly weird way to start a social relationship with a woman who Kate thought was cool enough to be slightly scary. Slightly scary could come in handy for this expedition, maybe. But she decided to leave it for another time.

Carol would've asked Monika, Kate thought. Sweet, guileless Carol. Carol didn't know about any of the cool new bands, but she didn't expect anyone to judge her for it. Carol had a great sense of herself and what she had to offer.

Maureen would've taken a man if she had a man on call at the moment. Kate considered asking Mesut, but that seemed more absurd than asking Monika. At least Monika was a co-worker. This was not-his-business Agency business, and there wouldn't even be electronica to entice him. Mitch had the excuse that he was in California. She did at least text him, seeing as this *was*-his-business agency business.

> Hey Mitch, keep your fingers crossed but I might have had a breakthrough on our film rights problem. Will let you know tonight how smart I am.

She hoped this would be mysterious enough to impress him, especially because the film rights were actually *his* problem, not *theirs*. But he was in a meeting with Flatfish, a suddenly very in-demand collective of young sketch comedians who were trying to Kickstart a web-only sitcom and wanted to offer a small part for Mitch as one of their stretch goals. He still replied to her, but only to tell her about what was happening to him at that precise moment, even more so than usual. His texts were all over the place emotionally, and she wasn't really sure if, or how, she was supposed to respond to them.

> im like a god to these
> young padawans ;)

had been a promising, if self-absorbed, start. Kate felt that a thumbs-up emoji was an adequate response. But that was followed in short order by

> no for real these dudes
> are all really young

and

> i am going to be the
> oldest person in this thing
> by abt 10 yrs :(

Kate found the Flatfish Kickstarter and followed the links to their bios. They were all her age or a few years younger. A few minutes later, he had moved on to other concerns:

> it turns out i really don't
> understand how kickstater
> works

and then

> do i have to pay my agent
> 15% if its a kickstarter

227

It seemed obvious even to her that the answer was yes, but instead she texted back

> I think that's a question for your agent?

And he countered with a quick

> haha yeah

There was no follow-up, which was good, Kate thought. Texting nonstop during a meeting would be rude, even if it was a meeting with a bunch of 26-year-old comedy nerds. It was possible, she conceded, that he had just started texting someone else.

In the end, when it was time to pick a comrade for her mission, she went the Eve route. Eve would pick a true, loyal friend, which is why Kate found herself standing at LaMont's cube, bag of donuts in hand.

"Wait, you want me to go *where* now?" said LaMont.

"Loudoun County," she said. "Virginia. Not very far." It was 1:45 p.m. on Friday, and the soporific effect of the encroaching weekend had descended on everyone at the Agency, wrapping them in a snug blanket of nonproductivity. The Agency wasn't like other workplaces, or so the Agents would tell you. So Christine would tell you, in particular. The Agency was uniquely about discovery and generation of passion and enthusiasm. Yet, here it was Friday afternoon and walking around the office was like walking through cotton. Time was going too slow, except for a few people for whom it was going way too fast. You could tell who was who: some people were leaning back in their ergonomic correct chairs, not seeing their monitors, thinking about weekend plans (sex, books, sleep, drugs, other vices), and some people were desperately typing at full speed, hoping to wrap things up by 5:30, 6 at the latest. The office would be open all weekend, but you didn't want to be there. The Agency was a compelling space, but that didn't mean that it was enjoyable to be compelled.

What Kate had in mind was exciting. Felicia, one of the newer Agents on LaMont's floor, was two cubes over, and she was talking in low, urgent tones. "I think Ms. Walker-Schwartz would bring a perspective to the table that's totally different from your other panelists," she said. "The work she's done with Moscow's feral dog packs can tell us a lot about human group dynamics in urban setti—yes, I'll hold." Felicia sighed. Felicia should have booked an appearance for Ms. Walker-Schwartz for next week by Thursday at the latest, Kate thought. The reasons she didn't were probably perfectly respectable, but could've been avoided with a little work. Kate's plan, on the other hand—an hour ago it wouldn't have made any sense. She didn't have all the information she needed to put it into place. Now, it was all she could think about.

"Look, can you just duck out for the rest of the afternoon? I'll drive, we leave now, and I'll get you home by 8, 8:30 at the latest. It's work-related, and I don't—I don't want to go by myself. It'll probably be fine, but it could be weird." She hoped that by being vague, she was making it impossible for LaMont to resist.

"Why don't you get one of your boyfriends to take you?" He was leaning back in his chair, legs extended and hands behind his head, and grinning up at her. He wasn't being mean-spirited about it. Still, she tipped her head forward and looked down her nose at LaMont, trying to look imperious. She thought about telling him she didn't have any boyfriends, or showing him the texts from Mitch (she would eventually; she knew he'd find them hilarious), or telling him how Mesut seemed to have blown her off, but finally just said, "Come on, Monty. You're the one I want to go with."

He grimaced. "Fine. *Fine.* Lucky for you *my* boyfriend doesn't want to spend time with me tonight, either." He rolled his chair back and gestured with a flourish at the GChat window open on his monitor.

> **me:** you are not serious
> **Nelson:** I know I know
> **me:** my dad keeps threatening to cancel his cable and then we wont have an hbo go password anymore
> **Nelson:** I know
> **me:** i have been avoiding spoilers for "the jinx" for so long
> **me:** you know it's a documentary, right
> **me:** do you know how hard it is to avoid spoilers for things that actually happened in real life
> **Nelson:** I have to stay late to re-revamp proposed water use regulations in designated drought areas
> **Nelson:** Because the chairman of the Senate ag committee keeps hearing from new lobbyists and changing his mind
> **Nelson:** Also, spoiler alert: even if these regs do pass the Senate they're gonna die in the House
> **me:** adlfjkdkfjdkdf

"Let's do it," he said. "I hope this crazy scheme is *extra* crazy."

᛭᛭᛭᛭᛭᛭᛭᛭᛭᛭᛭᛭

"Let me see the picture again," LaMont said to Kate. She was sitting in the passenger seat of his late-'90s Infiniti, a hand-me-down from Nelson's father that she had always found off-putting in its entry-level luxury, all leather seats and shiny faux-wood accents. She'd known she wouldn't have to make good on her promise to drive, since her car was in her apartment building's underground garage in Arlington, half an hour away from the office by train. LaMont thought public transportation was "gross" ("Don't tell the German boy," he had said, "he already hates me for trying to make his boss successful") and sat in traffic every day on 295 commuting from Hyattsville, singing along with his music or yelling at the hosts of *Morning Edition*, depending on his mood. She was grateful to have an hour to plan rather than concentrate on weaving through traffic, though she was unnerved by how often LaMont wanted to look at her phone.

"Come on," he said, "This light's not changing for a while."

She handed him the phone. "This is the guy," he said.

"Uh huh."

"The guy with the ferrets."

"Yeah, you can see the cage in the background, right?"

LaMont squinted at the screen. "I *guess* so? I see a little white face in there. Whiskers. Could be a lot of things. A gerbil. A raccoon. I'm not a scientist."

"Right, but I know what it is, though. And I know who it is in this picture. Because I called him."

"And you got his number how?"

"From the *phone book.*" The thought of it almost made her giggle. Kate had not, as far as she could remember, ever used a phone book before. But she knew that there were all sorts of arcana in the Agency's Research Room, a quiet chamber tucked away in a rear corner of the building, presided over by a real librarian, who Kate often wished was a stern-faced elderly woman but was a 26-year-old named Cooper who had recently graduated with his MLS degree and who smiled all the time. "If we ever had it, it's here," Cooper had said. "We never throw anything out. Advantages of working in a warehouse." He led her through a door into the still-sizable unfinished space that lurked in the rear of the Agency's headquarters, waiting for another round of expansion that, perhaps, would never come. There were rows of shabby metal shelving filled with the reference books the Agency had accumulated through the '90s and '00s, up until the point when reference books weren't a thing you accumulated anymore. There was a system, or at least Cooper seemed to be following a map in his head, and they reached a shelf stacked haphazardly with thick white and yellow volumes.

"Here's the most recent one we've got," he said. The spine read "LOUNDOUN COUNTY – VERIZON – 2003." She opened it there and thumbed rapidly through it until she found:

BARGEMAN, R. . . . . . (703) 555-0158

LaMont was merging into the traditional shitshow where 295 met the Beltway, and Kate looked down at her phone, where she still had open the Wikipedia article for Rex Bargeman, or, as Wikipedia called him, "Rex Bargeman (comics artist)," to distinguish him from "Rex Bargeman (Australian cricketer)." Rex was sitting with his drawing board behind him, but turned to face the camera; Eve, half-drawn, peeked out over his shoulder, bangs fetchingly mussed.

> **Rex Bargeman** (born June 2, 1928) is an American comic strip artist, comic book artist, and illustrator, best known as the artist for Charter Comics' *The Human Question*[1] and for his work as an illustrator for the NRA's youth magazine, *Young Marksman*.[2] Since 2004, he has been the uncredited artist[3] for the syndicated soap opera comic strip *Ladies Who Lunch*. He lives in Loudoun County, Virginia.

There were two ferret cages stacked up behind him in the picture, which had been uploaded by a user named BargeHelp, licensed as "Public Domain/Own Work." The article went on for multiple screens, and she flicked through them idly before snapping back to the top of the page to look at him again. He was white, with shaggy white hair and blue eyes that seemed younger than his weathered face. He was wearing a white button-up shirt with a black vest over it and was looking right into the camera and not quite smiling.

"You *talked* to him. Like, not even a text or anything."

"You've seen him. Do you think he *texts?*"

"I don't know what people do! My grandma lives in a tiny little town in Mississippi and didn't have an indoor toilet until she was 15, and she texts all the time."

Kate sighed. "I don't think he texts. I think he likes it when people treat him with respect. Respect is when you call someone on the phone to talk to them."

"Really? When someone calls me on the phone just to blah blah, my first thought is that they don't respect me or my time."

"It's different. He's a different ... age. From another era."

"Maybe you should've sent him a telegram. Ooh! A *singing* telegram."

Kate smiled a little in spite of herself. "Just ... just keep driving."

They rode in silence. Then, quietly, LaMont started singing. "Hello Mr. *Barge*man," he crooned tunelessly. "We'd like to make a *movie*. Out of the *comic* you *draw*. Why are you such a *diiiiiick* online to *everybody?*"

Kate was laughing. "I think you should probably stay in the car when we get there."

"Old NRA-member white man in rural Virginia? Way ahead of you."

When she'd found his number in the phone book, she had stared at it for a while, almost forgetting that Cooper was there. There was something about the physical weight of the book in her hands that gave the discovery substance, literal substance. She knew she was going to meet him in real life. She was going to talk to him on the phone first, and then she was going to look at him in the face.

"I don't think he's going to shoot me. Anyway, that's why you'll be waiting outside. If you hear gunshots, I want you running in to avenge me."

"This is the very worst Tarantino movie I've ever been in."

When she had found Rex's phone number, she had started over-thinking how she was going to handle calling him, then had decided not to overthink it and just call him. He answered on the second ring. "Hello?" Gravelly, wary.

"Mr. Bargeman?" *Mister* was instinct. She wasn't sure how he took it.

"Speaking."

"My name is Kate Berkowitz. I'm working on a project to turn

Ladies Who Lunch into a film—"

"Kate, huh."

He knows who I am, she thought. *He's been reading the LaWL-Chat forums, he's angry about this movie, and I've been posting under my own name. But we don't have to talk about it.* There was the whole sequence of coincidence and interaction that brought them together, a whole series of ugly, angry posts, but the best part was that she had found his name in the phone book. "I found your name in the phone book, and..." They could pretend that he never called her a *moron in over your head,* if he wanted, never called Mitch an *empty-headed hollywood he-whore,* never called all the people who dedicated hours of their lives reading and thinking about the strip he drew *human trash.* There was no need to make him acknowledge that he'd tipped his hand.

But he did anyway. "Guess you saw the posts on that damn Internet site and figured it out, huh."

They had danced around it a bit, but he wanted to meet in person. She'd hoped he would. "Would you like to come into our office, or...?" No, he did *not* want to come into any *office,* certainly not in the *District,* that was for sure. "Well, I could come to someplace near you, a restaurant, maybe—" No, his house was fine. He was working. She could come to him. "When would—" Today. Not like he had anything else to do. Why not now?

"I know you think I can help you with this dumb movie," he said, before he hung up. "There's about a 20 percent chance. Don't want you getting your hopes up."

Standing in front of his door, her hopes were not up. They were in a much different version of Northern Virginia sprawl than the carefully planned subdivision she and Mesut had trudged through to get to the WMATA meeting. The meandering lane she and LaMont had driven down had been dirt once, probably, and followed an ancient and self-emergent logic. The trees were old and huge, and hid the houses, which were even older. Rex's house was at the very end; big, rambling, covered with weathered wooden clapboard, with additions sticking out haphazardly. Kate turned around before she knocked and looked back at LaMont in the car. He gave her a thumbs-up, then rolled up the window and turned on the air conditioning.

She had visualized Rex sitting by the door, waiting for her (*with a shotgun,* in the moments when she allowed her imagination to get more lurid, despite having laughed off LaMont's worries). But she had to knock loudly, a couple of times, before she heard "Just a *minute,*" coming from inside. Eventually the door opened and there he was. Rex Bargeman. DOCTOR_FERRET. He was taller than she had expected, and, frankly, more handsome. The blue eyes were unclouded. His posture was great, despite a lifetime spent hunched over a drawing board. The vest wouldn't have been her choice, but it was a choice she could respect.

"Kate," she said and stuck out her hand.

His handshake was firm without being aggressive or creepy. "Rex." He sighed a little through his teeth as he looked down at her. "Never write what you think on the Internet, even if you really want to. Come in if you're coming in." She looked back at LaMont, but he already had his laptop open and was eating a candy bar.

Based on her experiences with ferrets in college—they were usually owned by white guys with dreadlocks—she expected the house to smell like an uncleaned ferret cage. It did not. There was a certain patina on everything she could see as she followed him up the hall—

probably what you'd expect from someone living in the same house as long she'd been alive. But it was all pretty tidy.

The eat-in kitchen was done up in yellows and oranges; she wondered if Rex had decorated it himself in the '70s, if there had been a time when keeping up with design trends had been important to him. Maybe he just liked the colors. "Hope you don't mind that I'm eating," he said. "You ever have chicken fried steak? It's steak, and you bread it and fry it, and then put gravy on it. That's four different things my doctor says I'm not supposed to eat, but I'm 87 and he's about 35, so what does he know, as far as I'm concerned. You want some?" There was just a hint of a waver in Rex's voice. The food smelled great, but she demurred. It was about 3:30 p.m., not time for any particular meal to happen. She thought about the odd times that DOCTOR_FERRET had posted screeds on the LaWLChat forums, and about what it would do to your schedule to live alone and work alone. She let him hand her a can of generic cola out of his refrigerator.

"So, you're going to make me go first?" he said, and she thought *Point: Berkowitz.* "Well, I apologize for ... some of the language I used on that site. Towards you, specifically. It was ungentlemanly. You gotta understand though, it's all just names on a screen to me."

"Apology accepted. Of course." His fulminations over the stupidity of the movie idea hadn't even been particularly abusive towards her personally, but he seemed genuinely contrite. She wondered how he would've felt faced with the other LaWLChatters at the focus group in New York, the ones he had gotten nastier with. He eyed her as if waiting for her to apologize for ... something. For being involved peripherally with what she assumed he saw as his humiliation. His shoulders slumped when she didn't, and he said,

"So how'd you guess?"

"Part of my job," she said, "is noticing how much people care about things. DOCTOR_FERRET cares about *Ladies Who Lunch* like he owns it."

Rex grimaced. "I don't though. I just draw it, that's all. The writer writes it, and I draw it, and they send me a check."

"You spend more time thinking about it than anyone else, though."

"More than most," he said.

"Anyway, I guessed from that. The rest was sort of dumb luck. I don't know if you thought about this when you picked your screen name." She handed him her phone, open to his Wikipedia page. It took him a moment to focus, but when he realized what it was, he laughed. He laughed in spite of himself and shook his head.

"This damn thing," he said. "This stupid thing. God, I'd like to pretend I have no idea what this is, but I do. My assistant wrote it for me. His idea. Yeah, I have an *assistant*, which I also can't believe. I've never actually met him, but he's a big comic book guy. Loves the classic stuff I worked on back in the day. He tracked me down, sent me a letter—a real letter—offering to help me get my stuff up on the *web*." He said the last word with a certain amount of contempt. "I send him checks when I can. I don't pay him enough for what he does and keep telling him that, but then he'll say, 'Oh, Rex, I wrote a Wikipedia for you last week, go look,' and it's three pages long when you print it out. He wanted a picture for it, so I sent him that one, with Sally and Laverne there."

He had a manila folder on the table next to him, and he opened it up and for a minute she thought he really was going to show her his Wikipedia article, printed out. But instead, he carefully started laying printouts from the LaWLChat Landerpalooza threads out on the table. They had the just-a-little-too-bright sheen of coming out of an inkjet printer, and recently. Mitch's face was attached to bodies drawn at various odd angles and topped with various silly hats.

"My assistant sent me the Web link to this ... this, a couple of years ago. *This* guy. I had to look him up. I guess he's a pretty big deal." He was sneering.

"He really does kind of look—"

"If you're wondering," he said, pretending not to hear her, "my model for when I want someone really handsome for the strip is William Powell, not this clown. I don't suppose you know who William Powell is."

Kate didn't really see the resemblance, but she thought it best not to say so. "Sure I do. *The Thin Man.* He always had a little mustache, though."

"Yeah, the, uh, writer for the strip says that looks too square for modern people, as if a lot of modern people read this thing anymore. I manage to slip a little mustache now and then on the ones who are supposed to be bad guys, though." He absent-mindedly rubbed a knuckle against his upper lip with what Kate guessed was nostalgia. "Anyway, you've seen it. I spend too much time yelling at these people. I'm not really sure what the point is, to be honest, now that you're sitting here in front of me. It takes the edge off sometimes, though."

"All these people," Kate said, pointing to the names on the printouts, "are really nice. I've met some of them! And they're very modern. They read the strip *religiously.*"

"This is as about as religious as when that guy used tax money to put a crucifix in a jar of pee," said Rex. "Not that I'm saying my drawings are Jesus or anything. But *Jesus.*" Kate wasn't sure what he was talking about, but it didn't sound good. "You know I've drawn this strip for 11 years, right? Longer than anyone else. Longer than Stan Gieselman did, in the beginning. So yeah, I have a lot of clip art lying around. I use it sometimes. It saves me time. My hands aren't what they used to be." He gestured at an image of Mitch grinning dreamily as an odd-looking, slightly lumpy bear loomed behind him, about to swipe at him with a malformed paw. The girls looked on in horror. "I still don't think I deserve this."

"They're not doing it to *you*," Kate said. He didn't get it. He had a big incentive to get it—getting it would make him feel less like the butt of the joke, probably—but he couldn't get past it. But what if he did, she thought. What if he did and started drawing his Powell-men even Mitchier? What if he started *trying* to make the LaWL-Chatters laugh? Would anyone even enjoy it anymore? The whole enterprise suddenly seemed to hinge on this old man continuing to not understand what the hell he was looking at.

"Sure they are," he said. "They're doing it to this comic, which is just this ... thing ... they know about. And that I happen to have drawn. For 11 years. You managed to get the film rights yet?"

He said it so casually, but this was the question the whole visit hinged on, and he knew it just as well as she did, she realized. *Point: Bargeman.* She opened her mouth hoping something would occur to her to say, but nothing came out. He took a bite of steak and let her stew. She couldn't lie, but she didn't want to admit the impasse they had reached, either. The silence didn't last very long—just long enough for it to be clear that it was silence—and then Rex said, "Fine, sorry, couldn't help myself. I know you don't have them, because I know who does. I'll tell you. You seem all right. You know what *The Thin Man* is. You drove all the way out here when you didn't have to, so I could check you out for her. I'm still pretty sure you're not going to talk her into it. But you can try."

LaMont drove her all the way home to Arlington. He didn't have to. "You can drop me off at a Metro stop," she said.

"Girl, you have to fly to *California* tomorrow. You need beauty rest."

She didn't get it, of course. She spent much of the evening packing, buying tickets, conferring with the Agency's 24-hour expense approval line (an Agent might be on duty at all times, and might need to spend money), texting with Mitch, fending off flirty emojis from Mitch, trying to impose the urgency of the situation on Mitch. Even when she was done, she was too keyed up to sleep. That's why she was awake and on her laptop when she got the message: scrolling through Twitter, enjoying the weird rhythms of people posting tweets at midnight, telling herself she'd check her RSS feeds one more time, and then go to bed, when suddenly a THEY'VE FOUND YOU alert popped up. *Probably nothing,* she thought. It was not nothing. It was a forum message from Jack, and it said:

> I know who you are.

LATER, KATE SPENT SOME TIME reconstructing how it had gone wrong. This was standard procedure for a live-site assignment where you lose your stealth. It was Agency policy to document and put your findings into a central database for reference. You wouldn't get fired, unless you were doing something illegal or unethical.

"Isn't just being stealth in the first place unethical?" Kate had asked Christine. This was towards the end of her time as a temp. The reports she had been writing on Los Mundos Del Cielo had been well received. By Christine, particularly. They had been *fun,* too, and got more fun the more effusive the feedback emails had gotten. *Really interesting insight,* Christine had emailed her. Or: *I'm not sure anyone here would've taken this analytical approach, but the results prove its value. Please send the spreadsheet around.* And then: *This assignment is ongoing, and we have the budget to add a new enthusiasm channel associate. Are you interested in full-time work here?*

YES YES YES YES YES she typed out on the grimy old keyboard in the cube assigned to temps. She gingerly deleted it, then typed: *Very much so. I've really enjoyed my time here and would love to stay. I can send you my resume tomorrow. Thank you for considering me.*

She stared at the letters on the screen, then deleted the period and added an exclamation point. *Thank you for considering me!* The job title was "enthusiasm channel associate." Being too cool to show excitement wasn't how she wanted to present herself. She thought about adding a second, after *love to stay,* decided she didn't want to come across as *too* excitable, then hit Send. She felt the message slip through the ether and land in Christine's in-box. (She eventually learned that Christine's computer and phone both emitted the same soft, vaguely new-agey chiming sound when an email or text message arrived.) She was very excited.

I already have your resume from your temp agency, Christine wrote back in short order. *Interview this afternoon? Not an ambush. Just trying to cut through overthinking and overpreparing. I'll answer as many questions as you have, of course. In a sense we've been interviewing you the whole time you've been here, and everything about that process has been positive.*

Everything about that process has been positive. It occurred to Kate, much later, that some people would've found it creepy to learn that they had been assessed, judged against some abstract standard, their references called without prior consent. She never could work herself up to be bothered or offended. The job, after all, was to recognize enthusiasm in a person before they themselves were fully aware that it was there.

To recognize it and to encourage it. It can't be summoned forth out of the void or out of outright hostility. But you can make it grow into something bigger, something that becomes different in quality, not just quantity. *This is much better than doing data entry for a defense contractor* becomes *Please hire me full-time* so gradually you barely notice it. Everything that had happened at the Agency since

Christine realized Kate had been excelling at her temp assignment was nurturing that enthusiasm.

So she was already pre-receptive in the interview when it came time for what LaMont jokingly called The Talk, the big reveal that Agency hands need to operate on a sliding scale of truthfulness in presenting their identity—*an* identity—to targeted communities. During their interview, Christine and Kate had spent an hour walking around Washington's southwest waterfront. It was a sunny day, and the odor from the river was detectable enough to know that something large and slightly alien was flowing through the middle of the city. Christine explained the kinds of assignments she'd be doing, the personae she'd develop along with other team members, the techniques for generating the strategic aspects of these identities and recognizing what parts of herself she would want to showcase. Sometimes, it's to present a best self to potential enthusiasts, bringing them up with you in a virtuous spiral; sometimes, antagonizing them produces the best result. Often, this would take place with a monitor and a keyboard safely between you and your subjects; occasionally, you will meet people in person, and you will not then be who you usually think you are.

"Stealth itself is not unethical *per se*," said Christine. "Certainly, people using those techniques can do unethical things. People who send out press releases signed with their legal names also can do unethical things. So can people who use hammers or accounting software."

It was early afternoon, and there were a lot of people on the street, government workers in khaki and blue button-downs and employees from local restaurants on break, wearing their uniforms and looking like they wished they weren't. Kate was surprised that Christine was telling her all this in public. She wasn't shouting about it, but she wasn't whispering it either. Kate supposed that was the point: here was impromptu training by example on how to act natural.

"Do nothing illegal," she said. "Obviously. Do nothing harmful. Your assignments will be tailored to boost enthusiasm, to boost *joy*, by definition. Within that framework, it's hard for me to find space for unethical behavior. Your own code of ethics may differ, of course."

"What happens if you get caught?"

As soon as she said it, she regretted the phrasing. It implied they were doing something wrong. Hadn't Christine just said she wouldn't have to do anything that was, in any meaningful way, wrong?

Christine took it in stride, though. Her speech was clipped, focused. "Be forthright. Acknowledge wounds. Focus on positive outcomes or attitudes already fostered among anyone who's upset. And when it's done, analyze the chain of inconsistencies that made the identity you presented unsustainable."

"And what happens to me then?" This was the intrusive memory that flooded into Kate's mind as she sat in bed, looking at Jack's message: that day by the Potomac, when she felt a gnawing certainty that if she had a stealth assignment, it would end with her exposure.

Christine smiled. "We don't leave you behind," she said. "It's not the CIA. You are expected to improve and to improve your understanding of what happened. Improve *our* understanding. If it keeps happening, then perhaps we should reconsider the sort of work for which you're best suited. But it happens sometimes to everybody. Well—" she paused for a moment. "Most people. It happens to most people."

She had had her chance to walk away but didn't take it. She filled out the intake paperwork that afternoon.

So: figuring out what had gone wrong. This was something you did at the first available moment, even if the assignment hasn't been wound down; once you're done tamping down the initial online shitstorm, or enduring one or more humiliating sessions of someone yelling at you over the phone, you start the autopsy. You want the evidence to be fresh: both the evidence your targeted community members may have picked up on that you were unaware of, and your own memories of the corners you cut, the risks you took, the hubris.

She had been ready for it to be Darius. Maybe he had started Googling her after the meeting in New York. The Agency's name, its actual name, the one its employees almost never said aloud, because it was bad luck, the way theater people never say "MacBeth"—it would've been on the paperwork he signed. Superstitions are based in reality. *MacBeth* is bad luck because it's full of stage fighting that can lead to injuries, and employees at Subconscious Agency don't say "Subconscious Agency" aloud because they don't want people getting curious and looking for its web site and thinking about what sort of projects it might be up to.

The name, in tiny print, but still there because it had to be. *Do nothing illegal. Obviously.* She wished it had been Darius. There were two enthusiast communities she was arranging encounters with in real space, but they had non-overlapping content focuses and were more than 200 miles apart. How could she have had anticipated that two different screen names, two identities in whom she had been seeding separate enthusiasms, would collapse into a single flesh-and-blood person, into a sweet, cheerful man in his early 20s who lived with his parents and may have been on the autistic spectrum and who loved trains and newspaper soap opera comics? "I'm not sure I fully believe in synchronicity," Christine would say. Kate imagined her saying this. In her mind, her boss's voice was heavy with a sort of rueful magnanimity. "Perhaps the difference between unlikely things and impossible things is that unlikely things do happen, sometimes." Plus, Darius was … Darius. It would be very difficult for anyone to be mad at Darius. Maybe that would apply transitively to her.

She had texted Mesut: I need you to call me tonight . He had told her, before she had left with LaMont, that he was going to see a late-night showing of a documentary with someone he knew from an EDM Facebook group, and she knew, because she knew him, that his phone was off. She pictured him sitting in the theater quietly and thoughtfully, listening to terrible, terrible music and interviews with the perfectly nice people who made it. He wouldn't see the message for another hour, maybe more. It is about the assignment and is important . She was continuing to kiss people she was working with and not giving a lot of thought, until after the fact, to the ways that might make normally straightforward professional communication unsettling and not straightforward at all. Mesut was even-keeled, though, especially when confronted with a scenario of particular gravity. She wasn't sure how she knew that. From having spent so much time with him, she supposed. She hadn't known how his mouth felt before the previous night, but she was pretty sure he'd be steady in a crisis. Worst-case scenario: exasperated. But he'd want data. She took a screenshot of Jack's message, then sent it off.

It was almost one in the morning by the time Mesut called her. She was in her pajamas, sitting on the bed, lights off, her laptop's glow illuminating the piles of dirty clothes. "This is an interesting and difficult situation," he said. "Hopefully it will not get us all fired?" He was still his sharp and sarcastic self, but there was a hint of softness to his voice that she didn't recognize. There was a brief moment when she thought that, maybe, he had taken ecstasy before the movie, until she realized, *no, he* likes *me.* "Did Darius figure the secret out? That would be the answer that is most obvious, though I doubt he would say anything to Jack. Everyone is slightly afraid of Jack."

Even as her mind was racing about how she was going to salvage this, how Siemens was going to still make a nine-figure sum selling trains to WMATA even though a cranky old trainspotter with too much time on his hands had figured out who she was, a small part of her was enjoying sitting on the bed with the phone jammed between her ear and her shoulder, talking to a guy she had recently kissed. She and her first boyfriend ("boyfriend") in junior high would barely make eye contact when they ran into each other between classes, but would talk for hours on the phone at night. There was something nice about having a disembodied voice that you liked in your ear.

"It wasn't Darius. Jack figured it out himself, sort of. He figured it out because—" She took a deep breath. "He wasn't even looking for us. He was paranoid about Rajiv, and he was right. Rajiv works for another agency, one hired by AnsaldoBreda. An agency called Ouisseauhai. He's been doing a counterplay. He's ... he's doing the same sort of thing we've been doing."

There was a long silence. "Hello?"

Mesut started to laugh. Genuinely laugh. It was a high barking giggle and, she admitted, not unpleasant. She had never heard him really laugh before, except for an occasional mournful or sarcastic chuckle. *Maybe he* is *on ecstasy,* she thought.

"I'm sorry, but ... well. Obviously this is bad. But I think we should confess to each other now that it is also extremely funny."

▟▛▟▛▟▛▟▛▟▛▟▛

Subconscious Agency began doing stealth work as Kate understood it by the end of 1997. The Internet was around—in fact, the Agency was a pioneer in online work—but its connection to the real world was much more tenuous, and easy to control. That connection, Christine would be the first to admit, was growing harder to manage as the '10s wore on and the Internet became real life.

"Here's how he did it," she said to Mesut. They were sitting together in her car, on the street outside the Agency offices, within the penumbra of its Wi-Fi network. It was seven o'clock on Saturday morning—an insane hour, but she had let Jack dictate the time and place of their meeting, so she and Mesut now had to meet even earlier to prepare. It was possible that someone was in the office working, but she didn't want to face them, and she assumed they'd also want to be left alone in their shame. She had her laptop open and was logged in to DCRailTalk. There was a new thread at the top of the discussion list.

> **The_Real_Jack** 12 hours ago
>
> ALERT: CORPORATE PUPPETMASTERS ARE MANIPULATING WMATA

"Oh dear," said Mesut. Kate's car was a used Jeep Cherokee her parents had given her as a college graduation present. The laptop sat in the middle of the dashboard, and as they huddled together, their shoulders brushed against each other.

"It's *interesting* at least," she said. Last night, when she had assured him that nothing was about to happen that would oblige them to wake up their bosses, he'd announced that he was going to go to bed and didn't want to hear any more details. "Can you really *sleep?*" she asked, and in her mind's eye she saw him shrug those bony shoulders.

"I can try. It's quite late."

She was eager to get him up to speed now, not just because they would be meeting Jack and Charlie and Darius in forty-five minutes at Dunkin' Donuts, but because there was a burden to being the only one who knew something. She had lain awake staring at the ceiling long after hanging up with him, feeling like she had to tell *someone*. LaMont? LaMont was home with his boyfriend. He didn't want to hear about work. He was probably asleep. Mitch? He didn't seem like he'd know what to do in a crisis, and anyway, despite his not-boyfriend status, she felt awkward about having introduced a new not-boyfriend into the mix. *Maybe I should call Christine?* she thought. *Bad ideas. Bad, bad ideas.*

"Yes. Interesting. This is a word to use for this situation."

The_Real_Jack 12 hours ago

As many of you know

"The thing I love about Jack," she said, "is that he really is the hero of his own story."

"You and I are sitting together in an automobile at seven in the morning reading his Internet manifesto. This is after he sent you a late-night message in which he announced that he has seen through your careful disguise. I am saying that he perhaps is not wrong?"

there was an incident at a WMATA public meeting several weeks ago in wich I was antagonized into a state of disruption. In what I now know to have been the plan all along, I was asked to leave. I believed at that time that there was an individual at this meeting who was not entirely as he seemed. Most of you know Rajiv from these boards. He was in attendence with his camera, mostly to

250

> capture on film the various display placards and vehicle
> mockups WMATA presented. They are notorious for not
> posting these kinds of materials on their public web site,
> despite the fact that they are a taxpayer-funded public
> agency.

"Oh, yes, I would definitely say this is interesting," said Mesut.

> I asked Rajiv to send me all of the pictures from the
> meeting. I didn't tell him why, but he knows I'm a
> completist. I believed, correctly, that he wouldn't think this
> was an unusual request. The relevant images are in the
> following post.

A series of photos from the public meeting followed: poorly lit,
badly framed. There was Mesut's face in the bottom corner of one,
his eyes glowing from the flash. There was one of Jack standing up
and gesticulating wildly, with Kate cringing behind him. And there,
in a picture that was vaguely centered on the WMATA's NextGen
Railcar Project placard, was a decent three-quarters-view portrait
of Ponytail, looking smug.

> **Railyard Ape** 12 hours ago
>
> Hey Jack I was at that meeting too. Another big
> performance from Jack. Not that you were wrong but
> Jesus man dial it back once in a while you know??

This was the only comment from someone other than Jack on
the thread. It was ignored.

> **The_Real_Jack** 12 hours ago
>
> Now those of you who aren't that computer-savvy might
> not know. But there are certain Internet search engines
> that can run what's called "reverse image search."
> Basically you give it a picture and it tries to come up with
> other pictures that are like it. I tried it with a picture of

> this individual's face. There were a lot of "false positives,"
> but in the end, I was able to successfuly identify him.
> What I found at the following links shocked me.
>
> http://www.ouisseauhai-consulting.com/about/people/
> charles-lecce

"Oh my," said Mesut, as they looked at his smiling face on his profile page. His hair was cut short, and he wasn't wearing glasses, but it was definitely the same guy. "It *was* a false ponytail."

"Ouisseauhai is a PR firm. They're..." Kate tried to figure out how much to explain. "They're probably the closest thing we have to a competitor. Bob Byrd, the owner, used to work at the Agency."

"Do they often do stealth assignments like you do?"

"Not that we knew about."

> http://www.ouisseauhai-consulting.com/news/press-
> releases/ansaldobreda

"See, and this is how you can tell. I can't believe they decided to do stealth and then put out a *press release* about it. Fucking *amateurs*."

"Well, the press release does not mention plans to put on wigs and antagonize railfans in public. It actually doesn't say much of anything at all? 'AnsaldoBreda is a worldwide leader in transportation infrastructure and Ouisseauhai is excited to help build brand awareness in the growing North American transit market.'"

"It's still bullshit," she said. She was fuming. She was grinding her teeth. Not because her own plans were derailed, or not *just* because of that. It was the *principle* of the thing. "Do you think that there's any press release anywhere linking us to Siemens in even the vaguest of terms?"

"We might have written one. Our Communications Department enjoys press releases and sending press releases to people very much, or that is my impression."

"I'm sure Christine told them not to in very strict terms. I'm sure she implied that if that happened she would *murder* someone, in a very calm and gentle way."

The_Real_Jack 12 hours ago

I made a thorough review of the individual who has posted here and elsewhere as 'Rajiv'. He is now confirmed to be Rajiv Pandit, a junior marketer at Ouisseauhai Partners and Associates LLC. He began posting on various railfan sites three days before the press release I linked to above was made public. Almost every single one of the discussions he initiated was negative in tone about other rolling stock manufacturers. I'd go so far as to define him as a 'hater.' And yet his own paymaster is never the target of his sarcasm, despite its well-known problematic

"OK, yes, so when does he get to us? Because if he is only complaining about Rajiv and Breda than this is all very excellent, and obviously this is not all very excellent."

Kate opened up the inbox for the kmacal1987@gmail.com account she'd created for the assignment in another browser tab. The only message was from Jack. Embedded at the top was a picture of four men in hard hats, standing in front of a train that looked almost, but not quite, like the S360. All were Teutonically blue-eyed and blond-haired except for olive-skinned Mesut, standing in the middle of the group, grinning almost as widely as he had at the Sons of UNIVAC show.

He let out a low whistle. "Ah, yes. Our Communications Department also enjoys adding photos to their press releases. They are very determined to do so, actually. They say it makes people more eager to read them."

There was text in the email below the image: *After unmasking Rajiv, which I'm sure you've read about by now, I thought I'd follow up on some other newcomers. This was an interesting find. And then I asked a few other people what they knew about you. Funny thing. Darius says you work for some marketing company. Doing comic strip movies, except I'll bet that's not all. And you and Mustafa are so buddy buddy. Except he's not Mustafa. Which you probably know.*

"So why didn't he put our faces in that thread?" Mesut asked.

"I don't know," she said. "I genuinely don't know. Maybe he just wants to gloat in person first. I asked him if we could all meet and talk, and he suggested Dunkin' Donuts this morning. Maybe he gave Rajiv the same chance to get yelled at."

"So we will go and be humiliated at breakfast and then ... I will go back to my hotel, I suppose, because you are flying to California for comics adventures at ten o'clock."

She shrugged. "I promise you that spending six hours incommunicado on a plane is going to be terrible for my nerves, if it makes you feel any better. Anyway, what have we got to lose?"

"Our jobs and millions of dollars for our companies. But other than that, why not."

▟▛▟▛▟▛▟▛▟▛

The Dunkin' Donuts was grimy, surprisingly large, and mostly empty this early on a Saturday; several years worth of corporate memos about updating the interior had been ignored by this particular franchisee. A few shift workers on their way home were scattered around, along with a few early risers. It still smelled great, though.

You can't go wrong with donuts. As soon as Kate and Mesut pushed through the door, they spotted the trio sitting all on one side of a booth in the far corner: Jack, Charlie, and Darius. Darius flashed them a smile and waved. *At least somebody still likes us,* Kate thought.

They slid into the booth opposite the trainspotters. There was a long moment of silence, during which Kate tried to summon up some avatar of support. What would Maureen do? Or Eve, or Carol? Nothing came. They were comic strip characters and this was real. "So," Mesut finally said, "Would it be OK if I get some donuts before we start, or..."

"The reason I picked this place," said Jack, "is that they don't give a crap how long you stay once you buy some coffee." He held up his cup of coffee and shook it, letting it slosh around meaningfully. "Now who are you?"

What would Christine do? *Be forthright.* "I'm Kate Berkowitz and I work for a company called Subconscious Agency. This is Mesut Özdemir and he's a mechanical engineer who works for Siemens. Siemens hired my company to help convince WMATA to buy the S360." *Acknowledge wounds.* "I completely understand that ... finding out what you found out must be very confusing and strange."

Jack cackled. "Strange? Oh, no. This is exactly how the world works. Wheels within wheels. I'm just glad people are actually going to start *believing* me now."

Charlie let loose a long exhale. "It's true. You guys are ... no offense, you really are one of his paranoid fantasies come to life."

"I almost stopped when I figured out who Rajiv was, but I just had this *feeling*," Jack said. "Like, every time something about Breda would get pushed out of my head, something else about Siemens would get pushed in. You know? So I did a little poking around.

Just a hunch. I figured, how many Turkish-Germans could there be working there, anyway?"

"Actually," said Mesut. "There are quite a lot of us. There's even an internal working group on discrimination issues that—"

"Why did you guys go watch the train with us?" asked Darius. "You know the people who built it. You could have seen it any time you wanted. You work for the company that makes it. It's *weird*, what you did."

"We did it because we wanted you to see it," said Kate. "Because we wanted you to know how great it was."

"But you could have just told us? You could have invited us to the factory or the railyards. And not pretended to be someone else."

"Darius," she said. "Do you remember how much *fun* it was?" She did. She remembered the thrill of trespassing, of sneaking through the fence. She remembered the wind of the train coming around the curve. She remembered the joy radiating off of them as it blew past.

Be forthright. Acknowledge wounds. Focus on positive outcomes or attitudes already fostered.

"She's right," said Charlie, "It was better than a factory tour. Not that we wouldn't like a factory tour as well, if we're bargaining." He looked at Jack with an exasperated expression. "Are we bargaining?"

"Jack," she said. "Why didn't you post our information on that thread like you did Rajiv's?"

He looked at her. "Do you even ride the Metro? Saw you pull up in some big SUV outside."

"I take the Orange Line in to work every day from Arlington, on the trains with the shitty broken air conditioners."

"You seemed real keen on the S360 air conditioners."

"The first time we met," Mesut said, "She asked if the new trains were going to have air conditioners that didn't break down. I told her if they worked in Mecca, surely they would work in Washington, D.C."

He turned to Mesut. "That stuff you told Charlie about the brakes? That a sales snow job?"

Mesut bristled. "I'm on the team that oversaw the brake systems. I'm not *in* the Sales Department. If I *say* something about it—"

Jack and Charlie started talking over him. "The tests they put those things through—" "The technical specs are online—" Discussion quickly hit an elevated level of technical detail that Kate couldn't follow. She sat there awkwardly, looking at Darius, who also wasn't talking.

"You know what," he said. "People sometimes think I know more about how trains work than I do. I don't really understand the engineering. I just think they look cool. And I like maps."

She smiled at him as the other three continued to tussle. "So do I, Darius. I'm sorry about all this."

He shrugged. "I still think it's a cool train. I hope WMATA buys it, and then I'll get to ride one for real."

"I just—*we* just wanted you to be excited about it, that's all. If you're excited, other people are excited. I don't know if you know that, but it's true. And when people get excited, they make decisions. They *do* stuff."

"But they paid you to get us excited," said Darius. "Right?"

She let that sit for a minute. "That's right. But the rest is still true." It was still true. It *was*. But they didn't say anything else, just the same.

"Look," Mesut was saying, karate-chopping the air to accentuate his points, "if you don't trust European testing facilities that have,

I don't know, decades of experience, on a continent that has more trains and fewer accidents than your continent, I am not going to convince you while I sit here and not eat donuts even though I want donuts."

"Fine. Fine. You know what? *Fine.* You've got jobs to do, I've got a job to do—" This was the first time Kate had ever heard Jack mention employment, and she couldn't imagine him holding down any job for long before blowing up at his boss and stalking out of the office, much as he appeared to be about to stalk out of this donut shop. Darius was sitting between him and the end of the booth, though, which significantly dampened the dramatic gesture. Mostly he just stood up awkwardly.

Mesut seemed taken aback. "So, are you going to ... are you going to post about us? On the website?"

Jack turned to Kate. "I can't speak for my friends, but I am not going to tell anyone about this, and I'll tell you why. Those other guys, Wisso-whatever, just tried to get me all riled up. They didn't know shit about what's a good train or anything else. But you brought an engineer into the mix. That shows *respect.* C'mon, Darius, I gotta go." Jack was practically climbing over him, even as Darius was trying extricate himself. "Bye, Kate!" Darius called out to her, and the two of them walked out.

Charlie was the only one left. He looked at them seriously, then laughed. "Weird morning," he said, then he left, too.

She sighed and let the tension seep out of her body, leaning into Mesut as she did. He put his hand on top of hers. "Well," he said. "Not to be smug, but it was very good that I was here this morning, yes?"

"Oh," she said, "I wouldn't have come without you. You're an engineer. It *does* show respect. Jack said it, and he's right. There's nothing that makes enthusiasm genuine like real topic knowledge, and real topic knowledge almost always engenders enthusiasm." She smiled. The words were coming out in a flood now. Jack wasn't going to blow their cover. She had pulled it off. "You were my ace in the hole!" Only as she said that last sentence did she realize that his face had been crumpling, that he had jerked his hand away and was leaning away from her back into the booth.

"Yes," he said, "The ace in ... yes. I see. I understand." She started to say that it wasn't like that, that she was happy he was here because she liked him, but they both knew that it *was* like that. She did like him. Of course. But he had done what she needed him to do this morning, because she knew him well enough to know that he would. She didn't even need to ask him.

And so she hadn't.

She wanted to hurry out of the sad, two-aesthetic-concepts-behind Dunkin' Donuts, just like Jack wanted to, and get to the airport. But like Jack, she was stuck on the inside of the booth, so she and Mesut just looked at each other.

14

IF KATE HAD TO PICK A MOMENT when it was clear the meeting had gone wrong—and she did have to identify that moment, immediately after it was done, when she wrote the First Impressions report that the Agency expected you to put together in the aftermath of a real-life encounter, when the pain or triumph was still hot—it was when Marie Redmond, frowning with increasing irritation at the iPad that she was flicking her finger across, said, "The problem with this, kids, is that I don't fucking *get* any of it."

First Impressions reports were supposed to be just that, and were more often than not tapped out on a smartphone in a parking lot before you went back home or to your hotel. Kate would write this one in the back seat of Mitch's car on the long drive back from Palm Desert, looking at the back of the heads of Mitch and Zach, the Producer, and taking in their variously flavored icy silences. "Original content creator not aligned with multilevel irony concept for deliv/ enthusiasm," she wrote, staring very intently at her phone. She had barely tapped the "m" before she started deleting.

If she were being really honest with herself, she would've admitted the sense of doom she felt when she stepped through the scrum and out of the secure area at LAX. The terminal was a dump, overcrowded and outdated and covered with a layer of grime that probably never washed away no matter how hard anyone tried. "Pardon our mess! Improvements are coming!" a few signs chirped cheerfully at her, but they, too, looked like they had been there longer than they should have.

Mitch was waiting. When he saw her, he flashed a tiny Magic-Markered sign that said KATE! with a little smiley face after it, and it did make her melt, just a little bit.

No melting, she thought. This was the deal she had made with herself. This was a salvage mission. No drama. No action. (Imposing a moratorium on drama was, of course, itself a sort of drama. But getting recursive was a recipe for overthinking, overthinking more than usual.)

She came towards him, panicking over whether to go in for a hug or a handshake or what. She was grateful when he took the lead, and was impressed at both the level of difficulty and the execution: reach out for a warm, lingering handshake with the right hand, a gentle touch on her shoulder with the left, which, once the handshake was done, became a subtle redirection—not a shove, not even a push, just a gentle, physical suggestion that maybe she should turn her body a few degrees to her left, so she could meet ... "Kate, this is Zach. I know you guys have chatted online, but here he is, in the flesh." And then Zach was shaking her hand, too, which managed to kill any romantic or sexual pulls she might have been experiencing. *Oh, right, fucking Zach,* she thought. *Zach who should've figured this thing out a long time ago.*

"Zach," she said. In person, he was short, shorter than Mitch, and a little bit doughy. His blond hair was short and neatly parted, and his glasses looked very expensive. Mostly he looked young, really young. Maybe 23? Not *that* much younger than her. But every once in a while, she wasn't the youngest adult in the room anymore, and, honestly, she looked forward to that happening more and more.

He also looked scared, which disarmed her a bit. She had been so busy convincing herself on the flight over that hooking up with Mitch again wasn't on the agenda that she barely realized how much taking vengeance on Zach was. But here he was, some blond kid who had made friends with Mitch somehow and was trying hard to do something that would impress him. Mitch had a soft spot for eager young people. *He likes you, doesn't he?* Maybe it wasn't worth her time, and just by formulating the thought, she knew there was no maybe involved. *This is a salvage mission. Let's not fight on the way. We go in with the resources we have.*

She looked at Mitch and Zach. *It's not going to be enough.*

"Hey, Kate, *great* to meet you, really stellar," Zach said, and it sounded so much like a parody of Hollywood smarm that her resolve almost slipped. Mitch offered to carry her bag for her, and she decided to allow him that much. They headed for the exit, and she saw Mitch craning his head, and she realized he was probably looking for paparazzi. Tabloids almost never put him on the cover, since he wasn't shockingly gorgeous or venal or insane; but there were a lot of square inches inside those magazines to fill with photos and cheerful two-sentence captions clearly written by someone who hated their lives and themselves. A likeable, handsome, easily recognizable comic actor would do great for a "Stars: They're Just Like At Least Some Of Us, Who Carry Our Own Bags" sidebar or a "Who Wore It Better?: Black jeans!" two-page spread. *Probably for the best I didn't go in for the hug,* she thought.

Zach had composed his features into an expression that he clearly believed conveyed sincerity. "I just want to tell you that I'm really impressed that you tracked down the rights-holder for this IP."

"For the who?" said Mitch.

"Intellectual property," Kate and Zach said together.

"You guys do the smart talk," he said. "I'll just carry the luggage."

"Seriously," said Zach. "It was crazy. Usually this is a straight-forward transaction. Either they want to sell or they don't. Either we can afford it or we can't." *How often have you actually done this,* she thought, but that wasn't charitable. That was not in keeping with the attitude of Zen-like resignation she had chosen for herself on the plane. She was sure he was right. "I would talk to different people at Monarch or Hearst, and it would be like, 'So, I hear you're interested in the book rights to our property,' and I'd be all, 'No, movie,' and then they'd say, 'Hey, do you want to do a series of 10-minute streaming webisodes,' and I'd be all, 'No, *movie,*' and they'd say..."

"I've had to listen to this for weeks, by the way," said Mitch.

It wasn't that hot, but Zach was sweating, and anything Mitch said seemed to make him cringe, and every time he did Kate's bloodlust faded into detached pity. *This was Zach's big play,* she thought. Zach wasn't a producer (or: he was not yet *the* producer) for anybody. Zach was mirroring what he thought Mitch might find helpful back at him. Which was great until he stopped being helpful.

"Do you have the address I sent you?" she asked Mitch.

"Already in my phone."

It was 2:30 in the afternoon. "Can we make it there in three hours?"

"If we're lucky."

"So is someone going to tell me why we're going out to Palm Desert? Is there, like ... a production company out there or something?"

Kate was genuinely shocked. "You didn't tell him?"

"Oh, Zach," said Mitch. "You kept *us* hanging for so long, man. I thought you could handle being kept hanging for a couple of days." Kate listened for hardness or anger in his voice and couldn't hear any. Even when he was doing his Magillicuddy shtick, Mitch Landers never seemed *mean*. Maybe he really did intend this to come across as friendly chiding, a little chops-bustin' for a bud who hadn't come through. Or maybe he was a really good actor. But still, either way, Zach was crumpling, and Kate found herself bailing him out despite herself.

"Honestly," she said, "Monarch and Hearst were stonewalling you. They'd noticed a forty-year-old screw-up for the first time because of all your questions. They were more scared of you than you were of them. Like bears. Bears that don't own intellectual property rights that they had been pretty sure they owned. The movie rights are still held by the strip's creator."

"Wait, by Hollis Houston? Is that a real guy?"

Oh, Zach, you keep making it hard to be nice to you. "No, the actual creator. Marie Redmond."

⫘⫘⫘⫘⫘⫘

"This trip is literally just for the day," she had said to Mesut after they had left the Dunkin' Donuts. They were back in her car, but sitting in their respective corners, the pleasant intimacy of huddling over the laptop screen vanished into the cool morning air. "I'll be back Sunday evening."

"Well, hopefully, Jack will not change his mind and denounce us to his legions of followers before you get back. I'm sure it would be a very interesting story for fanatics of Internet railfan drama, but it would be inconvenient if we were moderately fired. Is this trip involving your actor friend? What problems is *he* helping you solve?" That sarcastic edge to his voice was always funnier when aimed at other people.

"No, I solved one for him. Or, I figured out what we need to do to solve it. I just don't know if it's actually possible. Remember how we couldn't figure out who actually owned the legal rights to this movie?"

"I remember that you told me that it was not your job to buy those rights. Several times, you told me that. But then you kept talking about it."

"Yeah. Well, I found out they were owned by the original creator of the strip."

"Wait, I was understanding that the creator of the strip was a fake marketing personality. Like the kind you make for your job?"

"No, she's a real person." *And so am I,* she didn't say. "And she needs to get enthusiastic about this movie or she'll never sell the rights to Mitch. *That's* why it's my job."

This was what Rex had told Kate at his house in Loudoun County: when Ted Redmond got wind in the first heady years of the strip that a *Ladies Who Lunch* movie might happen, he convinced a lawyer friend of his to create a shell company, Ladies Film, Inc., without telling the syndicate or his wife. Ted was the sole share-holder, and the company existed only to own the movie rights to the strip, which Ted assigned to it. Nobody was left alive who knew his motivation, whether it was some kind of tax dodge or record-keeping OCD, but the financial records made it clear that Ladies Film, Inc., cashed the checks from Paramount, and Ladies Film, Inc., would've cashed more checks if the movie hadn't been a bomb and an embarrassment.

"You gotta understand, that movie was poison," said Rex. "Even though the strip was doing well in the newspapers, even though the girls were still celebrities, the film business was done with them." He said "the girls" with real warmth, and she realized that they'd been lodged in his headspace for more than a decade. "This was before you had your print publishers and your movie studios both owned by the same Japanese electronics company who makes them be nice to each other."

The three-cornered legal wrangle between Ted, Marie, and Monarch over the strip focused entirely on the lucrative rights to own and profit from the print strip and the supermarket-checkout digests. The movie rights, a still-fresh wound for everyone concerned, went untouched and unmentioned. In the end, both Ted and Marie ended up taking the payoff from Monarch in return for signing away "whatever rights to *Ladies Who Lunch* might pertain to any of the undersigned parties." Neither Ted nor Marie were forced to admit, legally, that the other one was right. As far as each was concerned, they had sold what was theirs and the other had sold a hot bag of lies.

"But Ted didn't own the *Ladies Who Lunch* film rights," said Rex. "Ladies Film, Inc., did. So that document didn't sign them away, because he signed as himself, not as CEO of Ladies Film, Inc. According to the law, those are two different people, or different things, or something."

"So who owns Ladies Film, Inc., now?"

"Well, Ted held onto it. Till he died in 2009. Then his estate took about four years to unravel; Ladies Film, Inc., was *not* his only shell corporation. It was the only one worth anything, though. We found that out the hard way."

"We?"

"Me and Marie. You know. Marie *Redmond*." This was his trump, what he had summoned her out here to tell her. "She was the sole heir in Ted's will. They never had kids, and he never remarried, and he never had a new will drawn up after the divorce. I don't know if he was sentimental or careless or just didn't know who else to leave all his stuff and his dumb fake companies to. Anyway, she and I have been friendly for a while. When my assistant put up the Wiki page, I think, is how she tracked me down. Interesting gal. Obviously has a lot to say about the strip. She's been writing it again for the past few years. A slot opened up, I suggested it to Monarch, they jumped at it."

This was too much. Kate put her hand to her mouth because she knew she was about to emit some ridiculous noise, a laugh-cry or a gasp-moan or something. "Why didn't..." And she couldn't help it: she immediately started imagining the buzz campaign she could build around this. *Marie Redmond, comics pioneer. Marie Redmond finally triumphs. Marie Redmond, feminist hero.* You wouldn't put out a press release. You never put out a press release. You tell somebody in the comics business, though. Maybe one of those guys who drew it in the '80s or '90s as their first comics gig, the ones who are elder statesmen who do art design for the movies now. They'd get the word out. People know. The newsreels of the trial get uploaded to the right YouTube accounts, show up on the right blogs. The glamorous pics—Kate thought they were glamorous—of her looking angry and badass on that movie tour, those go on Tumblr. Eventually it filters up to the mainstream press. Someone at Monarch defers.

Finally, someone goes to find her in her seclusion. She gives a single interview. It happens right around the time the movie comes out. "Why didn't anyone *say* anything?"

"Because she asked them not to." He cut into his steak, took a slow and deliberate bite. "All the drama with the divorce—that changed her, see? She never wants to go in front of a camera again. She's got a nice little place in the California desert, writes the scripts for the strip, doesn't get bothered."

"But you're blowing her cover."

Rex scowled. "Give me some credit, young lady. I talked to her right after I got off the phone from you. Told her I'd check you out for her. See if she should meet you in person. I guess you pass. On your honor, though: no reporters, no creeps, no nothing. You ask her for the rights, and she either says yes or no." He pulled out his wallet, unfolded a small piece of paper and pushed it across the table at her. On it was Marie's address and phone number, in a shaky handwriting that, after a moment of disorienting deja vu, she recognized as the same one used to letter *Ladies Who Lunch*. "Good luck. She's gonna bite your head in two, is what I think's gonna happen."

"I still can't believe you met Rex," said Mitch. They were on the 105 freeway, running into traffic as they approached the interchange with the 110. Kate's legs were up on the back seat, and she was leaning against the door on the driver's side. She could see Mitch's hair, spilling over the tops of his ears, and remembered what it was like to touch it. *Great hair,* she thought. *Real professional.*

"Sexy Rexy! LaWLasaurus Rex!" he said. These were the nicknames the LaWLChat posters had adopted for the strip's artist and deployed with various degrees of affection. "Did he say anything about me?"

"Said he'd never heard of you until a couple years ago. Said the guys in the strip are supposed to look like William Powell when he was young."

"That's not right," said Mitch. "That's ... that's factually incorrect. Jeez."

"Who's William Powell?" asked Zach. Nobody answered him.

━━━━━━━━━━━

Three and a half hours later, a bored security guard waved them through the gate into the seniors-only housing development where Marie Redmond lived. Since all Marie had was a landline, Kate had called, not texted, to tell her they had hit traffic and were running a little late. "It's all right, honey," said a deep, raspy voice on the other end. "I'm not going anywhere."

They drove slowly around the curved streets lined with neat little stucco bungalows. There were old people everywhere, in white shorts and pastel shirts and protective hats, waving at each other and walking from house to house. There were multiple barbecue grills going. Most of the men and some of the women had cans of beer or highball glasses in their hands. Golf carts sped by erratically.

"Holy cow," said Zach. "This is the life."

Marie was waiting for them on her front stoop as they pulled into her driveway. "Let me go first," said Kate, and she hopped out of the car before anyone could object. "Ms. Redmond," she said. At the last moment, she realized Marie had a cigarette in her right hand, so she offered her left to shake instead. "Kate Berkowitz. We spoke on the phone. Thanks for taking the time. I'm a fan."

"Marie Redmond," Marie said. "I doubt you are. I'm not even going to ask what year you were born in. I'm pretty sure it's way after anything interesting I ever did."

"Well, I'm a fan of what I've read."

"Ah, a history buff."

"Ms. Redmond," said Mitch, coming up behind Kate. "I'm Mitch Landers, and I love *Ladies Who Lunch*."

"See, this one I believe. I don't why, but I believe it." She looked him up and down and took a drag. "You're a good-looking specimen. They send you here to make an old lady's knees weak?"

"He's an actor," said Zach. "A famous actor."

"Yeah, I know who he is. That's what happens when you're famous. People know who you are. What's your story, number three?"

"I'm Zach, the producer." He fumbled in his wallet for his card, and there was a long, exquisite pause as she didn't take it. "Zach ... Merriman. I do production work."

"Merriman," she said. "I've heard of you. You're the one who kept sending all those anxious notes that Monarch would pass onto me, and I would ignore. You're all lucky Rex has a sense of professional responsibility about this shit."

A bald man wearing a white Kangol hat slowed his golf cart down in front of the house. "Hey, Marie," he shouted. "I'm grilling burgers, you wanna come over?"

"No," she yelled back, then took a long drag and glared.

"Suit yourself, you know where to find me." The cart took off with a whirr, weaving back and forth across the street.

"I swear to God, the men here think all they have to do is wiggle their dicks at you and you come running, just because there's half as many of them as there is of us. Fuck you, Bernard, I got a famous actor coming over." She stubbed out her cigarette in an ashtray she had set out on the cement walkway leading up to her front door.

"Can't even smoke in my own house because of all the damn rules. Come on in if you're coming in."

She gestured around the living room to the seats she had apparently chosen for them: couch, love seat, Eames chair. Everything was mid-century modern and a little tightly packed, like it had all been in a bigger place once and nothing had ever been sold or given away. "This is where the magic happens," she said, sweeping her hand around. On a desk in one corner was a CRT screen and grungy desktop computer; it was at least 10 years old and looked dated in a way that none of the 1960s-era furniture did. She sat down and picked an iPad up off the coffee table. "A present from Rex," she said, holding it gently and giving it a little smile.

"Rex seemed like..." Kate tried to choose her words carefully. "Not a big *fan* of technology."

"Oh, Rex is an old crank about everything, worse than I am, right up to the part where it lets him slack off more. He refused to do anything with email or learn how a scanner worked until he found out that he could send his art into the syndicate two days later if he did it over the computer. Then all of the sudden he's a big cyber-expert. At least when it comes to scanning and emailing." She flipped the iPad so they could see the screen. It was divided into three panels, and there were stick figures labeled CAROL and MAUREEN gesticulating at each other. "Look, I can sketch out the strip to send it to him to draw. I used to do it on paper for Stan, but this is easier to erase. And you don't have to wait for the mail." She put her finger on the screen and wrote "HELLO REX!" Then her smile faded and she abruptly closed the drawing app. "All right, you're late, so you've got an hour. I have a party to go to—not with that letch Bernard, if you're wondering." She brought up the Web browser and thrust the iPad aggressively at them. "Come on," she said, "which one of you is going to show me this website that you want to make some kind of movie out of?"

ⅢⅢⅢⅢⅢⅢ

Kate had suggested Mitch do it. "I hope you don't feel like I threw you to the lions back there," she said to him later, on the ride back. "Or, you know, to one particular lioness."

"I don't know, Kate," said Zach, whose opinion had not been requested. "Seems to me that's the sort of thing the talent pays for, not the thing that the talent *does*."

"The talent paid for me to build enthusiasm," she said. "The talent was also this scenario's genuine enthusiast. You have to build enthusiasm on *something*. It was our best shot."

"Well, I'm just sorry I fucked it up," Mitch said.

In fact, there had been a moment, a very long moment, when Kate had almost taken the iPad herself. She saw the FaceTime app icon on the screen and a name suddenly jumped into her head: *Darius*. Darius loved FaceTiming with people. After he had gone up to New York for the focus group, he'd post comments in LaWLChat asking if any of his new in-person friends were around and wanted to FaceTime. Sometimes they were and did. Often, it was right around this time of day, evening on the East Coast.

She imagined Darius's eager face popping up on the screen, imagined him talking about how much he loved making jokes about the strip, about all his LaWLChat friends. The strip, and the jokes about the strip, had made his life better. That would've been obvious. His sweetness would've cut through the unapologetic sourness of some of the LaWLChat posts.

Kate could've even set this up in advance, talked to him about it when she had seen him at the Dunkin' Donuts. That had been just this morning, though it felt like years ago now. But she had had other things on her mind at the time.

And if she'd asked, he wouldn't have done as good a job, would he? If she told him why she needed his help, he would've been happy to offer it, but his enthusiasm would have become goal-oriented. You don't tell your secret weapon it's a weapon.

She pulled her hand away from the iPad. "Mitch, this was your idea to begin with. Why don't you walk us through it?"

He'd done fine. He had sat on the sofa next to Marie, letting her hold the tablet, but leaning over and tapping and swiping for her, bringing up the LaWLChat forums, pointing out his favorite threads. The Mitch laugh and the Mitch smile were in full effect, and Kate had to issue more stern silent warnings to herself about melting. Marie seemed to be melting a little, in spite of herself.

There were a couple catches. One was that all of Mitch's favorite LaWLChat jokes were about him. His enthusiasm was no less genuine for being driven by his own self-fascination, but it made it less charming than it could've been. "You know it's supposed to look like William Powell, right," Marie said at one point, and Kate finally brought up a picture of him on her phone for Zach to look at. "Yeah, I kinda see it," he said.

The second catch was that Marie didn't understand the point of what the LaWLChatters were doing, and what she did grasp didn't make her feel like finding out more. "No, but I mean it," said Marie, "What the honest-to-god fuck is this. I don't get any of this."

"Marie," said Zach, "Your creation has taken on a life ... beyond what you could've ever imagined, I'm sure. All these years later, people are still reading..." *This isn't the right pitch,* Kate thought.

"Of course they're still reading," she snapped back. "I'm getting the checks, aren't I?"

"Yes, well. But you can see from those posts that the characters still..." He waved his hands around a bit. "Well, they've got a grip on people! Those folks online are interested in knowing what they're up to!"

Kate was starting to panic and waiting for Zach to shut up so she could get a word in edgewise. *He's patronizing her, pitching her what he thinks some notional nice old lady in his head would want to hear. Has he been here at all for the last twenty minutes? Has he heard all the swearing?*

Marie's thin-lipped grimace got broader. She fixed Zach with a withering glare and turned the iPad around so he could see the screen. They were looking at one of the more twisted LaWLChat Photoshop contest entries. Usually people pasted a photo of Mitch's real-life face onto the body of one of Rex's Mitchengängers; in this panel, though, the drawing of the character's head (it must have been from the storyline earlier this year in which the girls jetted off to Dubai for a shopping weekend, because it was topped with a flowing Middle Eastern headdress) had been plopped down atop a photo of a man's slim but quite toned naked torso. The edge of the frame was perilously low, with the tops of his hip bones peeking out. There were no visible pants or underwear. Nearby, on a bed, an also apparently naked woman was sitting with a sheet drawn up to cover herself; her face was covered by a fairly crudely Photoshopped image of *Ladies Who Lunch*'s Carol.

"Hey, that is ... also me!" said Mitch, sounding pleased. "Man, they are not stopping at the face anymore, are they? And the lady is..." He squinted one eye and pursed his mouth as he thought. "Kristen Bell! *Laying Pipeline,* surf comedy, 2013...ish? God, I had to not wear a shirt on that movie a lot."

"I never got a grip on the tone on that one," said Zach. "Was it supposed to be kinda dumb, or kinda smart, or kinda smart because it knew how dumb it was?"

"Yes, well, we all would've liked to have known that, Zachary," Mitch said, sighing. "You would have to ask the director and the three different screenwriters. None of them were talking to each other by the end."

"Oh, you two made a movie that was a disaster and everyone hated each other," said Marie. "That's an interesting tidbit."

"I did not work on that movie," said Zach.

"They love it," Kate said. "The people on the site. I know it seems weird, but they love the strip."

"I don't even know what it has to *do* with the strip."

Kate silently tried to take the measure of Marie. The steely eyes, the smoky voice. In the pictures she had seen from the early days of *Ladies Who Lunch,* she looked like Shirley MacLaine circa *The Apartment.* Now, she looked like Shirley MacLaine circa *Downton Abbey.* She was irritated, which probably masked being hurt.

"Look, you think of *Ladies Who Lunch* as your baby," she said.

"It is," she said. "Not legally. But it's mine again. Nobody stops me from doing what I want with it."

"Yeah, I know. But what I mean is ... you were there when it was born, you've seen it through its whole existence at this point." Marie's eyes narrowed, and Kate realized she needed to tread carefully. *Twenty-six-year-old spins overwrought and vaguely patronizing child metaphor to seventy-six-year-old with no children: not a good look.* It had to be done, though, she thought. It was the only way to get the point through. "You know what the strip is, how it's changed, for good or bad. But for these people"—she pointed at Mitch and Kristen Bell's torsos topped by Rex-drawn heads — "the strip is just, like, this fascinating cultural object from ... a different ... place."

The pauses had been a little too long. "From the past. From squaresville." She frowned at the screen.

"Speaking as a millennial," Zach said, "let me just say that there's a lot of respect, and a lot of *appreciation* for the milieu this strip came out of. *Mad Men* was huge among young people. We know the era's not square."

"*Mad Men* is a fucking theme park," Marie said, looking at Kate and not Zach.

"It's reverent," said Kate. "LaWLChat isn't. They're doing their own thing with something they found funny. They *found* funny," she repeated, something crystallizing in her head as she did. Darius could've made it clearer. His weird affection would've been less off-putting than Mitch's attempt to create a movie house of mirrors for himself. The narcissism! Imagine what it sounded like to a normal person. Kate realized how rarely she talked to normal people. She pushed on. "They feel like they discovered it, made it their own. People *like* having ownership," and just as she was finding her footing she realized that was wrong, a terribly wrong thing to say.

Marie pulled out a cigarette, looked at it, looked at the door, then put it away. "Like Columbus discovered America and made it his own. Just like that. Fuck 'em if someone else had it first."

There was a long, awkward silence. *Mitch will probably talk next,* Kate thought, and she was right. Mitch took an awkward silence in his presence as a cruel indictment of his own likability. "We all know this wouldn't be happening without—"

Marie was looking down at the iPad again. She made a few taps and brought up the strip that had been printed in a surprising number of newspapers that day. Maureen and her surfer boy (Mitch, or maybe William Powell, but blond) were staring into each other's eyes, with the Sydney Opera House looming in the background and the stars twinkling above them. "See that? Ted always said he'd take me to Australia, when he was less busy, which was never. Stan was scared to fly. Rex won't get a passport because he says there's a chip in them the government uses to track you everywhere." She shook her head. "Anyway. My girls are supposed to be your age, or around there, and I suppose I should really understand better what sort of things they'd talk about or like to do. I spent a lot of time thinking about it in the '60s. I read every letter. Jesus fucking Christ, people wrote letters, you wouldn't believe it. They seemed to care so much. I felt like I had a responsibility. Always 'Dear Mr. Houston,' which I hated, I don't think I have to tell you. They thought a man was writing it, so I worried even more that I'd make one of the girls do something a real single gal wouldn't do. I thought I was an old married lady who wasn't hep enough." She was silent for a moment. "That was another life. They were ghosts to me for a long time. Now I have them back and I honestly don't care what anyone else thinks. I write what's funny or interesting to me, or Rex tells me things he wants to draw. I'm having a blast, even if I'm just a hired hand."

Kate tried again. "Nobody thinks you're just—"

"Oh, I am, I am. The funny thing is that if you and Monarch wanted to do your strange jokes on Monarch's official Internet, you could. Or if you wanted to do it on TV, even. I mean, lucky you, you picked the one thing I'm allowed to say no to. And I've been waiting to say no for *years*."

"We haven't even made you an offer yet," Zach said.

She pulled an unlit cigarette out of the box and waved it around her tidy living room. "What are you gonna offer me that I don't have? No thanks. But thanks for driving all the way out here. You, you're a nice-looking young man, I can see why they put you in pictures." Mitch did the Mitch smile again, the one that made everyone like him so much. It was a real thing that came from a real place, Kate realized, or maybe from a place that had become real from constant use. "And you're a smart young woman. I'm glad you have this job you seem to like." Zach raised his eyebrows expectantly. "C'mon, get out. I gotta *smoke,* Jesus Christ."

Zach and Mitch were already halfway to the car when Marie grabbed Kate by the elbow and held her on the front stoop. "You two wait there, I want to talk to this one for a second," she shouted. Then, to Kate: "Look, that movie idea was ridiculous and stupid and I'm not sorry I said no." She lit her cigarette and inhaled gratefully. "But I am sorry if this gets you in trouble with your boss. I know girls have to work harder."

"The company is run by a woman, actually, though she still might be mad." *Are you certain you used all the resources available to you at this meeting in California?* Kate imagined Christine saying. *A long trip for a disappointing outcome.*

"A lady boss! Lucky you." She took another long drag. "Also, I think that guy likes you. The actor. Not the twerp, he's afraid of you."

Kate hesitated, then thought, *what the hell.* "Yeah, I, uh, I can confirm that. The liking me part." She smiled sheepishly.

"Lucky *you,*" Marie said. "God, I'm about to sound like my mother, but don't settle down, for Christ's sake. You're young. I got married when I was 22. Worst decision I ever made."

"I promise, I will *not* get married to Mitch Landers," said Kate, and they both giggled. Now she couldn't help herself. *She started it.* "So, you and Rex...?"

Marie picked up the ashtray and delicately tapped ashes into it. "Yup. He probably looked like an old man to you. Hell, he looks like an old man to me! He's got his charms, though."

"He's all the way across the country."

"Oh, that's the best, honey. You see him every eight weeks, fool around all weekend, and then you don't have to worry about cleaning his underwear or finding beard hairs in your sink. And he taught me how to send picture messages on that iPad. Don't knock it." She stubbed out her cigarette. "Now scram. I gotta girls' card game to go to."

On the drive back, she wrote and rewrote her First Impressions report. *Due to the legal structure of the potential project we were attempting to launch, the assignment hinged on the permission of a single individual, who also had a profound emotional stake in the outcome. She did not fully grasp*

She frowned and deleted, then rewrote

She decided the proposal wasn't congruent with her own enthusiasm for the universe she had created. Collective decision-making entities, such as profit-driven corporations and organic pre-existing enthusiast communities, can be influenced in largely predictable ways. Individuals pose a steeper challenge.

Another pause, and then:

I believe we exposed her to the full spectrum of enthusiasm vectors to the extent ethically possible.

And then she stared at it as they hurled through the desert.

THREE WEEKS BEFORE, when Kate and LaMont had gotten back from New York after the focus group, there were two prices she had to pay to get back into his good graces. The first was that she had to dish about Mitch. This was fun and was something she wanted to do anyway. Sleeping with a handsome yet approachable movie star is its own reward, of course. But assuming your goal is not to become a handsome movie star's long-term wife/girlfriend/sleeper-with, then what else do you get out of it? You get to tell a selected, discreet group of people all about it.

The second price, though, was listening to LaMont complain about Sigmar, *again*, and gush about how great Chuck Gindhart was, *again*. She tried hard to not feel impatient as she listened. It had taken a while for her to even admit to herself that she thought LaMont had been blowing it with Sigmar. She loved LaMont. He was her best friend at the Agency. He was definitely the person she spent the most time talking to, if you were tallying up the hours, and yet it was undeniable that this was the origin story of their friendship: they met in the break room and drifted together complaining about work. But something about LaMont's current difficulties had brought out something hard in her. He would moan about Sigmar stuttering on TV or his awkwardness with interviewers or any of the usual suite of Sigmar-typical behaviors, and Kate would hear a voice at the back of her head saying, *This is your job.* Of *course* Sigmar didn't want to argue with people on television. Arguing on television is *terrible.* Of *course* he sounded like he was trying to sell Siemens trains when he was doing a video interview for *The Wall Street Journal* website that was ostensibly about US-EU industrial cooperation. That's because he *was.* LaMont's job was to coach him through it.

Within a few days, though, LaMont had stopped complaining. Kate thought that he realized that she was fed up with him, or, alternately, that he had started realizing that *her* assignments were also giving her trouble and that it was time to start listening to her gripe. It embarrassed her, later, that the thought that he might be turning things around with Sigmar never occurred to her, and that she was getting too deep into her own problems to pay attention and notice this.

What she didn't know, because the two of them had agreed not to tell her, was that LaMont and Mesut had gone out after work one day, gotten drunk, and conspired to make Sigmar into a fully functional thought leader, a trusted voice whom bloggers and op-ed writers and sometimes even real reporters would keep in their contact list, tagged with the keywords TRAINS or INFRASTRUC-TURE or CAN SIMULATE HUMAN SMILE ON CAMERA.

This is how she found out: It was 8:30 Monday morning, and she had gotten back from California the night before. She felt foggy and jet-lagged and defeated, and went to LaMont's cube as soon as she got to the office. She had already texted with him Sunday while waiting for her delayed flight to leave Los Angeles, telling him about all the various ways her projects were imploding, and she didn't want to rehash any of that now. "Tell me some *good news,* Monty," she said as she turned the corner, and she was startled to see that Mesut was sitting there. She felt a bit of vertigo. They hadn't spoken since she had left Saturday morning.

The two men looked at each other guiltily. Then LaMont laughed. "Should we?"

Mesut shrugged. "You were the one who said it should be on the ... how did you say it? Down low?"

So LaMont told the story of how the two of them had gone to Balls, one of several fratty sports bars a few blocks from the office. LaMont had gone there when it opened last year, thinking, based on the name, that it might be a gay sports bar. It wasn't, but he decided it was one of the less bad places within walking distance.

"I knew he wouldn't help me if you were there," LaMont said to Kate. "That's why I didn't tell you." He turned to Mesut. "You were so hostile that first time I asked for help, like you were going to *impress* her by protecting Sigmar. You know where she *works,* right?" He was being funny, but Kate felt the sting.

"I'm sort of surprised you agreed to talk to him about it," said Kate. "You have been pretty negative about the whole idea."

"Well," Mesut said. "I am trying to make friends here, of course, because my hotel is very uninteresting, and I feel that you get bored of me if you see me all the time." Her heart melted a little bit. Just for a second. "But also, the day he asks me is also the day I learned from Sigmar that he is not actually in America to work for Siemens. He is on a leave of absence from the company at the moment. He is not even being paid!"

"He's not *what?*" Kate said.

"He's not *what?*" LaMont had said at Balls.

"Yes, exactly!" Mesut had told him, shoveling curly fries into his mouth. "I am reviewing these American regulations about crashworthiness, again, because they are very difficult to understand, still, and I go to the office Sigmar is using here to ask his advice, and he is watching these videos of people crying on chat shows—"

"It's his homework. I assigned that to him."

"He looked like *he* was about to cry. Then he tells me he needs to spend his time on doing well on these awful thought leader excursions you are sending him on, and that he does not have time to review anything about the S360 or anything else."

"He called them awful?"

"Not with words. But with his eyes, which looked very unhappy."

"Wait, I don't get it," Kate said, interrupting their story. "Hasn't he been acting like your boss the whole time you've been here? And who's paying for the Agency to make him a thought leader if Siemens isn't?"

"Yes, to your first question. In the sense that if I ask him for help he often provides it. Not in the sense that he tells me what to do or stops me from doing things he doesn't want me to do. It is shameful to me now that I did not notice. I thought I was just a very good employee who did not require much supervision? And, to your second question: he is. He is paying your Agency. To make him a thought leader."

"Sigmar's daughter," Mesut had told LaMont at Balls, "wants to go to university in America, very badly." He sipped his beer. "And he has been at the same level in the company for many years and the person above him is the same age as him and will never leave and he begins to feel inadequate. And he thinks getting a managerial job for Siemens in America will make these things better. And he thinks you can help him succeed in an American way. *The* American way, is what you say, I believe." He sighed. "It makes me sad that Sigmar feels like he has to go through all this. But he has been a good boss. He has been good to me here, even though he is secretly not my boss. So, I will help you help him."

After several beers and an order of mozzarella sticks, LaMont had asked Mesut what Sigmar "lived for." Mesut thought about it for a long moment. "Not his work, though he is a very dedicated employee. Sigmar 'lives for'"—LaMont could tell he was trying the English phrase out in his mouth—"his wife, and his children, and the Bayern Munich football team. The little village he lives in outside Berlin that he rides the train in from every morning. Half an hour, right on time."

"A Siemens train, of course."

"Well, there is still some older rolling stock from the East Germany times that is substituted on those regional lines occasionally..." He caught LaMont's glare. "But yes. I will say yes."

In LaMont's cube, Mesut looked vaguely embarrassed that his disloyalty had been revealed to Kate. LaMont was thrilled that he was finally getting to talk about it. His desk was a mess of candy wrappers and scraps of paper with scribbled handwriting, and he started hunting through the piles. "Here, let me find my notes from that night. Two hours of beer and Sigmar-talk, condensed. They've been my guiding star for the past few weeks." He found a piece of paper that looked like all the others, except that it had marinara sauce spilled on it, and held it out triumphantly for her to see.

COMFORT
↓
SECURITY
↓
PREDICTABILITY
↓
TRANSPORTATION
↓
SIEMENS
(DON'T SAY SIEMENS)

"That's it?" she said.

"That's *everything*."

LaMont never told Sigmar he and Mesut had spoken. But he abruptly cancelled the crying video curriculum. There were visualization exercises. Bookings were cancelled. Beloved items from Sigmar's little Brandenburg house were express-shipped to his sterile hotel room. The frequency of Skype appointments with his family were doubled.

"This was the first appearance under the new regime," said LaMont. He had hustled them into one of the Thought Leader Alliance's conference rooms. There was a monitor connected to the Agency's faithful digital recording service, which compiled videos of all of the TLs' TV appearances. "A late afternoon PBS cultural exchange show. They were talking about the romance of the German landscape."

"Is this ... relevant?" asked Kate.

"He's German, isn't he? I'm sure it wasn't easy for them, getting a German on short notice."

"They could've just called the embassy," said Kate.

"Yes, we are everywhere," said Mesut.

"For me," Sigmar was saying, "I have such good memories of green leaves and ... ancient trees." He looked nervous, but seemed to be slowly realizing that nobody was yelling at him. The host, an elderly woman with chunky jewelry, just nodded and smiled at him earnestly. "You know, during the Cold War, West Berlin was completely surrounded by the Wall. And inside this barrier was the Grunewald, a green forest park, many thousands of hectares, that was preserved for the West Berliners to go to, even when they could not leave to go to the real countryside, because ... because of Communism. My train to work goes through there every morning, and you know, I look out the window and think about those people and those times."

"Boom," said LaMont, pausing the recording. "Trains."

"Barely."

"Enough. And anyway, it was practice. Did you see how comfortable he looked?"

"Not very?"

"Yes, but *less* not very."

Next, LaMont had gotten him on a roundtable discussion on urban planning policy, which was only broadcast on C-SPAN 3 but seemed to have some DC-area transit pros in the audience; it got a nice write-up on Greater Greater Washington, in which Sigmar's Siemens affiliation was prominently mentioned. "He never said the name, though," said LaMont. "I told him he was not allowed." Most of the other panelists talked in abstractions about zoning variances and density tradeoffs; Sigmar waited until his opponents had blathered into exhaustion, then almost meekly described his walk home from the train station every day. "Ten minutes down tree-lined streets," he said. "It's a truly *heimisch* feeling, home-like, you would say. I know that this little village is mine, and that it can be mine and I can work in a big city, thanks to these steel rails and the rail station in the center of the village."

"Sigmar owns an automobile, you know," said Mesut. He looked sour. "A BMW. Not the most costly model, but not the least costly either."

The next week he was a guest on *FixItNow*, which had started out as a series of self-filmed YouTube videos put together by an eager tinkerer in his garage and had now escalated to half-hour segments put out weekly on Amazon Prime Instant Video. Chet Rincon, the host, had tracked down a Siemens light rail vehicle that had operated in Calgary until it was damaged in a collision in the '80s and scrapped; Amazon had paid to have it shipped to his Montana compound to restore or generally screw around with. Sigmar had been flown out to offer some sort of commentary or engineering expertise, with Siemens' blessing if not its subsidy, and he and Chet got down on their knees and were poking around the wheel trucks with a wrench.

"Sigmar has never touched a component in any of our manufacturing facilities in the entire time I've worked with him. Never." Mesut stood behind them, arms folded over his chest. Kate was losing patience with him. She was exhausted and felt terrible, and her two projects were spinning dangerously out of control, but she wasn't using it as an excuse to be *surly*.

"Did you know that Sigmar has a little workshop behind his house, and he likes to fool around with motors and other little gadgets?" asked LaMont.

"You know, Chet, I have my own little workshop behind my house, in Germany. Not as extensive as what you have here, ha ha!" On-screen Sigmar gestured expansively around the clearing that surrounded Chet's cabin. There were a *lot* of engine parts and other unidentifiable chunks of metal. Chet sure did love motors. He probably had a disorder.

"I guess maybe I've just gotten to know your boss better than you do, in some ways," LaMont said, smiling. He looked pretty smug. Mesut rolled his eyes and walked out without saying anything.

"Finally," he said. "I am in my moment of triumph here, and I don't need anyone being a pill, bringing me down. Even if he is the one who helped me crack the code." LaMont thought for a minute. "I'll make it up to him. Curly fries. Good lord that boy loves curly fries. Tomorrow, maybe." He turned back to the screen, where Sigmar had positioned himself in the rusted-out operator cab of the train and was giggling as he played with the controls. "Oh, yeah. That's the stuff."

ⵑⵑⵑⵑⵑⵑⵑⵑ

"Oh, my, Bob Byrd, what are you and Ouisseauhai *up* to." Christine shook her head. She had scheduled a mid-morning check-in meeting with Kate, which Kate had been dreading. It didn't help Kate's mood when she walked into Christine's office and found her waiting on her couch, not sitting behind the desk or standing up on the roof. Christine thought the desk created a hierarchical division between her and her employees, a division that would exacerbate negative interactions. Which was true, but when everyone knew how she operated, just seeing her knees as you came through the door was enough to send you into a panic.

Kate was sitting across from her, on a chair, and trying not to squirm. Christine had a folder beside her, full of printouts of emails and screenshots Kate had sent her; Christine loved paper, was a big believer in the tactile. She was looking over Jack's posts and emails. "Imitation is the sincerest form of flattery, of course, but it would be more flattering if they showed some respect for the quality of the services we offer." She sighed. "Sorry. Not your problem. Except in the sense that you allowed yourself to be guided by Ouisseauhai's fairly clumsy play."

Kate's brain was tired. It felt like a clay blob in her head. "I guess … yeah. I don't know. I wasn't *expecting* it, which I know isn't an excuse." It was the one she was using, though.

"Understandable, which isn't the same as acceptable, but still: this is the first time we've encountered another organization trying to mimic our stealth enthusiasm channel business. It won't be the last, no matter what a fiasco this is for Bob." She stared into the middle distance. "I ought to send him a condolence card. Anyway. Try to review your interactions with their agent for signs you shouldn't have missed and write it up. It's a whole new era. Spy versus spy, I suppose. You don't think this trainspotter, this"—she checked her printouts—"Jack is going to expose us online as well? Your notes on that interaction were a little spotty, but you seemed positive."

"I'm not sure of anything, but I'd guess not. There's a risk, though."

"All stealth involves risk. You brought your client-associate with you. Mesut. That was the right play, absolutely right."

"He was pretty mad about it, once he figured it out."

"Of course he was. That's a genuine reaction. Genuine reactions are what he's here for."

Kate breathed in sharply, despite herself. Christine glanced up at her without saying anything and then back at her notes.

"Well, obviously, you need to go silent on those boards for the moment. The good news is, solid groundwork has already been laid, and a decision could be close. We're working at it from the other direction, too, of course. Sigmar. That project's maturing in ways I didn't think were possible a few weeks ago."

"I thought that Siemens wasn't the customer there?"

Christine shrugged. "Not directly, it's true. But Sigmar is embedded in the superstructure of his employer, to an extent that he himself may not fully grasp. The enthusiasm LaMont is helping him awaken in himself will radiate outward into realms of interest for the company, who's also our client. It's a win for everyone involved."

Kate wondered how much Sigmar was paying, exactly. It was the sort of question Agents weren't supposed to trouble themselves with—there were other people who took care of that—but it suddenly seemed very important to her.

"Moving on. The California trip. Marie Redmond! That must have been *fascinating*. She seems like she'd be ... pretty vital. Negative surface affect?"

Kate nodded. "She was great. She was cranky and mean. I really liked her."

"But you had no success dovetailing her enthusiasm with the project, it seems. Understandable. Her relationship to that strip—it's very deep, very weird. How did Mitch take it?"

Mitch had taken it pretty hard, actually, for about an hour, as they drove glumly back through the desert. But Zach started pitching him ideas, and he perked up. *Say what you will about Zach, the Producer,* Kate thought, *but he knows what Mitch likes.*

"OK," said Zach. "What if you, like, inherit a chimp. From your great aunt. Or an orangutan."

"Sure," said Mitch. "Any of the more hilarious primates would work."

"And you have to road trip across the country with him. And then you have to fight a meth-dealing biker gang!"

"Wait," said Kate, "are you pitching an edgy *Every Which Way But Loose* reboot?"

"I have no idea what that is," Zach had said, and he meant it. Mitch laughed. "What? What is it?"

"Mitch is fine," Kate told Christine. "He's really fine."

Mitch was fine enough that after they'd dropped off Zach at his apartment building in Hollywood, he mentioned that his extremely nice place in Santa Monica would be *almost* as convenient to LAX as the airport hotel where she'd made reservations, which probably smelled like sad businessmen and industrial cleaning chemicals. She smiled and really did think about it, for a moment, before telling him that, no, probably she should go to the hotel. And he said, "Yeah, probably," and made a little disappointed look but didn't push it and then flashed that smile, and everything was fine, because, as she would tell everyone for years afterwards, Mitch Landers was pretty great.

"It would've been fun though, right?" he said, as they pulled up to the front of the hotel, which was exactly as grim as he'd predicted.

"Making a LaWLChat movie, I mean. Weird, but fun."

"I think so," she said, pulling her little suitcase from the back seat and opening the door.

"I still don't know if I've given up. I might have an idea or two. I'll send you a text!"

She leaned over and gave him a kiss on the cheek. "See you around, Handsome Dan," she had said, and then she got out of the car.

"He's already onto his next thing," Kate told Christine.

"I wouldn't be so sure," said Christine. "Mitch's enthusiasm for this idea is ... *unique*. There's a lot of fascinating things happening at once for him. He was drawn to a fan community for self-centered reasons, but then became a genuine member of the community without the burden of fame, and *then* saw an opportunity to creatively share his experience in his own medium. It's a heady brew. Plus, he wants to get into production and sees this as a way to do that while differentiating himself."

"But ... the project's dead. Marie's not going to budge on the rights."

"Oh, well, but it sounds like that situation is fairly dodgy, legally, yes? I'm sure Mitch could find a good entertainment lawyer who would find the whole scenario fascinating."

On your honor, Rex had told her, sternly. *No reporters, no creeps, no nothing. You ask her for the rights, and she either says yes or no.*

"I don't think Marie—"

"Marie is not our client. Mitch is, and it's Mitch's enthusiasm that we're trying to make something of. And an enthusiast is pleased by whatever perpetuates contact and interaction with the object of enthusiasm."

"Victory is an ending," Kate said. She had heard this one before, on her very first temp assignment at the Agency, when she and

Christine were discussing nonlinear online role-playing games. "Ending is not the goal." It had made so much sense at the time, but it suddenly sounded to her like a great way to maintain an indefinite, open-ended relationship with a client, one in which the checks kept coming in like clockwork, once a month. Kate realized that, back in her very first *Ladies Who Lunch* meeting with Christine, she had asked who the assignment's target was and never got a direct answer.

"You told me last week that enthusiasm within the LaWLChat community had begun to falter in the absence of specific milestone follow-ups to your focus group announcement," Christine was saying. "You'll need to stir the pot a bit, if only to maintain Mitch's interest. There was talk of soliciting story contributions from forum members, yes? Perhaps some kind of organized contest, to harness *their* excitement—"

Kate felt trapped, cornered. She wasn't sure why this seemed to be crossing a line. She had come into this meeting thinking she would have to justify why she hadn't used Darius to break through Marie's resolve, but now she felt like she'd been playing a different game all along without even knowing it. She didn't know why Mitch, of all people, was someone she suddenly felt the need to defend from her employer, from *herself*. Mitch was an amiable, emotionally indestructible millionaire who could've been doing *far* worse things with his money than indulging his enthusiastic fantasies. It wasn't that she had slept with him; she knew that much. Maybe it was because she had known him in person, seen him smile, caught his face in genuine expressions of glee or panic, visceral emotions she never got to experience with, say, the PartySweat salesbros. She thought about Rex, gruffly apologizing for being so cruel to people online who weren't really real to him. Kate had never been anything but nice to anyone online for her job. And yet.

What would the Ladies Who Lunch do? The question came to her mostly unbidden, as it had almost daily since she had found that folder on her desk. Maureen, of course, would have jumped into the assignment with gusto, since it would've given her the opportunity to literally profit from a romantic conquest. Eve would've done what she was told but held back her full enthusiasm, plotting a counter-move for a later date. Carol would've assumed the best of Christine and Mitch and everyone else involved and would've put a lot of frustrating energy into making as many people she could as happy as possible.

None of that was helpful. She fished around her exhausted brain for other models. *What would Christine do?* That was stupid. She was watching Christine do it. *What would—* And then she almost giggled in spite of herself. *What would* Jack *do?*

"I don't think we should do that," Kate said, interrupting what-ever it was Christine was saying.

"Do you have another angle for the play?" Christine said, tilting her head. "I'm listening."

Jack would have used a lot of swear words, but Kate chose not to. "The angle is that there is no angle. We shouldn't do it. It'll make Mitch happy, a little, for a while, but then just more disappointed later. And it'll make other people miserable. People who don't deserve to feel that way."

Christine looked as perturbed as Kate had ever seen her, which is to say not all that much, but it still was a little unsettling. "Kate," she said, "that's not your call to *make*. We're following the enthusiasm, amplifying it, so the money follows."

Kate stood up. She thought about how Jack practically had to climb over Darius to make his dramatic exit from the Dunkin' Donuts. "It's my call." There were no barriers between her and the door. It would be smooth sailing. "I'm making the call." And then she was out. She was crying, she realized as she walked down the stairs, but she still stood up straight and did it with panache. She was glad she didn't trip or fumble; she figured she wasn't going to do this very often, so it was good to get it right.

Or maybe she would make a habit of it. Who knew? She was still young.

▥▥▥▥▥▥▥▥

When Kate walked into Pickles Pub a week later, she didn't expect Monika to be sitting with LaMont and Mesut. She definitely didn't expect Monika to wave her arms in the air, jump out of the booth, and hug her. The non-work clothes she had on—a black sleeveless T-shirt and expertly torn jeans—were even cooler than her usual work clothes, which Kate didn't think was possible. "The fucking *legend* is here!" Monika shouted. She was a little drunk.

"The fucking *traitor*," said LaMont, but he barely seemed to mean it. She slid into the booth, and they pushed beer and curly fries at her.

"No, but seriously," said Monika. "This girl—*this* girl—you just told off the boss and then peaced out! That's punk rock as *shit*."

After walking out of the Agency, Kate had gone back to her apartment, turned off her phone, and refused to look at her computer for a full 24 hours. She actually watched broadcast TV to distract herself. When she finally did open her laptop, it was to review her budget spreadsheet and surf roommate-wanted ads on Craigslist.

"Yeah, I'm pretty much a badass," Kate said.

"Do you know who I have talk to at work now if I want to complain about things?" said LaMont. Then he lowered his voice to a stage whisper and pointed at Mesut. "This one!"

"It's true," said Mesut. "I am not very sympathetic about his problems, also."

"Did you ever hear from anyone in HR?" said Monika. "Like, do you even know if you actually officially quit?"

"A couple days ago," Kate said, "I got an email from Christine. Very ... formal. Polite. She said that the unusual nature of Agency work, especially stealth and in-person, causes us to encounter limits..."

"...that you don't know are there, very abruptly," said LaMont. "We've heard it."

"Anyway," said Kate, "She said that, you know, *she* didn't feel comfortable personally providing me with a reference in light of how I left, but HR would give a positive, nonspecific assessment to anyone who called asking about me. And my health insurance goes through the end of the month." She had cried when she read the email, but she didn't tell them that.

"She always liked you," said Monika.

"She's trying to keep on your good side," said LaMont. "She's gonna hire you back five years from now, when your soul is as dead as ours are."

"It's a double-blind, probably," said Mesut. "Maybe even a triple one." Kate felt so warmly towards all of them that she thought she would pop.

They left an hour later, when Monika's phone chirped to tell her that her Uber had arrived. "I can't believe you don't want to go to a public television studio to see them broadcast a transit roundtable discussion," LaMont said to her. "It sounds like exactly the sort of thing you'd be into."

"Sorry, nerds," she said, "I gotta go figure out how to break it to some aging indie rockers that their fans are super into 401ks and building decks now." She called out at Kate as she got into the back seat of the car. "Hey, call me, OK? I might have job leads for you."

The studio was a couple of blocks away. As they walked, Kate and Mesut let LaMont pull ahead. It was the first privacy they'd had since the morning at Dunkin' Donuts. "Hi," she said.

"Hello," Mesut said. "I just want to tell you ... I hope you did not do what you did because ... because I was mad. About Jack. I was perhaps overly ... petulant. I looked that word up, it is a good one."

"I didn't. I promise. I did it for me."

There was a long pause. "Have you been reading the railfan forums?"

She laughed. "I haven't, actually. That's why I needed to come to this roundtable tonight. To catch up on what I missed!" She had been keeping up with LaWLChat, though she didn't tell him that. With no new details about the movie, that topic seemed to have been forgotten, and everyone had gone back to their usual routines, which she hoped would never stop. She'd even seen a few posts from handsome_dan. Nothing from DOCTOR_FERRET, though.

"Being at the Agency is much less fun without you," said Mesut.

"Obviously."

"Which is just as well, because apparently Siemens does not have the money for me to live in a nice hotel indefinitely. So I will be going home soon."

There was a long moment of silence. "Can I come visit you? In a few months? Just for a long weekend, maybe."

"Of course. My apartment is quite large. Many famous people

have stayed there while touring Berlin. And obviously you will want to take in the city's electronic music scene. I know that is of great interest to you."

"Children!" LaMont shouted back at them as they smiled at each other. "Chop chop! We're going to miss my *finest hour.*"

⚏⚏⚏⚏⚏⚏⚏

Who comes to the filming of a transit roundtable? Kate thought. LaMont and Mesut had passes that let them stand to the side of the set, and Kate stuck close enough by them that nobody questioned her. She scanned the audience. Sigmar was telling a story about a date he had gone on as a teenager. The studio audience only filled about half the seats, but the people who were there were *enraptured.*

"And so we were stuck in the U-Bahn tunnel—subway, you would say—with no lights, for over three hours. And Liesl and I had had such an awkward dinner, but we had so much time in that train, we had to think of things to talk about. By the time the train started running again, we had made plans to meet the next week." He paused for dramatic effect, beaming. "And Liesl and I have been married 24 years, next month. Every year, we ride that train—line U4—on the anniversary of our first date."

The crowd *awww*ed. "Holy shit," whispered LaMont. "This is my actual fantasy come to life."

The other panelists were a woman from the WMATA Communications Department and a man from Save Our Metro, an activist group that issued furious press releases weekly about inadequate D.C.-area train and bus service. But the pleasant atmosphere Sigmar had created seemed to soothe them both. "Well, the next time

I'm stuck between Union Station and Judiciary Square for an hour," the Save Our Metro rep said, "I'll be hoping that the delay is at least helping along true love."

"WMATA is definitely pro-romance," said the agency flack. "But we're still going to try to reduce the opportunity for it to actually happen in our trains." Everyone laughed. There was no meanness to it.

"So," the moderator asked Sigmar. "Your company is pitching a new set of railcars to WMATA, correct?"

"It's about ... efficiency, Ray," said Sigmar, stumbling a little as he made the shift. But the goodwill he had built up was carrying him. "I'm not here to do a salesman call. New railcars from any manufacturer would be a generation ahead of what you have now and would probably be good. We do like to think that we..."

The segment was over soon, and the house lights came up, and people started milling around. Kate scanned the relatively sparse crowd. She'd assumed that at least a few railfans she knew would make an appearance, but she didn't see anyone familiar. Then she spotted him, after he had already spotted her. He hadn't been in the audience; he was part of the entourage that came with the WMATA representative. A middle-aged white man, blocky, bearded, head attached directly to his shoulders. He had been at the meeting where Jack had blown up at the Ouisseauhai agents, and he clearly recognized her. *Only woman at the meeting,* she thought.

"I suppose I cannot be upset if Sigmar is happy, which he clearly is," Mesut was saying to LaMont. "Who knew he liked to talk about himself so much?"

She poked him in the ribs. "Incoming," she said, and then, without really thinking about it, "We're on duty."

"Are we still doing this? Oh, this man, hello."

"Hey!" No-Neck said to them as he got within earshot. "Wanted to catch you before you leave." Neither of them had been making any obvious effort to go anywhere. "You guys are friends of Jack, right? Jack, shouty Jack? The real Jack?"

"I wouldn't say we're pals with him," said Mesut cautiously. "But we all respect each other."

"Well. I'm Frank. Frank Boyle. You guys on the railfan boards at all? I post as Railyard Ape."

"kmac1987," Kate said.

"BerlinZug," Mesut said.

"I used to be a maintenance guy at WMATA but they kicked me upstairs, and now I'm stuck behind a computer, and I barely know how to type. I was talking to that Sigmar about that a bit. He got it. Nice guy." Kate could see Mesut smile in spite of himself. "Anyway, I couldn't let *him* know, because it's still hush-hush, but if you see Jack, maybe pass along that this thing with the new railcars is going to go the way he wants. Probably. From what I'm hearing." He touched his nose. "You didn't hear it from me, though."

"If we didn't hear it from you," asked Mesut, "Why are you telling us?"

"I'm not telling you," said Boyle. "I'm telling Jack. I mean, he'll find out when everyone else does in a month or two, but something about the thought of making that cranky old fuck smile in spite of himself tickles me. Anyway, the new trains are going to be great." He grinned at them, and Kate knew that even though she'd made the right choice, she was going to miss this like crazy. "I don't know how to explain it. People just seem excited about it."

Afterword

My wife is a member of the Cash Cows, a women's investment club, and through it owns a small amount of Siemens stock. So I suppose it is in our financial best interest that I make it clear that nothing described in this book even remotely resembles how Siemens, or indeed any other rolling stock manufacturer, markets its products. No Siemens trains have ever run in the Washington Metro, nor have any from Adtranz, which despite its funny name was a real railcar manufacturer that was merged into Bombardier in 2001. AnsaldoBreda, which is also real, manufactured most of the cars in the system today. The opinions expressed in the book about the Washington Metro and various railcar manufacturers are held by the characters, not by me.

While I was writing this book, WMATA placed a large new order for modern railcars. The company that won the bid was Kawasaki Heavy Industries; their 7000-series cars entered service in April of 2015. They have a hexagonal cross-section and no carpets.

ⅢⅢⅢⅢⅢ

For more than ten years, I've run a blog called The Comics Curmudgeon (www.joshreads.com), which makes fun of daily newspaper comic strips, including soap opera strips. Readers of my blog and of the strips will recognize some details I've pulled from real life, but *Ladies Who Lunch* and the other soap opera strips I named in the book are fictional. In particular, all of the behind-the-scenes drama involving the creators of *Ladies Who Lunch* is entirely my own invention.

The Comics Curmudgeon has a large, boisterous, hilarious, and wonderful community of people who post in the comments section; this, obviously, was the inspiration for the LaWLChat community. Some of the LaWLChatters' user names are loose variations of real Comics Curmudgeon commenter handles; this is meant as an homage to this amazing group of people, as well as a way around the difficulty I experienced coming up with a bunch of user names all at once. However, none of the individual characters in the book are meant to correspond to any specific real commenter on my site.

Kickstarter Supporters

Carol Bondanza
Michael McGregor
Julieta Rivarola
Linda Helman
Matt Fisher
Braden Schlosser
Joe Stanton
Jenifer Zies
Patrick Lusk
Roger Hipp
kamalloy
Richard Nadeau
Chuck Kaufman
Richard Lahne
Aaron McCracken
Baka Gaijin
Jennifer Purdue
Penny Gross
Anne Phillips
Marie Stege
John Heins
David Teubner
Michael G. Hart
Shelby Franco
Helen Denman
Tom Nessinger
Nellie Power
Leah Marcus

Mark Fruhlinger
Freda Kirkham
Zeb Doyle
Ken Wagers
Jonathan May
Ryan DiGiorgi
Lindsay Guzowski
Steve Berlin
Daniel Laloggia
Ed Menze
Caroline Isaacs
Pamela G
Liz Martin
Patricia Lasusky
Jess Zimmerman
Thomas Carrington
Charles McGonigal
Austin Burns
Kevin Moreau
Michael Getzlaff
Howard Aronson
Don McHoull
Clare Peitzman
Brian Bergstrom
Karen Davis
Patrick Mulvanny
Chaunacey Dunklee
Andy Carle

Renee Hetter
Joe Fishbein
Grachakkla
Donna Normington
Thomas McCarthy
Paul Douglas
Allison Mankin
Casey Olson
Andrew Nelson
Lizzie Skurnick
Doug Waltonbaugh
Ryan Soto
Robin Currier
Terrie Sultan
Justin C. Taylor
Donna Asher
Lisa Lankford
Geoffrey Urland
Alex Hartzler
Nick Beary
Donald Newell
Reier Gotter
SMUGGCK
Shani N. Warner
Joe Nadenicek
Erik Grande
Danielle Juzan
Sara Carroll

Beth Chichester
Xwarzone
Wendi Roedema
Helen Chappell
Michael Isard
Dalton Rooney
Debra Wilkerson
Jason Pettus
Ralph Foster
Elizabeth Tinto
Duncan Sinclair
Gary Alvstad
Sue Trowbridge
Barbara Gilles
Katie Skean
Melissa Krause
Shannon Phillips
Gregory Gee
Marguerite
Kate Drabinski
Jeffrey Eaton
Sara Fulton
Nathan Borrebach
Mike Davis
Ann Wexler
Marion Delanoy
Charles H.
Alana Lenhart

Bronwyn Cerasoli Pucci
Andrew Reid and Erin Blake
Charles M Goodwin, D.Sc.
Valarie Perez-Schere
Christopher Sarnowski
David Noppenberger
Lester Todd-Schaefer
Rebecca Schoenkopf
Damian Hammontree
David Blankenbaker
Jennifer Arbogast Merlo
Daniel Ezra Moraff
Suzanne Geissler Bowles
Jonathan Elliott Blum
Rebecca Stanek-Rykoff
Clara Ribadeneyra
Chuck Baudelaire
Mackenzie Williams
Karen Vellacott-Ford
Anish Krishnamurthy
Samuel Douglas Miller
Philip Mackenzie Vogt
Katie Cunningham
Joseph Baneth Allen
MICHAEL P HERLIHY
ANDREA DENNINGER
Kerry Langkammerer
Peter Kacmarynski
Tiela Aldon Garnett
Sarah Katryn Adams
Niall J.D. Somerville
Carol (klio) Burrell
Greg Harrell-Edge
Matthew Goldman
Patrick McMahon
Katherine Hoffman
Elaine Froneberger
Douglas Woodhouse
Rose Sage Barone
Mackenzie Watten
Stephanie Koenig
Jessica Rosenblatt
Leslie Rosenblatt
Andrew M. Grossman

Annabeth Leong
William Malloy
Matthew Waslo
Lea Ann Wade
Meghan Hoffman
Scott Hildebrand
Jessica Murguia
Daniel Leonidas
Jennifer Califf
Charles Chrystal
James Hargrove
Derek Lessing
Marlys Amundson
Michael Duffey
Adam Snavely
Lisa Wishinsky
Jody Sollazzo
Marshal Blessing
Emily Chapman
Sue Breckenridge
Lynda Del Genis
Jennifer Kopp
Elizabeth Hendler
Angie LaPosta
Dave Horlick
Daniel Blackburn
Charles Kobbe
Jim Etherton
philosophymom
Andrew Blair
Jeff Newmark
Clinton J. Boomer
Steve Holzman
Seth Fitzsimmons
Nick Montgomery
Tristan Goss
Lillian Wood
Becky Coleman
Tony Bouquot
Charlie Ponyik
Bob Wardlaw
Pete Mattheis
GDRAEGER
Ryan Kasten

Simone Lorrain
Edward Bierhanzl
Brian Betker
Warren Sulcs
Jennifer Rauch
Carole Johnson
Keiren Havens
Jane Prescott
benedetta naglieri
Michael Fearnow
Jay De Lanoy
Leila Henley
Gwen Fremonti
adrian koren
Brian Compare
Nora Sawyer
Adam Lusch
Derrick Snelson
Brian Sebby
Maggie Hoop
Jim Herring
Twyla Mitchell
Wright Johnson
Garth Thompson
Bill Peschel
Jason Rideout
Skyler Gebhart
Kyle Burkhardt
Michael Broome
Robert Wininger
Leeann Pendley
Jon Fournier
Stephen Seiple
Barbara Baker
Aaron Bushell
Joshua J. Slone
Jodine Perkins
Michael Wallisch
Ed Dravecky
MICHAEL FLAIM
Melissa White
Nathan Wietbrock
Stephen Kohler
Devin McCullen

Chris Chambers
Ray Mescallado
Emily Davies
Kathryn Hartog
Jonathan Bogart
Diana Mitchell
david blankenship
Michael McKenna
Charles Henebry
John Harrison
Conor Lastowka
doug mayo-wells
David Lovely
Connor Moran
demaris howe
Ginger Huguelet
Molly Bauckham
Wrion Bowling
Joseph Abraham
Joan T. Sherwood
Karalynn Shields
Barbara Varley
Francis Fernandez
Benjamin Dodson
Michael Murphy
Stephen Murray
Greg Villepique
Michael Kelly
Kevin Arceneaux
Jeremy Fogelman
LeAnne Wintrode
Garett Auriemma
Katherine Warren
Emma Dinkelspiel
Ann Zimmerschied
Jonathan Bennett
Andreas Kjeldsen
Anjali Sachdeva
Corrie Savignano
Dori-Ann Granger
Eleanore Tebbetts
Benjamin Jones
Joseph Cornwell
Matthew Koelbl

THE ENTHUSIAST

Ian R. Beste
Jeff Knurek
Jeff Moore
Rob Carroll
Jan Forsyth
Sam Wylie
Mike Metrik
Jessica Green
AlFeelephant
Douglas Sopfe
charles firke
Jason Whisman
Zubin Madon
Cori Dulmage
mary rumsey
Laura Testa
Henry Hope
Ken Goodman
Matt Johnsen
Ryan Wyatt
Jessie Zimmer
Scott Robinson
Michael Duffy
Roy Zemlicka
Lauren Munoz
Dayle Steinke
Gabriel Danon
Jim Teece
Doug Wykstra
Mike Myers
Mary Jo Kirwan
K. Jespersen
Jason Clark
Orion Bawdon
Andrew Hatchell
Alan B. Combs
Luke Pacholski
Aileen Bennett
Zachary Prusak
Bruce Labbate
Harris Doshay
Ian Pylvainen
Jim Scott
Jim Ellwanger

Joseph Anderson
Linda Marshall
John Barton
Kate King
Eli Bovard
Kari Collins
Dana Smith
John Mara
Micah Smukler
Tom Wolper
Leo Breebaart
melissa sharlat
JoAnn Williams
Jo Eileen Sturgis
Carolyn Atkins
Grace Floros
Charles Boylan
Jon Bergdoll
Karl Freske
William Burns
Luke Smith
Dino DiMuro
Rob McPherson
James Bell
Jeff Pattillo
Ken Steiner
Ian Mond
David Glasser
Sal Giliberto
Max Blanchard
Kaia Dekker
Charles Berg
Jeff Norman
Chris Gibbins
Alex Balk
Nicole Osier
Tina Wood
David Thomson
Zach Shartiag
Susan Adami
Keith Watt
David Connolly
Aiden Carson
Mike Emrick

Jason Napora
David Brown
sharon jones
Michael A Rose
Jamie Bohr
Amy Denniston
Alicia Fansmith
Mike Steele
Alex Turnpenny
Kim Bissell
Tracy Vazquez
Scott Wickwire
Ryan Kertai
Peter Hall
Alice Huzar
Greg D'Avis
Colleen Fay
Bart Woolery
Erica Huff
Clayton Smith
Jeremy Singer
Mary Jo Redman
Michael Armor
Nathan McCoy
Jessica Griffiths
sarah Maltby
Allison Lyzenga
Matt Kouba
Brian Baresch
Jes Hansen
Jason Mann
Lora Volkert
Anthony Nelson
David Crowe
Katie Ansaldi
Norah Willett
Geoff Brown
Ryan McClain
Cene Ketcham
Wade Hassler
Jean Shaffer
jamesdowd
David Jensen
Dave Evans

John Mobbs
Will Nicholes
Blake Ewing
Robert Schroll
Mike Ricotta
Ben White
Emily Purcell
Emily Stark
Ted Nichols
Jan Werner
Mark Lunt
EJ Feddes
J Radziejeski
Matt Sell
Evan and Erin
Lena Olson
Robert Spillane
Deena Barrett
Joanna Kellogg
Crystal Rehder
Lonny Simonian
Cori Martinelli
Kerri Gibbons
Matt Thompson
Meredith Raley
Peter Voakes
Ann Finkbeiner
Bill Stilwell
Emily Sours
Mike Rosack
Patrick Lewis
John Wilson
Alex Reid
Paul Roub
Matt DiCarlo
matthurlburt
Julie Fountain
Matthew Ellison
Chris Hapka
Emily Philp
Matt Riffle
Mark Ryan
Rod Brady
david kueter

Paul Allred
Mike Cagle
Bill Way
Ellen Duff
Kim Wilson
John Roy
Ellen Stines
Rob Brock
David Young
A.M. Santos
Jay Dewey
Sam Raker
Arthur Close
Lisa Evans
Jim Corban
Janice Stark
Josh Gordon
Andy Ihnatko
harris smith
Steven Bolz
Matt Nash
Joe Bolin
Tili Sokolov
felix click
Luisa Hall
S Hackney
P.J. Stietz
Kelli King
Jeff Mills
Ben Gibbs
Beth Dunn
Mike Dang
Len Dueck
pam chozen
Andrew Tate
Joey Stern
Dug Steen
Mark Toner
Jason Gruber
Philip Elliott
Gregg Gaddy
Alan Maher
Bill James
Meg Ward

THE ENTHUSIAST

Will Wheeler
Ryan Mauldin
Jeff Fecke
Nicole Aptekar
Greg Cason
Merryl Gross
Mathew Walls
Lisa Hayes
Zachary Hill
Benjamin Goldner
David Burszan
Gayle Day
Dave Macfarlane
Daniel Mills
john nahajski
Brian Hayes
Scott Bowden
Todd Bennington
Dan Miller
Julie Woods
David Rothschild
Scott Simmons
Greg Knauss
Nicole Kenley
Andy Busch
Michael and Liz
Elaine Wilson
Brian Mitenko
Kevin Koeser
Tom English
Mark Fenster
Louis Inglese
Virginia Murray
Erin Wetzelberger
Andrew Malis
Craig Seanor
resonantcurves
Janet Cameron
Jamie Pierson
Kelli Brown
Andrew Schnorr
onesandzeroes
Miron Schmidt
John Biro

Scott Rowland
Kenneth Sharp
Michael Dunn
David Burkhart
seoman007
John Maline
Larry Lennhoff
Andrea Speed
Mike Beasley
Andrew Garrison
Aram Glick
Beth Haines
Melody Fohr
Marko Bosscher
Stephanie Martin
Trey Hart
Ryan Ridge
Amy Aitken
Dawn Greenway
Nicole Dieker
Kevin Grasso
Justin Stahl
Sean Bouchard
Jim Losby
Matt Leitzen
David Brewer
Carson Cooman
Landon Bradshaw
Will Metz
Alex Cabe
Jared M. Silver
Loki Carbis
Frank Mancinelli
Halcyon Snow
Rich Maltagliati
Joelle Thomas
Shelley Mcginnis
William Blevins
Ryan Vanasse
Utah Hamrick
Eric Pedersen
Ryan Alford
Alan Sheets
Wesley Farber

Ryan Wilson
Alexandra Petri
K Krub
MLScott57
Jade Hung
TomArmst
kirk is
Ashlea H
Michael G.
sthomson06
basherella
Notebooked
nyates314
paterbabe
mwchase
s marek
Sara
Lacey
Carol
Mike
Rachel
Alex
Brian
Ida
ckly
Chris
Rosan
Kira
George
jpb-ca
Zimty_C
Pete
Casey
Rowboat
Marcy
RS
Blake
Shawn
Hannah
Melanie
stacia123
Jeff G
Sergio
Rocketbride

Sarah
Travis
Ruuster
jaseibel
Annie N
Bill
Ayse
Erin
K T
Marly
Izzy!
Shane
Jo Dee
Mariana
konesaar
Lindsey
Adam T
Rebecca P
Nichole P.
Jason Y.
Alexander
Michelle
jriefler
jaymike
Lennon
ken k
Anna
Matt
Jaclyn
missgidge
Matt
JM
Rick
Stacy
Deborah
Jess M.
Eleanor
modernserf
coraa
Kristen
Josh
keshaw
Adrienne
James

Breanne
Nicole
jacob909
Taquelli
Martin
Steelneko
Bridget
Ariel
Allison C.
Alex H
Ruth
Julia Q.
GAZZA
Brock
L
Meg
Ari C.
crgulyas
Cletus
Kelly
Corinne
Sohna
Kate
Lisa
rochelle
kady
Thomk
L E
Brian
paul
cdragga
Megan
VZZ
Joggl
mary!
aaarizpe
Bryan
Brigid
Dagny16
Adam
Katkat
Aaron
Rafael

In 2004, Josh Fruhlinger created The Comics Curmudgeon, a blog dedicated to analyzing and mocking newspaper comic strips. Against all expectations, this made him vaguely Internet famous, and he still updates it daily. His writing has appeared online at ITworld, Wonkette, The Awl, The Billfold, and The Toast; with Conor Lastowka, he created [Citation Needed], a blog and book series highlighting the best of Wikipedia's worst writing. The Enthusiast is his first novel. He and his wife live in Los Angeles.

PHOTO: ALEXIS SIMPSON

Made in the USA
Middletown, DE
12 July 2020